DESPERATE LANDING IN
A STOLEN CRAFT

Cargo formed an image of the approach angle clearly. The maze balked and jibbered at him. It really wasn't made to cut endo, it didn't trust Cargo enough to risk burn.

He was tempted to swear at it, berate it, and then put it under his authority by force. Instead of whipping it he tried to seduce the machine. Centered in its heart, Cargo thought of the joys of flying sky, of riding the winds on the high plains of Vanity with the abandon of an amusement park ride. Images flowed almost tripping on each other, each more tempting than the last. Cargo got lost in them, in his own memories, the immense exaltation of skill that was only matched by combat.

He dangled glory glittering and the maze took the bait. They committed to burn, and then pierced the soft gaseous corona that could be so deadly.

Burning titanium flared violet, magenta, hot blue, and finally chromium yellow as the transport pierced atmosphere for the first time and rode it down.

Cargo's peripheral vision began to darken, then blotted out. He was blacking out, he knew, and for the moment he didn't care. If this was dying, then it was very easy. . . .

Dancing Vac

S.N. LEWITT

ACE BOOKS, NEW YORK

This book is an Ace original edition,
and has never been previously published.

DANCING VAC

An Ace Book / published by arrangement with
the author

PRINTING HISTORY
Ace edition / February 1990

ISBN: 0-441-13668-0

Ace Books are published by The Berkley Publishing Group,
200 Madison Avenue, New York, New York 10016.
The name "ACE" and the "A" logo are trademarks
belonging to Charter Communications, Inc.

PRINTED IN THE UNITED STATES OF AMERICA

10 9 8 7 6 5 4 3 2 1

Chapter

1

Dying is easy dancing vac. Even peace doesn't guarantee the angle entering endo, doesn't vouch for every plate and weld and bolt in the craft. To say nothing of the maze developing a leak and going mad or a backflow in the mag track launchers. And those are the safe parts. Pilot error is the real danger, the collisions when some barf-for-brains enswine screws the entry pattern or some old Joe keeping up his hours nods off to someplace the maze can't track.

Dying is very easy even in peace, and there wasn't peace yet. But Cargo had chosen the surest and most painful way to the Wall. He had turned in his wings.

"Discards and bid, bidding now," the dealer droned in a bored monotone.

Cargo blinked quickly and forced himself to concentrate on the here-and-now of the casino on Luxor. It was one thing to feel the eternal presence of the batwing when he was alone wandering through the gardens down by the Wall. But it wasn't smart at all to lose his focus on his one sure source of income. Especially since the hotel wanted a second week paid in advance and Luxor was not cheap.

He had thirteen hundred on the table, well below his usual standards. He'd been conservative. One king and two tens of spades had fallen and he held four more kings and six tens in his hand. Eight-deck khandinar was supposed to be impossible to count and impossible to beat, which only proved how stupid impossibility was. In the batwing he had done the impossible every day, for all that tourists on retirement vacation packages who frequented Luxor cared.

In a vague way he felt sorry for the old man with only a wisp of remaining hair sticking limply from under a beaten tweed cap. From previous bids and cards that had fallen Cargo knew he couldn't be holding anything higher than a queen of hearts. And the old guy had two thousand out. It was criminal to let people like that play. They should be kept in the first room with the five and dime tables and slots where they couldn't do themselves too much damage, Cargo reflected. Not only did they throw away their own money, it wasn't even any fun to beat them. They couldn't play worth a damn in the first place.

Cargo studied his cards as if he were considering his bid. In fact he had decided his strategy two rounds previously, but it was necessary to pretend that he was as inept as anyone else at the table. Slowly he counted to twenty and let out his breath. "Up two, spades seven," he said as haltingly as he could manage, trying to make the familiar phrases of the khandinar bid sound as if he were practicing foreign words, rolling the taste of them on his tongue and experiencing mild shock that they actually worked, producing the desired results.

The dealer's face didn't move as Cargo's choice flashed on the tally screen. Cargo tried to seem anxious. He'd done this enough times before to know that it was still good for another few hours. Maybe he could corner one of the really high rollers into a private game in the upstairs chambers later, when his stake was big enough to matter. He had to stay in character until then, the bumpkin flyer-on-leave who thinks he's hot.

"Mr. Ynglesias?"

This time the shock and disorientation were real. No one knew he was here under that name. The Bishop and Fourways would look for him under Mirabeau, and Cargo doubted they were looking at all. The Bishop had better things to do now, and Fourways should be relieved. There was no love lost between them.

Cargo swallowed hard and looked around. The man who had addressed him wore the formal blue drape and matching gloves that constituted the uniform of the Pyramid Casino. Behind him were two others, an Akhaid and a woman. Both were dressed like patrons of the place and seemed to be together, not noticing what was going on at the khandinar table. Cargo knew better. Their eyes were slitted sideways and they weren't looking at each other or the cards or even the other gamers. They were staring directly at him. Security. He'd been in the Second Directorate long enough to recognize the look.

"Yes?" he answered the uniformed employee, keeping the mask of innocence firmly in place.

"Mr. Ynglesias, would you please come with me?" The man in the blue gloves spoke softly, his very proper accent and soft modulation the model of tact. There could be no mistaking his breeding, his finesse.

Cargo affected not to care. He slid from the tufted velvet stool, gathered his talley, and followed the man past the glittering crystal-illuminated roulette wheels of the third room and the elegant baize dice tables of the second. The Akhaid and the woman were on either side of him, not close enough to attract attention but near enough to catch him should he make trouble. Real professionals. Cargo appreciated that.

The splendor of the casino took a dive as they mounted the marble stairs to the first room. The nickel and dime tables were surrounded by plain laminated stools and no one had bothered to mask the cheap aluminum casings of the slots. Not that it was his business. If things went the way Cargo thought they were going he wasn't likely to be back.

"Would you mind telling me what this is about?" Cargo inquired politely as they approached the door.

"Khandinar," the man said. "This is a gambling establishment. Your winnings over the past three weeks don't quite have the hallmarks of ordinary gambling, if you follow me. And, quite frankly, we were given some advice. Anonymously, of course."

"Of course," Cargo agreed, hoping the fury wasn't too evident in his voice. "I will take it to court if I have to. I wasn't cheating. I have never cheated in khandinar in my life."

The man shook his head sadly. "Now, I did not accuse you of cheating, Mr. Ynglesias. No one has. Only that card counters are not welcome in the gambling establishments of Luxor. Especially card counters who have published four articles on the game in the *Annals of Probability Studies*.

Professional statisticians are not welcome to try their pet theorems in our casino. Nor in any other in this MidCenter. I assume no further persuasion will be necessary."

Cargo sighed. There was one last chance, although he didn't set great store in it. Whoever had turned him in had done a good job of it. "I believe it was a Rafael Mirabeau who wrote those articles," he said, grasping at the last hope.

The Pyramid employee looked down momentarily. "Let's not make this more unpleasant than it has to be," he said wearily. "You had to print the register. We are not so naive to think that a professional stat gambler would use his real name here. I suggest you leave at once, or we will be forced to take stronger measures. I hope that won't be necessary."

The Bishop would have been proud of the grace with which he made his exit, Cargo thought. There was nothing else to say. He swept out under the central glitter-lit archway into the street with the cool hauteur of a Trustee of the Collegium, not entirely surprising since he had learned it from Mirabeau himself.

He chose to walk in the cloying darkness of the MidCenter, avoiding the obsequious cabs that stopped at five-meter intervals waiting for him to get in. No one walked on Luxor, at least not in the MidCenter. If a visitor wanted to enjoy the perfectly engineered night, a stroll by the river past the night-blooming jasmine, or through the pine grove to the Peaceful Falls, might be in order. Cargo ignored the cabs, ignored the stares directed at a visitor to Luxor in full, formal casino dress who chose to walk the streets like a common hotel employee.

The movement helped him to think, to sort things through. It was good to have been told that someone had tipped off the Pyramid. He would have guessed it, but might have lost some time trying to prove it wasn't so. Now there was no doubt. He had come to Luxor to escape but someone wasn't willing to let him go so easily. A second betrayal. After the first it wasn't so surprising, so horrifyingly painful.

Not worth it to speculate, he told himself. Like dancing vac, things either were or they weren't. Worrying or trying to figure out why it was so only wasted time, and at exo speeds in the maze there wasn't any time left over. Only the focus, the combat, that frozen moment that made all the rest alive, mattered. Everything else fell away.

So Cargo walked past the Seven Emperors and the Paradise, all facades matte and glitter in the night. None of the graffiti-burned titanium walls that had formed the background of nearly all his planet-bound nights. Not here on Luxor, where everything was made of wood and glass and brick reconstructions of ancient design, all prettied up and unthreatening. And unreal. Just like his own time had been.

Dimly he knew there was anger somewhere under the layer of fighter cold, loose and ready. When the time came . . . The thought burned pure and chill like the deadly glare of a Krait's Eyes.

He found his hotel around the next corner. Its pink marble floors and columns had seemed uncluttered, a fragment of the memory he had of his first trip to Luxor when he was a child. It probably was the same hotel. Now he had ceased to see it as he hurried through the grandly simple lobby and down corridors that bore more resemblance to the Trustee Palace on the Collegium than a mid-rate hotel ought to. The lift was slow, ponderous, as if programmed to slow him down. Cargo waited, paced, swore softly in a language no one else on Luxor would understand. And then the elegantly mirrored lift arrived, swallowed him by degrees, and began its torpid rise.

His door was locked, coded, and printed just as he had left it. That didn't mean it was safe. He wished he had followed his father's rule about always carrying a weapon when one gambled. Only his father had been killed in a knife fight during a khandinar game and Cargo figured he was better without one. Now he stood immobile in the rose-carpeted hallway staring at a mute slab door. Adrenaline coursed through his arteries, altering reality and time yet again. He was stronger, faster than he had been before the fear-rush began, the same as it had been in a Krait or a batwing, the same as it had been every time he had faced the uncertainty of an engagement.

He released the locks and stood under the hall light. No reason to make things easy for whoever was inside, waiting for him. That someone would be there he never doubted. It smelled too much of Fourways and the Directorate and the world he thought he had left. Deprive him of his one avenue to an honest if contested living, force him into their corner. No one should treat a pilot like that. Only they weren't pilots in the end. They were operatives in the Second Directorate. Just as he had been, had been trained to be. And he had been good at it, too. Just like all the others.

On the neatly made bed in the center of the hotel room's impersonal shadow sat Stonewall. Cargo half winced and half smiled at his own stupidity. Of course. If it would be anyone it would be Stonewall. Fourways wouldn't bother. Only the asshole from the Fourth Directorate would have both the knowledge and the impulse to use it. Someone else probably would have been more subtle.

"Have you checked the bar?" Cargo asked, his voice giving away nothing of what he felt. "I believe they have mint juleps here."

Stonewall smiled slowly and nodded his blond head. "I believe you are right in that. As a matter of fact, I did indeed try reconnaissance before my primary target appeared and begged me to assist."

Cargo raised his eyebrows. He thought he knew what Stonewall meant. For a moment he wondered whether he should kill Stonewall now. But that would only mean that someone else, someone he didn't know, would be tasked. Stonewall might be as low as they came, but he was predictable. He would have to learn a stranger's ways. Better a familiar enemy . . . at least for the moment.

That settled, Cargo relaxed his hands at his sides and casually crossed the threshold into what he had to remind himself was his own room. He took a seat in a chintz-upholstered chair, as far from Stonewall as he could reasonably get, in front of an expanse of glass, and turned on the light.

Stonewall smiled. "Are you showing off that you haven't forgotten, or do you think you can't trust me? Me, your good buddy from Vanity? I think I'll just assume that you wanted to show me that you are still Intel, whether you know it or not."

"You always were very diplomatic," Cargo sneered.

"Charleston breeding, good buddy. They always did say that blood would show, and that a gentleman is always a gentleman. And I assure you I would never in any case behave like rabble and humiliate you in public. My ancestors would never forgive me."

Cargo smiled unpleasantly. Stonewall pretended to misread his face. "I suppose you are curious as to why I have paid you such an impromptu visit," Stonewall continued casually.

"You could say that. And for forcing me out of a low-stakes game in a second-rate casino, where I hear I am now persona non grata throughout the moneymaking establishments in this region."

Stonewall smiled sincerely enough that it made Cargo queasy.

"A gentleman does not force anyone to assist him, and I do hope that the use of such mild persuasive inducements as I have at my disposal cannot be ranked with methods of coercion that I detest. Cargo, good buddy, you will be glad when you hear that I have been tasked with locating that scum that betrayed us all. I just want you to help. If anyone has a hint of where to find Ghoster, you would. And I do need the aid. I don't beg lightly."

Cargo sat unmoving, his eyes no longer focused on the tall blond who sat so comfortably at the foot of the bed. His gaze was fixed on the scattered dusting of stars visible just over the trees through his window. The Vinovi they were, wild and uninhabited. Once he had dreamed of going there and exploring. A stupid fantasy, one that would have been forgotten if they hadn't hung outside this hotel room in the early hours of the morning. The Vinovi, untamed and inimical, were less alien than the Akhaid with whom they shared more than one world.

Ghoster was alien, totally and irrevocably unknowable. It was something Cargo had never faced, not completely. They had been such a good team for so long, he and Ghoster, interfacing through the maze that had shielded both of them from the worst disorientation of touching truly different thought. They had gotten drunk together and taken annies together, had made jokes that the other never quite understood, had been friends. At least as much as a human and an Akhaid could be friends.

The worst was that Ghoster's betrayal wasn't for want of trust but of understanding. In the essential alienness of the Akhaid, Ghoster was convinced he was helping. He had even freed Cargo in the end, out of respect for the friendship they had both misjudged and shared in equal degrees.

Cargo couldn't hate his old partner. It would be so much easier if he could, if he could reduce what had happened to its simplest form and then act on that. In those terms Ghoster had killed his best friend, had tried to kill his mentor, and had passed secrets to the enemy. In the weeks on Luxor Cargo had tried to find that hate, had raked himself over again to discover any embers buried. None were there. Maybe it was some deficiency in himself that he knew Ghoster's actions made tragic sense of an Akhaid's highest level of morality. The screw-up had all been his, and every other human's who had ever worked with the Akhaid. It was too easy to pretend that their supple metallic-scaled skin and whiteless eyes indicated no more difference than blond- or black-haired humans.

"I thought I had resigned," Cargo said heavily. "I'm out of it."

Stonewall just shook his head. "I really think you need to reconsider. If you need a few minutes to think I can find my way to the bar. A mint julep in an iced-down silver cup is just exactly what I need right now. And there's something here from the Bishop for you. Which might help you make your decision. But to set your mind at rest, Fourways doesn't know I'm here. This whole job is strictly discretionary, if you catch my meaning. Leaving the Club and your personal debts of honor do not necessarily have to be identical."

"You're saying that I don't have to join up again?" Cargo asked more out of habit than real interest.

"That, my friend, is precisely what I am saying. I have full charge of this operation and a very nice expense account, and authorization to take on outside consultants. You can get that damned bastard and never have to play the military intelligence game again. If you want to."

Cargo blinked. In the soft hotel light, Stonewall's face was full of sincerity, his blue eyes wide and innocent. If he didn't know better, Cargo would be almost tempted to trust him.

As it was he knew Stonewall well enough to know that if Stonewall said it straight out there was a chance it could be true. And a very good chance it could be twisted. The Charlestonian's precious honor would not tolerate an outright lie to a former squadmate of Cargo's standing.

Stonewall coughed softly to get Cargo's attention, and then spoke again. "I would hate awfully to have to use any undignified method to persuade you," he said, standing. "I truly would. So I'll be down in the bar with a second drink ready to toast our partnership."

Cargo heard the door whisper shut as he left. He didn't have to wonder about Stonewall's ideas of undignified methods; he knew a threat when he heard it. And the last thing in the known manifold he wanted to do was hunt down Ghoster.

What he wanted to do was forget everything. He had come to Luxor because of the Wall and because it was a playground that offered every diversion he could have wanted. But the Wall shadowed all of it. Two names on it, two of the four people in the universe he cared most about, haunted even the brightest afternoons, and their ghosts drifted through every casino and every cabaret.

Just the wrong place, he told himself. He should have left after he had paid his respects at the Wall, should have hopped the first scheduled transport to anywhere in the Collegium. Only it was all too much effort. There was no place he wanted to go, nothing he wanted at all except for unceasing numbness.

Stonewall wouldn't understand that, he thought, looking at the rumpled spot where his one-time colleague had sat. And then he saw the thick white envelope for the first time.

He hesitated, trying to tell himself that he was just imagining things, but the paper didn't go away. And Stonewall had said that the Bishop had sent a communication. He should have been thinking. The usual channels, the mode and the screen mail, were out. The Bishop was on Marcanter, a Cardia world, and all his transmissions would be monitored. And Cargo had to assume that this was something the Bishop wanted to keep silent.

How the hell did Stonewall get to Marcanter, to the Bishop? But it didn't have to be Stonewall at all, he remembered. Anyone in Intel could have passed it through the Club until it reached the right source. Typical of Stonewall to have been there in time to catch it.

Maybe he no longer wanted anything except oblivion, but the Bishop wanted the whole manifold even though he was old enough to have been through two careers, Cargo thought. And there was no fighting it. Andre Michel Mirabeau, Bishop of Mawbray's Colony and ex-Trustee of the Collegium, always won. Even when he lost he managed to twist it to advantage. Cargo had no doubts at all that if the Collegium lost the war, the Bishop would win back more at the treaty negotiations.

There was no choice. He picked up the envelope and ripped the thick paper.

The letter was written in the Bishop's elegant hand in French, not the ubiquitous Indopean of official communication. Cargo had learned French long before the Bishop had adopted him, and Mirabeau had insisted on using it exclusively between them.

The first paragraphs were only personal notes, condolences on Plato's death and Ghoster's defection, a description of a reception for the negotiaters. It wasn't until near the end that the Bishop got to the point.

Rafael, he read, *you have endured many difficulties and painful moments in the past weeks, and my heart is with you. But it is also with all those other beings, both human and Akhaid, who have also suffered so needlessly. What I want you to remember is this: you are uniquely capable of changing the balance of power. Now that you have completed several types of training and have experienced many of the joys and some of the cruelty of life, you can be the fulcrum on which the whole of the manifold turns. I have been your father for this reason as well as my own. However, in order to use your gifts and knowledge, it is necessary for you to get back in the game.*

Believe me, you will not be happy again until you do. And remember that any situation can be used to your advantage. Although you must be in the game, do not be of it. Keep your goal in mind and there is nothing you cannot accomplish.

Your loving father, Andre Michel Mirabeau

Cargo swore softly under his breath. That was as close to a direct order as the Bishop had ever given him. Didn't the old man know when he had gone too far? It was one thing to get back in the game; it was another to hunt down and kill Ghoster.

Then it hit him totally by surprise, so obvious that he knew he was a moron, an idiot, a candidate for the brain tubs not to have understood from the first.

It was Stonewall who wanted Ghoster dead, and Stonewall would in the end find him. But if Cargo went along he could somehow protect his erstwhile partner and friend. Ghoster had saved his life once in violation of whatever loyalties had made the Akhaid betray the Collegium. There was no reason why Cargo couldn't do the same. And in doing that find the fulcrum the Bishop mentioned.

Because, Cargo's mind raced on, if he found Ghoster he could explain the misunderstanding. And they would stop. That was the key.

Cargo looked around the room and smiled grimly. The window and the stars no longer held his attention. He wondered that they ever had, that he had spent so many hours staring blankly wondering about them. Instead he noticed that, for all its comparative luxury, this was still a smallish room in a mid-rate hotel. Mid-rate for Luxor, at least. The prints over the bed were reproductions of some innocuous landscape, the grey and rose colors bland and inoffensive. There wasn't even the piquant scent of poverty lurking around the corner out of the bright lights, the exhilaration of the unknown. The only excitement on Luxor was the casino. The only danger was to the wallet. The only life was on the Wall among the dead.

There wasn't even anything he needed to pack, Cargo thought with disgust. Nothing that mattered. His luck, the Ste. Maries-de-la-Mer medal, was around his neck. Everything else was worthless. He turned and left the room without a final glance, forcing himself onward before he lost his nerve.

He had promised Ghoster that he would never give his Eyes away, promised at the moment when the Akhaid could have left him to die in an explosion that never happened. They had gotten the Bishop to Marcanter, to the preliminary negotiations with the Cardia peace faction. Ghoster hadn't been scheduled to go along. The Bishop hadn't really needed Cargo to fly his official vehicle so much as to instruct Cargo in the politics of the moment. But Ghoster had shown up and no one had ever questioned it. After all, Cargo and Ghoster always flew together.

The Bishop's official vehicle had been sumptuous, all blue carpets and bulkheads and soft cream leather upholstery. There was even a galley full of paté and caviar ready for the Bishop's reception that evening. He remembered dipping into one of the iced silver bowls of caviar with Ghoster. Caviar was one of the few human foods the Akhaid had liked. That and anchovies and coffee. Decaf, really, Cargo recalled. Coffee got Ghoster higher than any three annies combined. Finding that out hadn't been pleasant.

Still, they had landed the Bishop on Marcanter together,

gone off to a Quartermaster's mess together, Cargo all unsuspecting. Ghoster was the one who insisted they go with the Quartermasters, that they would have the best food. And they had. The memory of that feast, tainted as it was by other recollections, still stood out as one of the most awe-inspiring culinary feats Cargo had ever witnessed. And that was including the fact that he had eaten at the Bishop's table for several years and Mirabeau was no dilettante. Then they had gone drinking.

Somewhere in there Ghoster had gone missing. Cargo remembered his fear of having to drag Ghoster out of some public park, cover for him making a nuisance of himself in front of the Cardia officers. There had been enough times when the damned Akhaid had gotten drunk or annie blitzed and crawled under a shrub or fell into a flower bed. Like the bank of African violets Cargo had pulled him out of after the Ghost had gone and stolen the plans for the batwing. If Ghoster hadn't told him about that Cargo never would have known, and now wished deeply that he had been left in ignorance.

He had returned to that luxuriously appointed shuttle to find Ghoster wiring a bomb under the maze. Ghoster, his buddy, his good friend, his only friend still alive after Two Bits and Plato were gone, was the traitor they'd been looking for all along. And out of friendship Ghoster had let him go. Both him and the Bishop, and in return Cargo had promised not to follow.

Cargo felt the engine vibration through the bedding struts of the cabin he shared with Stonewall. That didn't happen when they were out-manifold, not even in military transport that didn't have any of the meager cosmetic niceties of the *Melesse*, by no means the Royal Lion Line's showpiece. Either Stonewall's expense account wasn't quite as large as he had intimated or he didn't care about the amenities. Once Cargo thought Stonewall did care, but he was no longer certain. During their passage to the Cotrato Complex, Lionsport Hub, Stonewall had been quieter than Cargo had ever believed possible.

Now, though, the subtle vibration that made the bedding shudder indicated they were back in the manifold. Cargo heard Stonewall whistling some tune he couldn't name and refused to open his eyes. No reason to let Stonewall know he was awake and had noticed their shift out of the Six and back into the normal universe. Cargo couldn't decide if it was worse having Stonewall talkative or quiet, and then decided that having Stonewall at all was bad enough. Especially since the cabins aboard the *Melesse* weren't any larger than the staterooms allotted to junior officers on any carrier.

"You can't fool me, Cargo, old buddy. You are awake and ready to roll. I know it surely," Stonewall whispered from above.

Cargo groaned and opened his eyes. Stonewall stood over him, already dressed in the kind of tasteful slacks and sportshirt that anyone from a Zhia Bau miner to the Presiding Trustee would own. Behind him the yellow-burned bulkhead rose monotonously. The whole ship was that monochrome yellow, the Royal Lion Line's eccentricity. Cargo had never seen monoburn before, and was grateful for it. Now he hoped never to see that particular shade of yellow again.

"Now if you are decently dressed in time for breakfast we can get some real work done," Stonewall insisted.

This penetrated Cargo's pre-coffee consciousness. "You mean we're going to discuss the mission?"

Stonewall's eyes grew wide with amazement. "No, we're going to get started. This scow has been docked for almost four hours, and we've got Collegium authorizations. No customs. And the *Andronika* leaves in seven hours."

"What?"

Stonewall sighed. "I knew it would be impossible before you had any coffee. The *Andronika*. Which you will be on. Or rather, which a Mr. Kore Verdun, native of Marcanter, will be on. Is that perfectly clear?"

It took all of Cargo's self-control and then some to keep from slamming Stonewall into the vile yellow titanium bulkhead. The fact that he had a second birth certificate under the name Kore Verdun was privileged information. Especially the fact that it was just as real as the one issued to Django Ynglesias of Mawbray's Colony.

"I'm real sorry to do this, good buddy, but in seven hours both Django Ynglesias and Rafael Mirabeau have to be killed. We just don't have a whole lot of time."

Chapter

2

The entire reason for Contrato's existence was the Hub. There were four in the Collegium, great port stations completely devoted to moving freight and passengers, making connections and interlocking schedules. The outer shell of the Hub bristled with docked ships. Every class of merchant vessel was represented, from tiny orbit runners to giant heavy haulers. Luxury liners were berthed next to overloaded colony ships, and even a few pleasure yachts dotted the moorage. From the approach screens Cargo could even make out several fast frigates and one diplomatic craft among the military ships in the restricted area.

Next to him, Stonewall grinned unpleasantly. A soft, mechanically feminine voice announced disembarkation was under way, would all passengers prepare to disembark at the nearest marked exit and thank you for choosing Royal Lion, the gold service of the Collegium. It has been a pleasure having you aboard.

Emerging from the *Melesse* was a relief. The station walls had been burned in the same brilliant hues as every shred of titanium he had ever seen, hot violet shading into a horrific magenta, screaming blue and pink and chromium yellow like the whorish junk jewelry rich kids wore slumming. Cargo knew he was back in the Collegium again, back home, and no longer locked in cramped spaces with Stonewall.

At the end of the connector, as they entered the Hub proper, they were confronted by every kind of mercantile inducement Cargo had ever imagined and a few he hadn't. An annie bar was wedged next to a boutique that shared frontage with an expensive gelateria. A glass door had been squeezed between that and an exotic floral display, painted with a flat palm. "Sister Delores, readings of the future, love, luck. Only six C.S."

Cargo shivered slightly.

"Want to go in and have your fortune told?" Stonewall inquired maliciously.

"No," Cargo replied abruptly and turned away. Stonewall knew well enough to know it was cruel.

Then his companion softened slightly. "What about a coffee? On the expense account."

Cargo didn't need to reply. The *Melesse* had absolutely the worst coffee he had ever drunk in his life. Neither he nor Stonewall had touched the stuff after the first day, and he was feeling the effects of withdrawal. The low-grade headache from caffeine deprivation couldn't be improving his thought processes any and he needed to think quickly. Seven hours on Contrato. Six and a half now, and take off a half for checking in at *Andronika*. Somewhere in there Stonewall planned to kill off two of Cargo's identities, leaving him with only the Cardia citizen Kore Verdun.

Kore Verdun was an identity he had used only once before, for less than a day. He and Ghoster had gone down to Marcanter before the Bishop's diplomatic trip. There had been reports of Cardia stealthcraft massing on Marcanter's isolated western base. He and Ghoster had infiltrated almost too easily. The base was huge but there weren't enough pilots rated on the black batwings the Cardia called Scorpions to go around. No one questioned his ability.

He remembered the horror of it, meeting and chatting with Cardia batwing pilots like his own group. It was one thing to take out a fighter, a piece of machinery like a target in a game. It was something very different to have to wonder about the individuals, to know their names and their voices, to have seen their shards of luck scattered like his own.

Unthinkingly his hand went to the Ste. Maries-de-la-Mer medal around his neck. His luck. Two Bits, his oldest friend, had given it to him. Then they had drawn patrol at Azar Community, he and Two Bits both, and had been ambushed by four Cardia fighters. Two Bits was on the Wall now, but it wasn't a gomer who'd put him there. It had been Ghoster, firing from Cargo's own fighter, Ghoster who'd been his partner since they'd begun training.

It was the last thing Ghoster had told him before the Akhaid had disappeared on Marcanter. It was the one thing Cargo knew but fought knowing, refusing to comprehend that he had been piloting the craft that had brought Two Bits down.

They found a cafe several doors down, one of the fancy expensive types with seventeen varieties and a case full of puff pastry and whipped cream in several different shapes. Stonewall ordered espresso and napoleons for both of them and took the tray to a table in the corner against the window. He left Cargo the window seat.

"*Andronika* will take us far as Zhai Bau," Stonewall muttered into his cup. "Then we pick up the ore run to Marcanter."

"I thought there was a law against that," Cargo said, disinterested. In fact, he knew there was a law against it. Trading with the enemy had been outlawed within the first days of the conflict.

"Not too many Collegium authorities bother with Zhai Bau," Stonewall replied. "And they need the currency. Besides, it ever occur to you that they never seem to have any trouble, all the way out there near enough to the Cardia you could spit? But for once it's going to help us out, since that's about the only way we could get there."

Cargo grinned. "We could fly."

"Now that's an interesting thought indeed, good buddy. Something to ponder on, I don't wonder. But how could we requisition a ship big enough to go out-manifold? And take it out, just the two of us?"

Cargo remembered C. L. Wong's yacht and snorted. At thirteen he had been able to steal it and pilot it out of the dock alone. Oh, sure, his friends had been with him, but the boy who became Two Bits and the rest of their gang hadn't taken the controls. At that time he hadn't even had the biochips inserted in the back of his skull.

It had been a very long time since he had done anything quite that illegal, or quite that stupid. It occurred to him that it might be about past due.

"Oh, no," Stonewall said before Cargo had said more than six words. "I have some nice all paid up tickets and a few little games I learned from those assholes down in the First Directorate. Shouldn't take more than fifteen minutes to kill off two out of three identities as far as Contrato Records is concerned. And then we're home free. So long as those same aforementioned barf-for-brains cyberspies do what they damn well promised so sweet before I left and make good and sure Kore Verdun has all his shots for the Records."

Cargo's eyes raked Stonewall once. "Boring. Very boring. No one could ever make an entertainment series the way you operate. And to think that we were told the very first day we reported to the Second Directorate that there were no such things as spies anymore. That everything was all ELint and that those shows were so much turtle dung."

Stonewall blinked and Cargo read surprise on his pale features. It took a moment to connect. Then he realized that the phrase turtle dung was something he'd picked up from Ghoster. No one who had used Indopean for over half his life would have learned that off the streets. Cargo wondered if it was a direct translation of something slightly nastier in Atrash, the accepted major language of the Akhaid.

Stonewall recovered his equanimity rapidly. "The point is not drama," he slurred phlegmatically. "The point is efficiency. And simplicity."

"Might as well add truth and beauty to that list," Cargo replied and then fell silent. The idea grew inside him, first playing around the edge of his consciousness with amusing little scenarios.

No reason you can't do it, the voice whispered seductively in his head. *After all, it's the same job. And will look better too. No reason to be dull just because Stonewall has no imagination.*

That wasn't really true. Stonewall did have an imagination. Just not real well developed. After all, this was the person who decided that because a light was connected to the switch in church that there was no God. That was perhaps a reasonable assumption based on the data, but that was where Cargo decided that Stonewall fell short. No, it wasn't nerve or imagination the tall Charlestonian lacked. It was intuition. Stonewall always had to go by the numbers. He didn't have the facility to look at a problem and see the solution, perfect and complete, before him.

But just because Stonewall had no intuition was no reason to discount it, Cargo thought reasonably. He dug into the napoleon to hide the smile that threatened around the edge of his mouth, and nearly gagged. It tasted like sugared cardboard, too sweet and heavy without any real substance.

It would be easy enough. After all, he'd done essentially the same thing when he was only thirteen. And this time his motivation was better.

He had promised the Bishop that he wouldn't steal anything again, and had kept that promise faithfully. Only this wasn't stealing exactly, he told himself firmly. This was requisitioning for military purposes. Not that the Bishop would draw such fine distinctions, but Cargo frequently did. Otherwise there would be no possibility of keeping any promises at all.

"You wanted me as a consultant, Stonewall. So here's what I think we should do. Simple and efficient, and all very, very reasonable."

Stonewall leaned over, ignoring the scraps of puff pastry that clung to his plate. His espresso grew cold as he listened to Cargo explain, as if to a child, once and then once over again.

"Yes," he finally agreed, his eyes glowing with excitement as he considered Cargo's plan.

Cargo didn't even smile. He didn't want to. No matter how he liked the solution to infiltrating Marcanter, there was still the matter of Ghoster. He wondered again, idly, why he wasn't planning on using his own idea without Stonewall's knowledge. It would be simple enough to warn Ghoster off, perhaps.

The coffee had become slightly bitter and the cream had begun to form an obscenely greasy film on the skin of the liquid. He set the cup down carefully. The moment for denial had passed. There was a time when he could have backed out, changed his mind, and no matter how much Cargo insisted to himself that he could still cut and run, there was a place where he knew he was committed.

In combat there was a moment when the run was committed, when there was no turning back. The titanium-burned shell of the Krait couldn't take the stress, even a combat maze fully in mode couldn't respond fast enough. But there was a strange moment hanging between the commitment and the engagement, the split space of time when it was possible to still believe that combat was not inevitable. In that strangely distant second when all choice was gone there was still the illusion of choice.

Cargo recognized the illusion and was still seduced by it.

Stonewall mumbled something about Accounting and slipped his expense-account card into the check tally at the table. When the cost of the espressos and napoleons had been deducted he stood with a studied casualness. "Guess it's time."

Cargo nodded. Like an Eyes run dancing vac, the engagement had begun.

A batwing would have been best, but Cargo would have even preferred a gaudy-burned Krait that had been used a little too hard endo. Either one would have had the speed and the tight turns, all the moves for dancing vac the way he had fought it for the past four years. Passing by the berthing cradles in the Hub, Cargo felt a pang of desire. They were pretty, loose, and elegant with the proportions of a vacuum ballerina. All light and grace, the fighter craft close up looked almost fragile tethered in their locks.

Cargo paused, struck hard by a combination of sadness and desire. He had learned to survive in a Krait, how to scissor it wide from defensive to aggressive stance, to roll it down the blue axis of the enemy craft through the blind spot so they didn't see him coming. Mental reflexes fired and he could almost feel the wide receptive congruency of the maze responding seamlessly as he imaged the fighter's response to enemy coming vis on red-six, Eyes ready to spectraprint his tail.

Or he could slip out of the jaunty Krait and strap on the void black batwing. The stealthfighter had been his truest love, all curves and quiet made to slip under the high winds running endo and ride them on its outstretched wings. And then to emerge again into the night, disappearing into the endless fabric of space.

He could taste the freedom of that movement, of the membrane-thin maze interface in the batwing where he and Ghoster had so often been yoked together, alien thought rubbing the connection raw but still feeding into the maze. Together both the Krait and the batwing had responded to their linked minds, enhanced and augmented in cybermode. The faintly sour taste of Three-B's teased at the edges of consciousness and the pain of the memories nearly drove Cargo to abandon the plan. He had not expected to feel bereft, severed from his own life. For a fraction of a second the longing for it all threatened to overwhelm him and Cargo stumbled against the stiff sheeting of the cradles.

No more. Never again. He had made that decision when he had turned in his wings. He wasn't a flier anymore. Just one more gambler, one more veteran demanding the dole, one more statistic to report in the flims. He had done it because that day at the Wall, looking at Two Bits' and Plato's names engraved in the rock that was all that remained of them, he had decided that it was all absurd. The whole concept of flying and killing, of combat and negotiation, became transparent in their meaninglessness.

There on Luxor was the Wall with the names of all the dead, those who had died in combat and those who had been hostages of the Cardia, those who had died of infected wounds in hospitals and those who had been executed in prison camps and those who had starved in the siege. All those names lived here on the Wall, in the shadow of the MidCenter casinos and bars, the sidewalk vendors of new annies and the Garden attendants dressed in revealing costumes, strategically located in picturesque turnings in the path. Cargo wondered once again how many of those package-tourists on Luxor had passed by the Wall without once giving it a thought. It wasn't worth it to die for the old ladies, retired and wearing pastel slacks and large buttons that said Galaxy Tours or Andreson Vacations, who pursed their lips and elbowed their way in front of him on line, who talked in voices that were too loud and cut through the background roar of the MidCenter. It wasn't worth it to die for the Garden attendants who were really politely labeled whores whose eyes were velvet soft with decadence and whose thighs were slick with greed. It wasn't worth it to die for the grubby kid in the stained striped tee shirt who had grabbed his belt in the terminal and said, "Hey, mister, gimme a stad."

So he had left his matte black wings for Plato's memory, a gift at the Wall, and he had walked away. Even now, confronted with the beauty of the multihued craft stowed in delicate-looking banks like a collection of rare butterflies, he knew he had been right. If only the desire would stop, end, with his heart torn out. Like Ghoster had torn him and Plato, who had been Beatrice Sunday. There was no question that he had done right, but the sacrifice was unfair. It boiled in him and he kept it close inside and continued to walk.

Getting in to the military sector of the Hub had been almost laughably easy. His old authorization from Intelligence's elite covert operations group, Second Directorate, gave him unquestioned access to the entire complex. And because of the Directorate's particular mission, no one questioned the fact he was out of uniform or that he requested an SBR-119 cargo transport on demand. He signed the release form as Rafael Mirabeau, the name that had been on all the military documents in his file. Django Ynglesias might have been the name his parents had given him, but the Bishop's adoption had counted for more. Especially when the name was Mirabeau and the old man had once been one of the best known and most powerful Trustees the Collegium had ever had.

And justice it was that he had to take a cargo transport for what he privately had figured was his last run. It was, after all, his namesake. Perhaps Noritane and Lowe would be amused their prediction had come true after all. They were the ones who had dubbed him Cargo way back after his first flight in a Krait, and it had stuck. Some people chose their own call signs (and Cargo suspected Stonewall fell into this category) and others were bestowed by classmates and instructors. Frequently the latter were not particularly flattering, but Cargo, like most others in his position, knew better than to buck it.

He had been trained at Kallitori in a class that had started with one hundred fifty pilot candidates and had graduated fifty. Of those fifty only twenty finally qualified in Kraits and were assigned to a squadron. Cargo had been plain old Mirabeau there, one more who hoped to make it a fancy dancer, and more than likely one more who would fail. He and Storrey Lowe had been linked in the maze the first time he had ever gotten into a Krait. It had been one of the ancient O-9 series, burned so bright that it almost glowed in the dark. Lowe was in the Eyes chair and already bitching about it.

"Gonna get the wrong idea about me," she'd griped.

"Gonna get me back here aiming Eyes and then it's all over. That's what I heard back on Mneuser and I'd bet money it's true."

"How much?" Cargo had asked a little too quickly. Lowe was one of the stars of the class, a pure natural in mode.

Storrey had laughed. "Not enough to interest you," she'd come back quickly. "Or maybe we should put down money that I got put with you to test my nerve. Nothing coming at me could possibly be as bad as what you could do in a Krait. You pull that kind of shit in a Krait like you did when we worked out on the Box and you're going to be flying cargo for the rest of your natural life."

He'd snorted, which didn't read through the maze and turned his attention to the magtracks. The Krait had responded to the force of his image and immediately began to barrel down the dark chute to the outside.

And then he was jerked backward so hard that he thought he was going to fly through the back of his seat. "Wait for authorization," the instructor's voice came through dryly.

Cargo responded with a few choice words. "No data under that heading," the maze had responded politely, the way it always did whenever he swore at it. Vaguely he wondered when someone was going to teach a maze to understand the fuller aspects of the language. Although that was stupid. The maze, after all, used only Indopean, and as an artificially constructed language there were no colorful terms. Those had all been imported from the mother tongues of all those who used Indopean together, and shared freely.

Cargo ignored the maze's ignorance and continued to recite his entire choice vocabulary in Russian, Greek, and Romany. One of Noritane's tricks, no doubt. The tracks were supposed to be locked until authorization was granted to an entire flight. That had been on page one of the current manual, a work Cargo read with the respect and dedication the Bishop gave his Bible. Not that it would do any good to remind the instructor of that. Cargo had long ago decided that Noritane's job consisted mainly of finding ways to flunk student officers out of the program. Teaching them something about Kraits, about combat, about how to dance, to fly exo on three axis and stay alive, was definitely secondary in Noritane's book.

He had waited for the all-clear to sound through the chatterbox for what seemed like half the morning. But when something did come it was Noritane again, this time meaner than usual. "You waiting for an engraved invitation?" the instructor inquired, and Cargo had no trouble visualizing his sneer in the coordinating office.

This time he checked his anger and went through procedure carefully preparing for track launch. That was all, launch and landing, for the first time out. They had waited on the track longer than they were exo.

When he got back, he realized that Noritane must have been listening in. "You ever do that again, lunchmeat, you're going to fly cargo for the rest of your career." Quoting Lowe, who'd always had a mouth on her.

It had stuck. By dinnertime everyone in the group was calling him Cargo. Rafael Mirabeau had been annihilated by a few well-chosen phrases.

And now, after his career was well and truly over, he was going to fly cargo for the first time. There was some kind of poetic justice to it, he figured, but he couldn't really see it. If Plato were here she'd smile and point it out if he asked. Or just be quiet with that knowing glow in her Bishop-grey eyes.

"Hangar nine, bay three one one," a young technician in spec stripes informed him. "All set to go, sir. Clearance waits."

"Thanks," Cargo said, smiling. He wondered if the wideness in the tech's eyes was for the Second Directorate or just the change in routine. Had to be the Directorate, he decided as he walked down past the bays of transport. Covert glances from the men and women, Akhaid and human working on various craft, followed him. He never caught their eyes, only the too-sudden glance back down and away. The Directorate had that effect. Most people half believed that the whole of Intel was mythological. They shrank from the ordinariness of the individual who was part of that shadowy organization, pretending not to see that Cargo was only about average height and the unconscious arrogance of his expression was exactly the same as they saw every day in every pilot who danced vac.

He found the transport easily enough. The system at Contrato was no different than it was at any base or on any military station. The vessel, though, took him back.

Cargo was supposedly rated on the transport, had passed his

check flight in that before he had ever even seen a Krait up close. That didn't mean he had any recent hours in one. Which only proved the strength of the Second Directorate once again. He shouldn't be permitted to sign solo on a craft without a hundred hours in the past year, and since he had joined the batwing he hadn't seen the insides of a Krait, let alone a clunker like the thing he was going to take out-manifold.

Maybe Stonewall was right. A nice easy ride on a commercial cruiser to Zhai Bau, no fuss no worry. And no flying, none of the freedom of the void. Even a clunker was better than nothing. Besides, Stonewall was qualified as a pilot, but he wasn't a flyer by blood. Cargo was certain he didn't break into a smile every time he broke exo, more at home in the jaunty color-burned dancing suit than with his feet on the ground. Stonewall didn't understand.

Cargo climbed into the pit and dry swallowed two Three-B's to open the link between the maze and the DNA chips planted at the base of his skull. At least he still had his own helmet, the microwave link specifically calibrated to his personal preference, more delicate and responsive than the common stock.

And then his mind blossomed, flowing into cybermode with the alacrity of desire.

Mode felt different, unbalanced, as if something were missing. He could taste/see/know the maze-brain of the ship and the computer complex beneath it, responsible for the physical body of the vessel. Only the scent of the Akhaid was missing, the faintly irritating alien touch that had meshed in with all the other components to become the single force that was a batwing. But Ghoster was gone. The bereavement hit Cargo fresh, the unaccustomed unalien maze too sterile for the pleasure that was flight.

He pushed the realization aside. There was no time to waste and he was a professional with a job to do. Coldly he closed his mind to the absence of Ghoster and went through the checklist with his full attention. It was a little different from the checklists he knew so well, Krait and batwing alike. The maze had to prompt and Cargo followed, focus forced completely on the task at hand.

Then the magtracks opened, energy rippling down the double lines. The transport was poised, ready, and then a thought on the surface of Cargo's mind sent them hurtling out into the void.

Fully meshed with the ship's systems, Cargo wove through the Hub traffic by rote. For the first time since he had left the batwing he knew he was fully alive. Reality was the harsh demands of exo, of the maze keyed in to his mind, even the Three-B's racing through his body that he suspected were responsible for the edge of rapture that could so easily seduce him from courage to recklessness.

He permitted himself the merest tease of ecstasy before icing down his feelings to professional calm. It had been a long time since he had taken a craft out-manifold and even with the maze prompting it took his full concentration. The maze could calculate entrance and exit points but it took a mind with visual imagination to guide the ship through.

Cargo had enough book knowledge of the way the manifold worked to have passed his ground examination, which meant the whole thing was completely theoretical to him. He knew that the universe was twisted into a shape describable only by the most arcane mathematics and that the drive used the Other Six dimensions as the particle strings that *were* all that composed reality oscillated through to break the fragile foam-like microstructure of the universe.

Usually Cargo hated to be out-manifold. Usually he distrusted the blank unformed space that did not exactly contain his vessel. Usually he took his frustration out on piles of paperwork that never seemed to get done. This time the out-manifold was merely neutral, because this time when he reentered his own universe it would be in enemy territory.

Stonewall reported to the boarding bay for *Andronika* with a slightly sour stomach and a metallic taste in his mouth. The blazing bimbos in the First Directorate were right as usual. It had taken maybe fifteen minutes of computer time to fake the death of Rafael Mirabeau in a stolen military transport, and register the unregarded passing of one Django Ynglesias, Walker. Walkers were dying all the time. It was what they did best.

But now Stonewall was going to have to say something to his superiors. He had not wanted this assignment, not the way it was given to him in the Fourth. There were things even the

Directorate of counterespionage did not know about Greydon Beauford Randolph, III. There were things he didn't know about himself, even, as he had discovered over espresso and bad napoleons in the Hub. Like he was ready to disobey orders for the first time. That much as he might despise Cargo, he still counted as a comrade in arms, a buddy, the way the stinking math-brass didn't. So he had gone along with Cargo's scheme even though it violated all his training and some of his common sense.

Gantor had tasked him. Stonewall had been called in to that impressive wood and leather office in the unmarked building opposite the Department of Health and Hospitals on the Collegium itself. Oz Gantor, as Prefect of the Fourth Directorate, would normally never even meet someone like Stonewall. Indeed, Stonewall had been more than a little shocked to find out that Gantor was short, overweight, and had the bad habit of fidgeting with an expensive personalized gold pen. There was nothing military or even vaguely Intel about him. Stonewall suddenly realized that he was facing a political appointee, a bureaucrat who had served his time, picked the right friends, and successfully defended his turf.

Almost eight years of a career with the Fourth Directorate had been washed out in a tenth of a second. Before Gantor even opened his mouth Stonewall had lost his faith once more. In other circumstances he would have resigned there and then, the way he had with the church, but he was already committed to whatever this overstuffed cretin wanted.

No, not a cretin, he reminded himself rigorously. Never underestimate a person because he is fat or dresses poorly and clearly is no gentleman. Rabble trash can still be dangerous, sly, his daddy had told him, and his daddy had been right more than not. No, Grey Randolph, Jr. had made certain not only that his boy was a gentleman but that he never trust anyone not approved by Charleston tradition as well. It was a gift for which Stonewall had never adequately thanked him.

So he had sat in the tufted brown leather wing chair and listened while the Prefect of the Fourth Directorate spoke in a thin voice. "Of course, if you can take care of the Akhaid, do so. I certainly wouldn't want to discourage you. However, that is not the major objective of this mission, as I see it. You know that Mirabeau elder, the Bishop Andre Michel Mirabeau, that is, is currently involved in negotiations with the peace faction of the Cardia. Your job is to eliminate the younger Mirabeau, Rafael. You already know him as Cargo, I think. You can use the excuse of the Akhaid Ghoster if you want to."

"May I inquire as to why I should eliminate someone who until this time has been nothing but an admirable Collegium patriot?" Stonewall asked, careful to keep his tone casual.

Gantor smiled and, for the first time in his entire life, Stonewall knew stark terror. He had been afraid before, many times, had seen himself dead or dying in the service and displeasing his daddy, which was worse. He had known different forms of fear in many unrelated circumstances, but he had never before been faced with the danger of losing his self-respect. That was most horrible than all the Eyes and all the batwings and all the spies he could imagine. People who played the game usually played clean.

Gantor's smile was not clean. It was an invitation to the kind of political intrigue that, centuries earlier, a Randolph would have been so angry to be even considered for that a perfectly white glove would be lying on the desk before the smile faded. Stonewall deeply regretted the fact that dueling with such overt weapons as pistols was no longer in vogue.

"I suppose it might be to your benefit," Gantor said, his voice as sly as his face. "Naturally, officially, the government wants peace. Mirabeau's faction has been using that for leverage ever since the Bishop left the Trustee Palace. What you might not realize is that Mirabeau caused the break in the first place. His first adopted son was Ki Shodar's brother. It seems reasonable that this Rafael was adopted and trained for the same reason Aliadro was. To manipulate various factions to keep the Mirabeau on top."

Stonewall managed a nod. He had heard several versions of this story before.

"The fact is, a settlement with the Cardia will only enhance the influence of the Mirabeau. As a matter of fact, there is a Vice Minister of Defense, a character named Agular, who is one of the Bishop's lackeys. The Padaron faction, though, have nothing at all to gain from a peace. Most of their resources are tied up with military contracts, and do you know how many people would be out of work if even a tenth of those contracts were rescinded? And it is the Padaron who have given the most support to Intel. If it weren't for the Trustees Chaing and Stanos, we would still be a little back office in Defense that no one ever listened to. Instead, here we are at the center of power."

Stonewall wanted to say that a building across from Health and Hospitals was hardly the center of power, but managed to restrain himself. Not because he was afraid of the consequences, but because he had made a decision. Or rather, the decision had been made and now the means had been presented to him.

The fact that pistols at dawn was now considered rather passé had nothing to do with demanding satisfaction. The honor of the entire Randolph family had been offended. Stonewall could not let that pass. It was not in his genes or his heritage to ignore the insult Oz Gantor had offered him.

The Prefect dismissed him, with instructions that further information would be delivered through the usual channels. Stonewall had smiled and left. But somehow he managed to lose one of his uniform gloves in the deep pile carpet under a very elegant leather wing chair.

Chapter
3

Breaking sky over Marcanter took all Cargo's concentration. He had come endo here twice before, once in a batwing that the Cardia forces couldn't detect and the second time with an invited diplomatic mission. Obviously they had spotted the transport well before Cargo even got close to endo, but he hadn't seen any recce. That rattled him just a little. There was still a state of war last time he looked. Nothing should approach this close without a once-over at least.

Don't fight luck, he told himself, and brushed the holy medal he always wore. Only experience and suspicion told him that if this was luck, it was the wrong kind.

Even with that faint anomaly nagging at him, Cargo set up the approach the way he had decided with the maze during the blank time out-manifold. There were two major continents on Marcanter, the maze had informed him. The larger eastern one had been settled from the beginning and contained three major and five minor cities, as well as most of the industry. This was where he'd taken the Bishop for his peace talks. The other was where he and Ghoster had infiltrated the Cardia stealth group on one of the largest installations Cargo had ever seen.

After a good bit of deliberation Cargo had chosen the eastern continent. It was where he had last seen Ghoster, so if there was any trail it would start there. Besides, Cargo didn't think that Ghoster would be likely to try and join the Cardia forces.

Higher probability that he was already deep in Akhaid territory,
protected by the Walker faction. At least, that was what Cargo
called it to himself, partly as a reminder that it was misinfor-
mation that created them and not malice.

He had wanted to follow a dodge-and-dart pattern for
entering enemy territory that he had learned in Intel, but the
transport maze simply denied any ability to comprehend the
maneuver. It had not been built for combat and refused to react
as if it had. Finally he had settled on a standard commercial
approach, not because he wanted to. The maze suggested other
alternatives that it was prepared to implement and none of them
were even close to reasonable. Cargo hoped that a transport
following a commercial pattern would simply fade into the
background. Every monitor would pick it up and none would
judge it hostile. He hoped. The one major advantage he had
was that the Cardia had only split fifteen years ago and most
classes of spacecraft were pretty standard, Cardia and Collegium alike. Or at least the differences were minor enough to
be local variations.

That was what the First Directorate had released and what
Cargo had studied when he was in the batwing. Now he only
hoped it was true. He wasn't sure he trusted the First
Directorate anymore. After all, hadn't they been the ones
overseeing everything else? First Directorate had all the data
everyone else gathered. Weren't they the ones who had told
Stonewall where he was? Certainly it wasn't the paranoid
counter-intelligence agents of the Fourth Directorate. Unless
Fourways had had something to say about that.

Now, though, he was closing in. He could see the distortion
of the atmosphere halo around the planet, the clouds soft and
white over an expanse of tumultuous ocean. The storms on
Marcanter weren't quite as bad as the winds of Vanity where he
had learned all the tricks of currents and drift and lift and drag,
but only because there wasn't any place as bad as Vanity. He
stiffened slightly, thinking about cutting endo, the angle of
burn, and how to catch the lift on stubby wings.

The transport was not really designed for flying sky. It
could, but only because everything could, at least theoretically.
Some politician who owed a favor several centuries ago had
made that law. Any craft, no matter if it was never supposed to
get near an atmosphere, had to be at least minimally air-

worthy. For safety reasons, it was stated. And still was. No matter that the law made no sense, especially designing the great carriers that were small planetoids in themselves (those had been reclassified as proto-base colonies in order to avoid the ruling). It also meant extra expense, more equipment, and more things that could go wrong. Like most pilots, Cargo did not consider the nearly vestigial avionics of the majority of spacecraft to qualify them as truly transatmospheric. The batwing had been the real thing, but it was one of a kind. The transport clearly was not.

He formed an image of the approach angle clearly. The maze balked and jibbered at him. It really wasn't made to cut endo, it didn't want to trust the stunted wings to carry the craft, didn't trust Cargo enough to risk burn.

He was tempted to swear at it, berate it, and then put it under his authority by force. Damn all mazes anyway, and damn their programmers who were responsible for such civilized indispositions. Instead of whipping it he tried to seduce the machine. Centered in its heart, Cargo thought of the joys of flying sky, of riding the winds on the high plains of Vanity with the abandon of an amusement park ride. Images flowed almost tripping on each other, each more tempting than the last. Cargo got lost in them, in his own memories and the sensations he had experienced so briefly in the batwing, the immense exaltation of skill that was only matched by combat.

He dangled glory glittering and the maze took the bait. They committed to burn, and then pierced the soft gaseous corona that could be so deadly.

It burned. The maze reacted at first with surprise. Cargo had overridden logic and consideration of friction and stress. The transport's hull, pristine vacuum virgin, began to take on the hues of experience. Burning titanium flared violet, magenta, hot blue, and finally chromium yellow as the transport pierced atmosphere for the first time and rode it down.

It was not a comfortable ride. Cargo was slammed back into the less than well padded seat. The restraints around his waist and chest pulled fiercely. Though he hated the webbing used in combat craft with a passion, Cargo missed it here. He was not well secured and his forearms were thrown hard against the rests, then slammed against the bulkheads. Only the mode collar held his head in place and he was grateful for the necessity of linked contact with the maze. Otherwise he was sure his neck would have snapped from the rattling he was getting. Every bone was bounced and sore, and Cargo knew that it wasn't going to be easy to climb out of the cockpit.

This craft has not been fully tested in atmospheric conditions, the maze informed him.

Cargo had to suppress an urge to laugh unpleasantly at this useless information. Someone had made damn sure that the maze had its priorities exactly upside down. Too much personality was not exactly welcome. Only one being could dominate a craft, and it had damn well better be the pilot. Dancing vac or sky, there could be no democracy in the cockpit.

Fuel down to one-seven. At current consumption rate we have two hours of atmosphere or seventeen hours vac. Instruct.

Cargo drew a deep breath. An unhappy maze was an annoyance. The reported level of fuel consumption was a disaster. In two hours he could barely hope to locate an adequate landing strip, let alone bring the ungainly transport in at the proper angle and set it down on gear that had probably never been checked, let alone used.

Two hours. He slammed his fists against the arm rests. Why the hell hadn't the maze told him earlier?

Insufficient data on fuel consumption in atmosphere, it replied to his clearly thought inquiry.

Anger vied with cold logic in Cargo's mind. After the batwings, with their broad curved wings designed to glide for kilometers on the barest trace of fuel, the transport was quickly devolving in Cargo's mind from barely functional to political pork barrel. Only the coldness won. He had too many years of combat, too much sheer arrogance in his own skill, and too much of a desire to live to let the craft rule him. Deep in the maze, he didn't know that his face had a nasty smile.

He thought gently to the maze, reassuring himself as well as the interface, and brought the craft down as abruptly as he could without losing control. The transport plummeted out of the sky like a gaudy inert buzzard diving for prey. Cargo lost his breath and then slowly began to ease up the nose, pushing against the force of the high thermals. Air pressure was his enemy and his friend. Deep in mode, unified with the actual shell of the transport, he could feel the atmosphere pressing down like a hand.

The transport fell. Time distorted into speed and then there was no time at all. Cargo's peripheral vision began to darken, then blotted out. A black tunnel appeared in front of his eyes, narrowing slowly. He was blacking out, he knew, and for the moment he didn't care. If this was dying, then it was very easy. No fear, no pain, only the black tunnel growing, the light at the end dissolving into a single point. In the center of the fury Cargo was perfectly calm.

Almost lazily he accepted the transport's downward plunge. He had seen something like it once at an air show when he was a boy, he remembered. Only in the aerobatics demonstration the pilot had managed to twist the craft around so that it was falling trailfirst.

He remembered watching this unable to breathe, the Bishop at his side shaking his head. Then, almost miraculously, the craft had turned, rolled, and flew on. A hammerhead, the announcer had said, and the audience had responded with polite applause.

He could see the movement with a clarity that he had rarely experienced. There was a kind of joy in the memory, a single thing that had been beautiful and pure and painless for the moment before he lost consciousness.

The tunnel became blacker and Cargo could feel the blood puddling in his abdomen and legs. They didn't issue poopy suits with transports and he hadn't thought to ask. After all, he'd flown without one on Vanity more than once. Necessary part of training, Fourways had said. Just in case. And this was the case.

Under him, around him, the transport shuddered and fought into a spin. Up, reversed, just like . . .

He made the image of the air show once again, instructing the maze carefully, reinforcing every point. It fought with him, not pulling against pressure but falling, permitting the spin to get wilder, more dangerous. Only it couldn't be more dangerous, Cargo realized.

The maze had not been built for aerobatics. Neither had the transport, and somewhere at the edge of consciousness Cargo knew that the hull couldn't stand the stress. The metal shell would reach yield and collapse. Still, that way he could be no more dead than he already was. He taught it, held the instructions firm, not because he thought it would help but because it was better to do something, no matter how idiotic.

The brilliance at the end of the tunnel became a mere pinprick of light. Then it began to fade. He could feel his body being tossed against the restraints as the transport struggled to obey, but he couldn't feel any bruising. His body felt far away, like pain, and already gone. The darkness closed, warm and soft and calm against the tumult of the sky. Cargo wondered at it briefly, then accepted it. The Bishop had been right all along.

Query. Landing, query. One hour seven minutes fuel. Conserving.

Cargo blinked rapidly. Under the extreme smoothness of the ride he could sense the microvibrations of the engine. The maze requested landing data yet again, updating the fuel situation.

Disoriented, he looked around. He was in the transport and there was Marcanter below him. Not so far below anymore, either. The plunge and hammerhead combined to bring him within range to spot a likely place. It took a moment for him to clear his head finally, and then Cargo realized what must have happened.

The transport maze wasn't nearly as hyped as the Krait or the batwing. When he had blacked out it had followed through on his orders. A miracle that it had been able to do so.

"Scan," he thought into the maze, instructing it to monitor several Cardia frequencies. Reluctantly it obeyed.

For the first few moments there was nothing. Cargo looked through the canopy to the ground below. He was over a large red-colored plateau. Desert or cropland he couldn't tell, only that it went on nearly forever. At the edge of the horizon stood a single structure. From this distance Cargo couldn't tell what it was, only that it was exceptionally high.

He swept his eyes over the red once again, then focused back to the surrounding sky, scanning automatically for birds. One of the biggest problems on Vanity had been birds crashing into the canopy of a batwing. Nothing could be done about it, and the situation was almost embarrassing. All that technology knocked out of the air by something with the intelligence of an earthworm.

Looking for bird-spots, he noted them only subliminally at the very edge of his awareness. Then they closed on both sides, tiny jeweled darts in the expanse of sky. Fighters. They had him flanked, outrun, and outmaneuvered.

Cargo demanded the message from the maze furiously. There had to be some communication. Besides, he could not believe that he had survived that insane fall only to die in a more premeditated manner.

"Identify yourself," came through, translated into the voice of the maze by the machinery.

Cargo sighed. Now it was time to begin. "Kore Verdun," he answered, "native of Marcanter. And I'm in bad shape. Less than an hour of fuel with any safety margin and this thing is a pig in the sky."

Even the maze couldn't mask the surprise of the reply. "Holy fucking Deckmejian. This isn't some kind of joke, is it? Because you are in big trouble, buddy, no matter how much fuel you have. Kore Verdun? Jesus. We're taking you in to the base."

There was no option but to obey. The Cardia fighters were shepherding him in tight formation on the one hand, and on the other he didn't have enough fuel to evade even if he could have slipped out from under their guns.

The tall building marked the edge of a superstrip. Not even the shepherd guards worried Cargo more than landing the transport. Between burn and approach he still hadn't bled off enough speed to avoid an impressive fireworks show if he had to pull a slide.

The maze remained slightly smug, and only got more so as the landing gear moved effortlessly into place. The one piece of real luck he'd had, Cargo thought, and then guided the transport down.

Even as they came to rest on the edge of the strip facing the building the two fighters flanked Cargo's craft. There wasn't much power down in the transport, and besides, it was ringed by security guards. Not that he knew the uniform, but the stance and polish and weapons were identification enough. Language and culture and political affiliation didn't change those marks of authority.

He closed his eyes gently against the glare. Down here somewhere the Bishop was talking to the Cardia peace faction, trying to set up a cease-fire. Somewhere else Ghoster was either holed up or had left a trail. Somewhere on the surface of Marcanter Stonewall was due to arrive. And somewhere on the Western Continent on the Cardia batwing base was a squad he had joined for a single flight, the very first time he had ever been Kore Verdun.

And now it was right. The transport should have fallen from the sky, crashed in a glory of flame and killed him. Only by a miracle was he alive, and Cargo had to acknowledge the fairness of it. Here on Marcanter he was being born again. Kore Verdun was becoming real, taking shape in the shell of those who had died in the transport accident. Or should have died. It made no difference. Only that he had died and been resurrected and that being reborn he should be new.

New name, new identity, new allegiance even. Cargo only wished it had come with a new past. No matter what name was his now he couldn't blot out the people he had loved and the enemies who had killed them, and the fact that sometimes they were the same. Not even the spin in the transport, the escort down to Marcanter, whatever they could do to him here, none of that could erase the past.

Knowing that, feeling all his *mule* around him, Cargo left the transport and placed himself under arrest.

"Holy fucking Deckmejian, you were supposed to be dead! I mean, we figured you had to be. No properly filed prisoner report or nothing, it was pretty obvious. But where's your Eyes?"

Cargo shook his head and smiled. It had taken a minute but he had remembered the man's name. Mike Allen. One of the Cardia batwings he had flown with. Now Mike looked totally bemused.

The visit had been a shock. He hadn't really thought that any of them would be here, let alone remember. Or rather, he had hoped they wouldn't. It was hard enough to create a persona without having to fit in with the memories of the dry run. He'd only met three of the Cardia batwings, fair chance that he'd never run into them again, and here was Mike all decked out in the very pale blue of the Cardia's forces. The only thing that indicated his stealth training were his wings. Exactly like those of the Collegium, they were painted out an almost infinite matte black that recalled the void.

Besides, it was bad enough to be in a detention cell. The hard light glanced off the shiny walls and burned his eyes. Conventional detention dress consisted of puke green pajamas and paper slippers. The whole point was humiliation. Cargo understood that perfectly well, but knowledge didn't make it any less effective.

Having Mike see him in this state made it worse.

Mike had made it clear from the start that he had just been assigned back to here at Hoyle to train the incoming batwing class. "Finally got production of these babies up to where we need a regular training program and I got stuck at the desk. Assistant commander of the program, no less."

"Congratulations," Cargo had replied, smiling. "So you're out of the action."

Mike winced and Cargo knew he'd touched sensitive ground. "Not much choice," Mike had said, then tapped his right leg. In the uniform it didn't look different from the left.

"What happened?"

Allen just shook his head and smiled sadly. "How the hell did you manage to get out? And where's your Eyes?" he asked again.

Cargo had told the story to the interrogators twice already. For one sickening moment he wondered if Allen had been called down specially to play the "soft" role and reveal whatever they thought he could be hiding. Then he dismissed the whole idea. There wasn't anything about Mike's visit that wasn't perfectly reasonable. And besides, he'd have to tell the story to someone other than interrogators sooner or later.

He had made it up in the time it had taken to walk from the transport into the single base establishment and be introduced to the Security Chief. No one else, Cargo thought, really could have done so well in so little time. Training counted. A boy who could steal C. L. Wong's yacht, who had made the holotapes for the crystal ball, that person could tell a story the authorities would believe. After all, he was Sister Mary's son, and she was the best *boojo* woman among all the Tshurara tribe. Con artistry was in his genes.

He leaned back against the white tile wall and tilted his head back, as if remembering. "I don't know where the Ghoster is," he started honestly, his voice echoing spectacularly in the confined space. It was the last completely honest statement he made. Old Pulika had taught him that lying was a great art and he must be worthy of it, to delicately weave the fabric of story on the stretch loom of fact. *Always use the facts you can,* Old Pulika had told him. *Then it is easier to remember, and easier to convince yourself that it is true. That is the real secret. If you can believe the story when you speak it, it will be true at the time. Not even the scan will dislodge it. If you can really believe.*

"I guess you know that we were captured in that sneak attack. The Scorp was damaged, the aft converters gone, and holes in the wings like Swiss cheese. Picked us up and packed us into that carrier. The *Horn,* the name of it was. Horn and Hardart they called it. They separated us from the Akhaid, then broke it down again." Cargo let his voice develop a slight hitch and gazed blankly at the white wall. "Wasn't like this, when they brought us to Mnueser. That was the base. I remember it. Big. Huge, even. There was an entire quadrant that was a prison camp. Holding camp, actually, for interrogation. After that nobody knew. You got sent somewhere in the Collegium. Or maybe killed. There were all kinds of stories. Most of them were worse. I didn't believe most of them, either. I mean, it would be stupid to use us for labor. Sabotage is too easy. And I really don't think they'd kill prisoners, not with the Neutrals Oversight Committee around, especially not if they ever hope to come to terms. It just didn't make sense. Only on low rations and all crowded together and not knowing when they were coming for you, sense wasn't what it used to be either.

"You know, the very worst was that we couldn't really stay clean. That's the whole base of civilization, I sometimes think. Only one room with ten toilets and three sinks that didn't work half the time. And two showers, no soap, no towels. It's hard to keep your self-respect, to remember you're an officer, a technician, a sentient being when you can't sit down to eat with your hands because they don't give you any utensils and there's a layer of muck on your palms. The first couple of times you cringe and wait until you're starving. After that you hardly notice.

"The interrogators behaved like we were less than human because we stank, even if it was their fault."

"But how did you get out?" Mike asked, trying to turn the conversation.

Cargo sighed softly. The camp conditions business was pretty standard anyway. He'd hardly had to elaborate on anything there. He'd seen enough when he was stationed out of Mnueser on the *Torque* anyway. The rest of it was a carefully embroidered version of how he'd stolen C. L. Wong's yacht.

"It wasn't really that hard. The whole camp was oriented to keep us from escaping from the base. Getting to the base was almost a joke. I mean, I think they maybe even set it up that way. Rations details, to and from the interrogation areas, the whole thing was poorly guarded. And the guards never got real close and tried to turn away as much as they could. Not that I blamed them.

"The whole idea seemed to be that if we couldn't leave the base there wouldn't be any trouble. I mean, where could we go? I guess they don't get a whole lot of pilots there, or else they might have thought about the setup a little better, you know? So it was easy enough to get on ration detail, hauling garbage wrappers out to the reclaimant plant. And faded away.

"I knew I couldn't leave the base with all the Eye beams and everything else, but that wasn't where I was headed. There were hundreds and hundreds of repair sheds on Mnueser. I mean, there must have been nearly twenty square kilometers or so, and crews going all the time."

Actually, Cargo knew the exact dimensions of the Krait yard on Mnueser, twenty-seven square kilometers including licks, and the exact number of Kraits serviced every three days, which was three thousand two hundred thirty-one, on average.

"Well, you know that whole area can't be patrolled. And there's more than enough space to hide. So, to keep a long story short, I found this transport and took it out and here I am."

Mike raised an eyebrow. "No problem getting out?"

Cargo's smile was more genuine this time, which both fit the story and the way he felt. After all, there had to be a little brag in a good story.

"I'm a Scorp, right? Even that goddamn ration can pig of a transport can look like a test run, right? Got everything together, the bubble gum will hold a couple more runs. Come on, get creative."

He glanced over at Allen once more and shrugged. "So when you think I'm getting out of this joint? Gonna spring me like you did from the hospital?"

Allen shook his head. "Don't hate Security near as much as Medical. Besides, once they pull your file there won't be any problem."

And Mike Allen had left. Cargo thought about the visit for a while, turning the whole thing over in his mind, tasting it from various angles. He couldn't be sure, but he really thought they maybe had sent Allen to break his story. Or something else, only Cargo couldn't think what. His head was pounding miserably from hot light and glare and exhaustion. Exhaustion finally won and he was able to block out the worst of the light by throwing his arm over his face. He didn't even realize that he had done so before he fell asleep.

He didn't wake up until the third time they called his name. He cursed himself for it, too. He hadn't prepared well enough. Old Pulika had taught him that people will automatically wake at the sound of their names and that it was a good way to make sure someone was telling the truth. Only it didn't look like the guard who was waiting in the corridor had ever heard that theory.

The Eye bands across the tile access were dark grey. Off. Cargo didn't question it. He followed the guard past the room where his previous interrogations had taken place and found himself deposited in a working office. The furniture was battered and functionally grey. No care had been taken to impress either visitors or those who worked here.

Three of the four desks were empty. A woman in pale blue with shiny wings sat in the corner staring at the one working terminal. He prayed Stonewall hadn't been joking about setting up a history for Kore Verdun.

"Oh, Verdun," she said, not glancing up. "Allen told us to pull your record, and you know the bastard was right. Looks like you've got just the profile to pull that shit on the Collegium. Great stuff. You're out of here. And even Shodar is interested in meeting you. Hero shit and all that jazz. Don't take it too seriously. You've got a whole lot of leave coming to you and a nice bit of back pay plus combat bonus plus an additional award for I don't know what."

Her fingers flew over the screen and a dysfunctional-looking printer that had been old well before Ki Shodar had ever thought of the Cardia hiccuped a couple of times. The woman shrugged, walked over, and nonchalantly kicked it. The noises that emerged sounded something like a protest, and then the official pink flim papers began to emerge as if the machine were reluctant to part with them.

"Everything you need to know is here in triplicate," the woman said, smiling. "Sign all three copies and give me two and get your ass over to the bar."

"Only three copies?" Cargo asked innocently. "Not fifteen?"

The woman laughed and he signed, leaning on one of the unoccupied desks. He skimmed the papers, winked at the woman, and Kore Verdun left the complex, born for the second and only real time.

Chapter 4

None of it was what he expected. There had been stories of Ki Shodar living in some great deep vac palace surrounded by exotic gardens and even more exotic "aides." But if those stories had any grain of truth to them, it surely wasn't reflected here on Marcanter.

Unlike the pure classical proportions of the Trustee Palace of the Collegium or the imperial fist of the stadiats sprinkled liberally through the colonies, Ki Shodar's official residence and headquarters on Marcanter was at the very least unimposing, a square, unwindowed box, an unpainted bunker set precisely in the center of an unrelieved lawn. Marcanter boasted finer homes and more impressive public buildings, the local library being currently eclipsed by the new technical middle school in popular opinion. Even the bunker's ugliness was unremarkable.

Like the Cardia, like Marcanter itself, the Deckmejian ideology invaded even the cracks between the spaces so that all that was left was plain to the point of hostility. Suffering was good, the Deckmejians said. Suffering was the whole and paid the price of entitlement.

All Cargo knew was that he found the city depressing. He wished he'd at least had a glimpse of the MidCenter, Spin Street, any of the cheap and lively sectors that catered to the older pleasures at a basic, if unrefined, level. Even on

Marcanter such places existed, but on the street in front of
Shodar's official headquarters he suddenly doubted he wanted
to spend much time on the local entertainments.

He was escorted down the rigidly geometrical white path to
the plain titanium doors burned a solid, uninspired indigo. It
took real work to burn a color that avoided any hint of
brilliance; long, long hours had gone into layer after layer of
spray to make sure no spot hinted of magenta or fuchsia for
being too thinly treated.

His guard changed twice as he was led through utilitarian
corridors. He could feel his heart and his throat grow dry.
Somewhere behind one of those doors sat the one being he
knew was the most evil in the entire manifold. Evil, and mad.
Ki Shodar.

It was not, the Bishop had explained carefully, exactly
Shodar's fault. The splice-life group had intended only the
highest good, the merging of the best creative levels of humans
and Akhaid. It had taken the group more than twenty years to
learn the technique, and then work had begun in earnest.
Genetic material from six individuals of each species had been
used, people of exceptional genius all. The first wave of the
experiment were all going to be brothers and raised apart to test
various theories, as well as let each of them exercise their full
range of creativity.

Of the eight embryos created in glass dishes, only half
survived long enough to bury. One died less than three months
after "birth" and another of strange complications at the age of
twelve. The two who lived long enough to become adults had
broken their isolation, become allies and maybe friends, and
fought a revolution. And won.

Then one was, according to official sources, assassinated.
Aliadro Mirabeau had been found with his eyes gouged out and
his throat cut. Ki Shodar, the last survivor of the experiments,
vowed revenge. And had it.

Shodar himself had led the raid on Luxor with a handpicked
team of his revolutionary forces, killing hostages in front of the
flim teams with butcher knives. Shodar had said they were
lucky they didn't pull out the hostages' eyes first.

After Luxor, any schoolchild could recite the rest. How
Shodar had used the Deckmejian Heresy and his own blooded
troops to pull the Cardia into line. The Cardia Group had

always been a little apart, separated not only by philosophy but by history, waves of colonization, and language. Indopean was not a necessary evil, a common construct language among them. It was anathema. The Cardia had legally made Greek their official language. That was the only policy Aliadro Mirabeau had ever made.

Shodar must have recognized that the Cardia was very close to splitting from the Collegium at that point, the Bishop had said softly. A single individual can take charge of a historical imperative and mold it. But he cannot create it. If Shodar had been born a century earlier it would never have happened. But history creates its own vehicles, Mirabeau said. Then he had opened a bottle of wine and poured silently.

It had been during one of their usual meetings that the old man had told Cargo all this, had explained that it was not the individual alone, but that person's interaction with the whole of history that created greatness. And he had used that word carefully, Cargo remembered, and smiled when he said that maybe great evil is less to be despised than nothingness, even if that was the rationale of Lucifer's fall.

Cargo could almost taste the crispness of the wine, his first experience with a Sancerre, and see the gleaming white tablecloth turning softly pink in the sunset that flooded the window of the Bishop's study. There had been something strangely distant about Mirabeau that time, and it was the first time Cargo had been able to see age in the old man's eyes.

"I knew them, you know," the Bishop had said quietly, mournfully, as if he were half a ghost already.

"I knew Aliadro from the time he was maybe ten, maybe eleven. It was hard to tell, the way the combination worked. They were beautiful and horrible at the same time, but I didn't think that way about Aliadro when I met him. He was just a little boy, and alone.

"And Shodar, Ki Shodar I first met at Aliadro's funeral. A beautiful funeral, for a Hero of the State I believe they called it, with music and elegies and millions of flowers. It was hot and humid and the flowers stank like death on the heavy air.

"That was the first time I met him, but not the last."

The Bishop hadn't said any more and Cargo didn't ask. He'd heard enough on the streets, remembered enough from the news, and he was a bright youngster. He had put it together easily enough. Besides, he knew Andre Michel Mirabeau, knew what he believed in and the simple courage of his decisions. To his adopted son's knowledge, Bishop Mirabeau had never moved on a principle in his life. And it was this courage more than anything else that had impressed the youngster, had made him want to emulate the old man. Rafael Mirabeau had never known a person of principle before meeting the Bishop. And, from his experience since, had concluded they were even more rare than he had supposed. The Bishop, and Ghoster, who had betrayed him and their friendship for a principle. According to current theorists, Ki Shodar was also a man of principle.

Cargo smirked to himself. The Rom found the whole idea laughable, but the Rom had never been a people to fight grimly to the death of millions for some point of honor or belief. If Shodar and the Bishop and Ghoster had all been Rom, they would be sitting on an overstuffed cut-velvet sofa drinking perovka and laughing over what a fine stunt it had all been. Perhaps principles weren't the best thing for a being to have. Except, Cargo acknowledged ruefully, he had his own. And he was facing Ki Shodar because he wanted to save a friend. No matter that Ghoster had tried to kill him. That was something Cargo understood. No, it was because Cargo was Rom and friendship was sacred.

The guard indicated a door and rapped sharply. Cargo heard no answer, but found himself propelled in anyway, before he could fully consider that he was about to face the being that was responsible for more death and misery than anyone else in the past five hundred years.

The room was so deeply shadowed that it took Cargo some time to adjust to the lack of light. Then he noticed that, while functional, the whole created an ambiance both rich and cruel. Nothing about the place indicated that it was the office of a head of state and the leader of armies. The atmosphere reminded him more of the *ofisa* he had grown up in, elegant in the cloying dark but dusty and tattered in sunlight.

A pool table dominated the center of the space. It was a fine one, solid as the bunker itself and gleaming with the polish of use. Balls were scattered over the thick green felt randomly, as if someone had broken only minutes before and had not set up another shot.

"Do you play?"

The voice came out of the shadows and focused Cargo's attention on the being. Now that he looked, he found it amazing that he hadn't noticed Shodar immediately. The Cardia leader's silver-tinged Akhaid skin seemed to absorb all the illumination in the room, directing it all inward, hoarding.

At first Shodar appeared entirely Akhaid. The reflective quasi-scaling of the skin and the whiteless eyes owed nothing to any human genes. The normal Akhaid body-type, lean to emaciation in human terms, was in Shodar's case reminiscent of whip cables and wild dogs only lightly restrained. The tension that seemed to hold his body together seemed to create an energy that radiated from him. Cargo was fascinated.

And then Shodar smiled. It was mocking and sad and weary at the same time, as if its owner had lived for a million years and had seen the birth of galaxies and the death of hundreds of civilizations. It was an entirely human smile, and utterly unhuman as well. It was the smile of a god.

"Do you play?" Shodar's voice was low, sonorous with just a touch of gravel hoarseness.

Cargo was rooted to the spot. His mouth was dry, and besides, he couldn't think of anything to say anyway. Something in Ki Shodar appealed to a part of his personality so primitive it was unaffected by even his Romany lore. He wanted to follow Ki Shodar. He could feel the mantle of power on this being, knew that he could hope for no more than to please this master. It called to him with a yearning that made him nervously aware that his shoes weren't perfectly polished and that he was overdue for a haircut.

So this is what the Bishop meant by charisma, another part of him thought, a part that observed and remained unaffected by Shodar's overwhelming presence.

A strange gift, the Bishop had called it on that cool afternoon when he had begun to instruct Cargo in the rudiments of statecraft. The being who has it creates an image of itself within you, and then you create that being for yourself. It is not intellect, nor physical beauty nor great powers of speech, although it has pieces of all of them. The Bishop had blinked and looked slightly perturbed for a moment. No, he had gone on, it is something emotional and fundamental, as if these beings are catalysts of our feelings, our hopes and fears. They are the ultimate parent, the great teachers, the leaders. Only a gift, and those who have it are not always the best suited to its use.

Cargo remembered dutifully, but the essence of Ki Shodar threatened to drown out the voice of reason still clamoring in his head. Once a long time ago he had thought that the Bishop had had charisma. Now he knew better. The Bishop had a kind of moral authority that emanated from the depth of his being. Ki Shodar had no morality at all. He needed none. Or rather, anyone in his presence would accept whatever Shodar wanted as a moral good.

"When I lived on the streets I made a living in pool halls," Shodar was saying conversationally, inviting Cargo deeper into his magical being. "I find it relaxing. It helps me think."

"I play khandinar, sir," Cargo sputtered.

Shodar smiled again to exactly the same effect and leaned against the polished wooden borders of the table, the cue resting lightly in his hand. "Yes. Khandinar. I've heard something about that. A few casinos on Luxor, I believe."

Cargo felt as if he were literally falling apart. Whatever had been water in his body had dried up in that instant and he was no more than a collection of four pounds of chemicals. He wondered why he didn't simply collapse into a small crystallized heap.

Shodar's smile became only a shade more sardonic, but Cargo read into that expression an aptitude for dispassionate and almost limitless cruelty. "And to what do we owe the pleasure of your current visit, Mr. Mirabeau?"

Cargo felt physically stricken. There was, there should be, no way Shodar could know. But he did.

It was not that the glamour was gone. If anything, Cargo could sense it more acutely now. No, it was only that he had to retreat to the single vestige of pure intellect left, the one corner of his mind that was not entranced by the Cardia's strange splice-life leader.

Shodar balanced the pool cue lightly on his fingertips and rolled it toward Cargo before snapping it back to the palm of his hand.

The whole thing had been a trap. He saw it all clearly for the first time. Ghoster, Stonewall, all of them, even the Bishop himself. His entire life had been beaters in the bush heading him up against this being who was more the Wall than any structure of stone. If only the charisma wasn't so great he would at least know that he had done right. He had not revealed anything. He hadn't even been working against the Cardia. But the force of Shodar's magnetism changed that knowledge, warped it, because he knew even in that cold and unaffected place that he was in danger of succumbing. The very worst was that some part of him wanted to give in and go over to the enemy. And the idea that he could even consider anything so unthinkable made him tremble and brought a cold sweat to his palms.

"I am Rafael Mirabeau . . ." he began to recite permitted information by rote, but Shodar waved a hand and cut him off.

"I know," Shodar said, and his voice was still seductive. "I know all that. I even know that you accompanied your Bishop here when he arrived at my invitation."

Cargo hesitated. "I thought it was the peace faction that invited him."

Shodar's face expressed indulgent contempt. "I am the peace faction. Of course, I am also the war faction, and the conciliation faction and the dispersal faction. The fact is, I know perfectly well what your Bishop is doing and exactly how he's going about it. And if it were anyone else, he might actually have a chance, too. And, I suspect that whatever you are doing here is more for his sake than for your Collegium." Then the leader's vivid purple eyes refocused and became both softer and more dangerous. "In fact, I know perfectly well that you resigned from the Collegium military. You are a civilian now, although you don't seem to realize that. And you are a citizen of Marcanter. You are not only a fraud, you're a genuine one at that. So why don't you tell me why you're here."

Cargo blinked. It was perfectly degrading to be proven truthful in a lie. What was even worse, he could tell Shodar. In a single gestalt he realized that whatever Ghoster was up to, whatever the misunderstanding was, he was facing the one being in the manifold who could comprehend and maybe do something about it. And it was more dangerous for the Collegium, for the Bishop himself, if Shodar did not know.

In the back of Cargo's mind a small but glistening hope was born, that Shodar would listen to him and be ready to make a

peace immediately. The Bishop was an honorable man. And
knowing that they had all been manipulated by an insidious
third force, it would be an honorable peace.

That fantasy managed to live for almost a full second before
it shriveled and burned under Ki Shodar's withering gaze.

"Rafael Mirabeau, I suggest that both you and your Bishop,
and even your precious Collegium, have very little to gain from
your silence." Shodar's voice was soft and laced with threat.

Cargo swallowed hard. "It's a long story, sir," he started
lamely. Shodar merely nodded and gestured with an open
hand.

"I don't know what you know about the Collegium military," he continued, gaining more confidence, "but the Kraits
are designed for an Akhaid and a human to work together in the
maze. It seems that there's something about the interspecies
synergy that improves efficiency. Not that I understand it
particularly, but it seems to be there."

Shodar made a humming noise in the back of his throat and
his face hardened with mockery. Cargo was embarrassed. The
Cardia leader looked so Akhaid it was hard to remember he
was genetically half human. And knew a whole lot more about
interspecies synergy than any being living, too.

"Anyway, Ghoster and I were assigned in training and it
worked. The maze link was as near perfect as it gets. And
outside, too, we were one hundred percent. We were individuals, if you follow me, not just generic human and Akhaid. We
did the bars together, joked, I never did get his jokes, even
tried each other's food. Which was what I guess they wanted.
We were assigned together. We were friends, really. I guess I
never thought of Ghoster so much as Akhaid after that. He was
just Ghoster, if you know what I mean.

"I guess that's where the trouble was, too. I forgot that he
wasn't human most of the time. Some of the brass think that's
better on both sides, but I know they're wrong. I would have
known earlier if I'd been thinking. Anyway, to make a very
long story a little shorter, Ghoster and I joined the batwing, the
Intel section. And I found out it was Ghoster who had sold you
the stealth technology.

"Only he wasn't your agent. He's a member of something
else, some Akhaid group that thinks this whole thing's a Walk.
They're trying to keep the sides even so no one can win,

sabotaging peace efforts all over the place, because they think we need to fight each other to Walk. And they think they're helping us humans by doing this. I understand it intellectually, but on some real level it doesn't make any sense at all.

"Except for one thing. Ghoster and I are still friends. I know that, the same way I know that he thought he was helping me by doing what he did. And I'm here to find him and tell him that the Collegium is tracking him down for selling the batwing designs.

"On the one hand, it makes me sick when I know what he did. But he's not going to be killed for an interspecies misunderstanding."

Cargo breathed deeply at the end of his recitation. He wanted a cup of water. He wanted to sit down even more. Telling the story, even leaving out the worst parts, had drained him. Telling it to Shodar, whom he didn't trust at all, drained him even more. But he wasn't invited to sit.

Indeed, it seemed as if Shodar had forgotten him altogether. The Akhaid-looking Cardia leader was leaning over the pool table, eyeing a shot. In a single fluid motion he snapped the cue forward and the white ball rolled across the green felt and smacked another ball with a firm knock.

Shodar made his way around the table and repeated the process, his movements economical and completely sure. There was no hesitation in his judgment or execution of each shot, even the one Cargo thought nearly impossible.

Four balls disappeared in rapid succession before Shodar straightened up and looked at Cargo. Cargo thought he seemed very pleased with himself and might break into laughter. It was a laughter he did not want to hear. The pleasure in Shodar's face was saturated with cruelty.

"Thank you for your information, Mr. Mirabeau," he said. "We'll have to talk again sometime. I suppose you won't be offended if I suggest that you might want to stay here for a while before continuing your search for your Akhaid friend. A heartrending story, to be sure."

Cargo pressed his lips together in a firm line. "I suppose that means you're sending me back to the camp," he said tersely.

Shodar laughed, then looked very pleased with himself. "No, not at all. I'm going to do something very much worse. I'm going to make you a hero. Good day, Mr. Verdun."

* * *

Shodar was right. It was much worse.

He couldn't walk from Flight Ops to Headquarters without every being in twenty meters pretending to ignore him. Two media types were on duty most of the time, trailing him at a distance respectable enough that he could possibly have an almost private conversation, but close enough that he couldn't just sit down at the piano bar in the O-Club and drink enough to forget them. Suddenly all his meager personal effects were catalogued and reviewed.

"The public really wants to know," one of the offending gossip mongers assured him. "It makes the whole story so much more poignant, how little you were able to salvage."

And there was no way he could protest. Cargo recognized a propaganda campaign when he saw one, especially when he was in the middle of one. He even remembered the Bishop plotting such coups from the cathedral office on Mawbry's.

"Make them associate with an individual," he remembered the Bishop saying one hot afternoon just before he left for his third year of university. "Most people don't think in abstract terms. Perhaps they can't. I'm more easily convinced they don't want to. People want easy answers. You have to be able to give the entire situation and the answer in eighty seconds with lots of good visuals. One individual that people can identify with is worth all the advertising in the universe."

At the time Cargo hadn't thought much about it. He was a probabilist, and his major concern that year was finding an adequate topic for his graduation paper. And he remembered that he had wondered, all through the Bishop's discourse, how he was going to tell his adoptive father that he was not planning a career in politics. It was no different than the world of the *ofisa* that he had left.

The only possible course of action, at least for the time being, was to give in to the inevitable. In the name of Kore Verdun Cargo had drawn a dress uniform on the pretense that his other was for winter. Stores had made a face and snorted, but had been pleased to inform him in a nasal voice that the tailor would need at least two weeks to make all the alterations. Cargo had cursed, paid, and told Stores to forget it.

When he tried it on, the pale blue pants had fit poorly and the cropped dress jacket was even worse. Mike Allen hadn't been able to recommend anything, so Cargo had gone on his own into the MidCenter to find a private tailor. The price had been at least five times what Stores had quoted, but this tailor promised the uniform back in three days.

In the end, he had to admit the extra expense was justified. The ice-pale jacket fit like it had been custom made and the pants clung as if they'd been painted on. Which was exactly how they were supposed to look according to the reg book.

"Give me the name of that tailor," Mike had said. "I don't care what it costs."

"We'll all be better dressed than the admiral," Miep van Rooijen said, sipping her coffee. "But that's all right. For the ceremony you want to be."

Cargo shook his head. Allen had invited Miep because she was the only pilot on base who knew anything about the protocols of such public awards. Her father had once been Ambassador to Zhai Bau, and Miep had served as his hostess. Or so Allen had told Cargo when he suggested that some coaching wouldn't be such a bad idea. After all, it reflected on him, his base, and the entire Cardia stealth corps. At Ki Shodar's command, the ceremony was going to be broadcast live to every Cardia outpost, to encourage the people was the way the release had been worded.

So far nothing useful had come from standing around Mike's living room and having Miep and Mike inspect him. They were supposed to have dinner and Cargo was starving, but it didn't look like any food would be forthcoming soon.

"Have you written your speech yet?" Miep asked.

Cargo shook his head.

"We'll have to work on that," she said, raising an eyebrow at Mike. "And you'll have to get a haircut."

"I know that," Cargo snapped back. "Do I do that on base, or am I supposed to pay a fortune for that too?"

His tone was slightly nastier than he had intended. Hunger, he figured. And being forced to pay too much attention to the surface of things. He had thought he had escaped that once, when he had been forced out of his home and declared *marhime*. That, and being forced to be concerned with the inanities of ceremony and circumstance.

Ki Shodar had to be a genius in more ways than he was normally credited, Cargo thought ruefully. One didn't usually think that being named as the recipient of the highest honor the Cardia had to give was a punishment, but it was a prison far more effective than bars. His face had been on the news every night for five days, and on the base he was treated with a respect that verged on discourtesy.

He couldn't rage against it. There was no way to rage against honors. And he couldn't talk to anyone. Even Mike, especially Mike, had been so congratulatory that any other attitude was unthinkable. The only bitch Mike did understand was that Cargo had been taken off the rotation.

"Just for the time being," the clerk had said apologetically. "Mr. Shodar doesn't want anything happening before the ceremony."

"Just for the time being," Cargo had spat back in Mike's office. "What the hell do they think I am? A stuffed display mannequin?"

Mike had looked abashed but had said nothing. A gilded cage to be sure, but nonetheless a cage. And one that might never end. So he had just paid serious money to alter a uniform both he and Shodar knew he had no right to wear to accept an honor he had no right to accept to keep him under very careful wraps.

"The speech should be more inspirational than factual," Miep was saying. "And short, naturally. And a few humorous anecdotes. Everyone loves humor."

"Can't I just say thank you, I don't deserve it, every other flier out there does the same thing every day? That's maybe three sentences."

Miep shook her head firmly. "You're scheduled for at least five minutes. Probably five exactly, if it's anything like I remember. And if you don't talk long enough someone's going to have to fill in the empty space."

"What empty space?" Allen asked.

Miep sighed. "In the broadcast. The whole thing is built around the news schedule. Shodar will speak first, then give you the medal. Then you'll speak for five minutes, and then someone else for at least five or maybe ten. That'll give Jace Arzimanian enough time to get together the commentary on whatever Shodar says so they can have an instant analysis after the break. Damn."

Cargo blinked. It had never occurred to him that he had been scheduled to make a speech so that the political commentary would be right on time. "Then they're doing this live?" he asked naively.

"Of course they are. You already know that," Miep replied, obviously exasperated. "Do you want my help or not?"

Cargo hesitated. The nucleus of an idea was beginning to form, but it was vague and not quite reliable yet. Still, he'd made it up as he'd gone along before. The risk was half the fun. "Well, I'm going to write the speech myself."

"Are you sure?" Mike asked, pained. "Are you good at that kind of thing?"

Cargo shook his head. "I don't know. I've never tried it before. Only, we're supposed to be big and dumb and inarticulate, right? I'm just a fighter jock doing my job. So if I don't sound like a politican it'll be just fine. But could you tell me a good place to get a haircut? One that won't charge me the rest of this month's pay would be nice."

Chapter
5

Andre Michel Mirabeau, Bishop of Mawbry's Colony and ex-Trustee of the Collegium, leaned back in the white leather seat and refilled his wine glass. The white was not a true Cobrisse '27, of course, but it was adequate and not pretentious. More important, it wouldn't travel well, and the Bishop knew that he had less than a day left on Marcanter. Around him on the official transport were stowage reports for most of the important documents generated by the first round of negotiations. The rest had gone down the trash and had been reduced to their component atoms. No matter what any Intelligence service said, the Bishop dared any of them to reconstruct that matter. Confidentiality was important in such delicate affairs, especially now that the mission was being withdrawn. Indelicately.

The old man sighed and sipped his wine slowly as if his only concern in the universe was to see the broadcast where his son would be made a Companion of Aliadro, the highest honor in the Cardia. He smiled gently, knowing just exactly what kind of honor was intended. Ki Shodar had always been a worthy opponent, an able player. That was what had made the game so interesting for so very long. The only thing that was needed in order to complete it perfectly was Shodar's redemption.

That he was being dismissed did not disturb Mirabeau. He had expected it, in fact. These things were done carefully and over long periods of time. Talks took place in series, one following the next, each being broken off as if some slight had been offered or suffered on either side. This had only been the first round. The second would come sooner and last longer, and there would be three or four more before anything was officially recognized. That the process would eventually lead to a settlement Mirabeau did not doubt. The practical evidence as well as the sentiment indicated that the Cardia could not survive another fifteen years of conflict. They most likely could not survive another five. It was simply a matter of working out appearances so that nothing would look like withdrawal or surrender.

No, none of that worried him anymore. Only the individuals, Ki and Rafael and the others, they worried him. And that made Mirabeau think that perhaps he really was becoming an old man. It happened to the best. His mentor had warned him nearly half a century ago of that, that someday he would be more concerned about the people he knew than about the future history of humanity. And on that day it was time to retire.

But he was already retired, technically at least. Only technically. The day he was out of the game was the day he died. It was something Mirabeau had acknowledged a very long time ago. The youngster who had taken the luxury liner to the Collegium with the aim of becoming a parish priest had been gone for three quarters of a century. And yet, vestiges remained. And so he worried about Ki Shodar's redemption.

Not that he ever wondered about Shodar's contrition. It was only that Mirabeau knew that Ki would do it again, given the same circumstances. That much hadn't changed. And that much saddened him.

The face on the broadcast was essentially no different tonight than it had been fifteen years ago. And not terribly different than Aliadro's. That was not surprising. Genetically they were brothers. In other ways they had been much less and far more. It should have been Aliadro there, the first of the Bishop's sons, and the first he lost. Now only Rafael was left, and Mirabeau couldn't say he wasn't the best. Aliadro, for all his gifts, had failed to survive.

And the only other person who knows it all is Ki Shodar, Mirabeau thought with a wry amusement. And one thing alone reassured him. Shodar knew better than to kill another one of his sons.

Ki Shodar was speaking, and even over the broadcast his voice carried an authority and charisma that very few people ever projected. The Bishop wasn't surprised by what he said, but he listened anyway. Sometimes there were more subtle messages coded into public speeches, things that had to be understood and analyzed in light of developments. And sometimes there weren't, but he had to listen all the same. Andre Michel Mirabeau, after all, was not immune to Shodar's spell. He only behaved as if he were.

"After the reports we have had from our escaped hero, Kore Verdun, it is impossible for us to believe in the good will of the Collegium embassy that even now is trying to convince us they mean an honorable peace. How can we accept their terms, knowing full well they are in the process of developing a viral genetic weapon? Can we honestly believe that it is simply science, in the interest of research? Can they convince me?

"Believe me, I know more deeply and surely than anyone could about genetic experiments. And the Concord that outlawed them has been obeyed by even those worlds outside its jurisdiction. So we are to surrender, to ally ourselves with an enemy that permits such experiments? I say never. I say we are less than beings with souls if we permit ourselves to be blinded by our own expediency and forget the generations to come. For their sake it is worth every drop of blood to keep this evil from our door."

Mirabeau blinked twice, nothing else on his face changed. He had disciplined his features over too many years through too many crises to let his fury show now.

It was one thing for Shodar to use Rafael badly. Rafe had made a mistake and had gotten caught. At least he was alive, and as safe as he had ever been. But to accuse the Collegium of conducting interspecies genetic experiments was a lie of such hideous proportion that it was guaranteed to set the peace initiative back on Luxor.

He had miscalculated Shodar again. Mirabeau thought that all those years, those experiences, and his own knowledge of the being would have prevented that. But he believed, totally to the depths of his soul, in some form of mercy. He could not make himself believe that Ki Shodar had none at all.

The Bishop had met two sociopaths when he worked in an institution, and at least one more in the Department of Development. The Shodar he had known was not one of them. He was something else, driven by a demon only he could name. But Mirabeau had hoped that time and responsibility and maturity would teach him the disciplines of pain and not the uses of it. The Ki Shodar he had known fifteen years ago was still very young, with the cynicism of the young. Fifteen years should have been enough time to have taught him faith.

The medal was handed over, followed by polite applause. Then Cargo, Rafael Mirabeau, Kore Verdun, stood alone swallowing hard. Looking just like a hero should at that moment, stunned and inarticulate. The way we like our heroes, Mirabeau thought. Just the way we like everything. Very simple and served up already boned.

Cargo, Rafael Mirabeau, Kore Verdun, tried to say something. He opened his mouth once or twice, but no words came. Finally, after a moment staring at the floor, his eyes became vacant.

"I would like to thank the Cardia, and especially our leader Ki Shodar. But I want to point out that I didn't do anything out of the ordinary, anything that any other pilot doesn't do every day. Maybe they just decided to make me a symbol, and I'm grateful for that. But for all of us, not for me alone. And I just want to get back there, dancing vac."

There was a blank space in the broadcast. It lasted only the merest second, but the Bishop had enough experience in political use of the media to spot it.

That had not been Cargo's arranged and rehearsed speech. He himself had taught the youngster public speaking, had coached him in the finer points of delivery and composition. It took no special knowledge to realize that whatever Cargo had planned to say had been preempted by Shodar's announcement.

"And you will go back," Shodar was saying smoothly. Already he had stepped into the frame next to Cargo, beaming as if the pilot had read a statement prepared by his own staff. *"As of tomorrow, you will take your new job as group leader in the twenty-third. We wouldn't keep you planet-bound longer than absolutely necessary, that I promise. Because for all our pilots, like Kore Verdun, dancing vac, as they call it, is dearer than life. As they should be to all of us."*

The Bishop gently replaced his wine glass. It was still close to full, but he hardly noticed. Shodar had done it, condemned his last son. And all to create an impression, to keep the aura intact.

Cargo had let him do it, too, although his reasons were stranger to the Bishop than any political ploy would have been. Cargo believed in flying, in dancing vac. When he had graduated from the Faculty of Probability, the Bishop had an excellent position as an analyst on the Tactical Staff all arranged. Cargo had been sad when he had said no. He had always hated disappointing his adoptive father. But he had already been accepted to pilot training and refused to give it up. All his life, he had told Mirabeau that night, always he had dreamed of that perfect freedom, that complete aliveness that was flying.

Mirabeau did not understand, not really. He supposed in its own way it was like power was for him, an addiction. The Bishop never felt so alive as when he was making things happen, pulling the strings behind the events of the age. That, he supposed, was how Cargo felt when he flew.

That, and something else, something Cargo would never say but the old man suspected. There was something honest about flying. Like mathematics, it was pure and clean in its own way. There was wrong and right, live and die and nothing was grey. Cargo had grown up with all different shades of grey and nothing else. Mirabeau suspected that he secretly craved absolutes to cling to, since he had had none as a child. And he further suspected that Cargo had no idea at all that this was true.

"Holy fucking Deckmejian. I never said one word about experiments. I'd bet two months pay, with combat supplement, that it's all a fucking lie." Cargo was angrier than he had been in a very long time. Angrier than he had ever been at Stonewall or even Ghoster, and that was a fact.

"Some hero," one of Shodar's aides said with heavy contempt.

Cargo took a ragged breath and tried to calm down. There were still guards at the door and, public hero or not, they wouldn't let him get much farther.

He hadn't been happy about the broadcast being done in the

bunker in the first place. It was too much like a prison, too impersonal for him to feel comfortable. And there were too many guards, too many Eye beams all over the place, and too little cheer.

Even the lounge they were using as a green room had only four padded chairs, already occupied by civilians with brief-cases and superior airs. The rest were an amalgamation of seating units that would be ashamed in the roughest hot shack and the decaf-only coffee service was purest disposables.

He didn't know which made him angrier, the allegations of experiments or being assigned to a Cardia fighter group. Damn, that was one thing he hadn't expected Shodar to do, especially knowing about Rafael Mirabeau. And how the hell could he get back? Oh, it was too perfect, for him to defect over to the Collegium in a Cardia fighter when he was known as a batwing? The universe reeled and made no sense.

The guard came back and escorted him back down the endless corridors. For once he was grateful. Even walking took some degree of thought that he couldn't spare at the moment. Other things were taking precedence. Like how to use this double situation.

No doubt that it could be used. In fact, he should be able to reconnect the Bishop with whatever underground faction that didn't include Shodar. Maybe with the Collegium's assistance a coup was even possible. Only, Shodar knew who he was and would have him watched every moment. That was one thing Cargo didn't doubt.

He didn't bother to register the trip back to the base or his own blank decision to have dinner. Those were merely automatic functions of the body. His mind was somewhere on the border between the warring factions, twisting them around and challenging the way the Bishop had taught him.

The worst was, this all had nothing to do with finding Ghoster. Stonewall was out there somewhere, and Ghoster was his prey. One thing Cargo felt pretty sure of was that Stonewall was not going to let go lightly. Not even if Cargo found some way of using the situation to their advantage. And that was something he'd better not forget, he told himself severely. He had come out here to save the best friend he had left, and Ki Shodar, Mike Allen, and the whole Cardia notwithstanding, that had to be his first priority.

Only it was so easy to forget the simple things when the possibilities for other layers of rich complexities of con games abounded. His mother would have found some way to use them all and make everything work.

It had been a very long time since he had thought of his mother, and the image startled him. She had been one of the greats, he thought with a mixture of pride and shame. And one of the reasons was that she acknowledged no morality, no authority, other than the thousands-year-old code of the Rom. That gave her the freedom that gave her strength.

Just as he thought that he pushed open the double door to the officer's mess. When he entered, everyone in the room stood together and raised a glass.

Cargo was stunned and disoriented, catapulted back to present reality. The confusion lasted no more than a fraction of a second. Cargo saluted them all, and applause broke out, loud and spontaneous.

He had never felt like such a fraud in his whole conniving life as he did as he walked down the center of the formal dinner room between the long white cloths to the high table. Mike stood with the rest, alternately clapping and tapping his knife against his water glass, as Cargo came forward. There was an empty place at Mike's left, the place of honor, Cargo remembered the protocol from all the Bishop's various functions.

And being a fraud, he didn't dare let the aura slip. Not for himself, but for the concept of the hero which he honored as much as anyone there. More, maybe, he decided, since he knew exactly how dirty he was willing to play. Which was as dirty as he could. No, his only choice was to play the part for the sake of the part and not for himself.

It seemed an eternity before he reached his place at the table. The wine glass was already full, he saw, a white. Slowly, he took it and raised it in his right hand. The crowd hushed. Since they all knew the protocol that forbade anyone drinking to himself, it was speech time.

But Cargo didn't make a speech. "To every pilot who ever died dancing vac." His voice rang out in the silence that continued as everyone present, including the three chefs and servers who had come out of the kitchen to witness the event, considered his tribute.

The silence choked and overwhelmed him. And although

this was the first formal meal he had attended on base, even the duck swimming in black current sauce and saffron rice on the fine china didn't tempt him. He stared down at his plate, unable to move.

"Hey, that's probably the last decent meal you'll see in a long time," Mike whispered to him. "You're going out on the *Younger*, and they have the most notorious human chef in the fleet. I've heard veterans of that carrier call it the Ptomaine."

That struck Cargo as extremely funny. "I thought the best food always went out with the fleet. Sort of compensation," he said when he stopped laughing.

Allen regarded him like a schoolmaster with a particularly dull pupil. "The food is fine. But the chef ranks just about every noncom in the entire service and isn't about to leave the *Younger*. And what he does to it, well, mutilation would be a polite term. I've heard of people who got very interested in Akhaid cuisine on a long cruise, let me tell you."

The tension broken, Cargo attacked his dinner like a point target in a shooting exercise. The Bishop hadn't taught him to appreciate good food for nothing.

It wasn't until later when, so stuffed he could hardly move, Cargo and Mike made their way over to the Club. The bar was in a post dinner phase, not yet quite rowdy enough for the crazy games of Smash and Teaser, but working with true dedication to overcome sobriety. The din was just below the pitch needed to drown out a companion's conversation and there were a few shreds of decorum left. Certainly enough so that they recognized Cargo. And it happened again.

Not everyone in the bar had been at dinner. In fact, Cargo figured that most of them hadn't. Those on the flight line tended to eat at the earlier seating. But this dead quiet on his entry and everyone standing up, that was getting ridiculous. It was one thing being a hero and the symbol of a hero on a live broadcast for the civs. It was quite another thing here in the bar. Cargo knew that he had to stop this craziness once and for all.

"A round on me," he yelled, throwing his hat in the air. "Anybody ready for a game of Smash?"

The *Younger* was very much like the Collegium carriers he had served on all his career, and in some subtle ways very different. There were moments when the differences skewed his perspective, and suddenly everything seemed alien all at once.

Last night for example. He had reported aboard that afternoon when the ferry dropped him with seventy others who were joining the ship's complement. Cargo had been able to follow the lead of a slightly senior pilot, checking the register and getting settled. Accommodations were not much different than he had been accustomed to before. Three roommates, their belongings stowed in the most desirable spaces, were out. Old timers on the *Younger*, he figured. That would be helpful. They could clue him in on whatever bits of tradition applied here, things that changed from ship to ship and group to group.

He was more concerned about meeting his Eyes. A new ship was one thing, but a new partner, especially an alien, was quite another. His friendship with Ghoster had been built carefully over a period of years and a series of incidents that were off the official record.

There had been the time when Ghoster had caught him out in a palm reader's shop in the MidCenter on Taler. He had wandered in more out of homesickness than anything. The familiar smell of wax candles and stale cooking under the cheap heavy incense had been comforting. From her looks, Cargo had thought the woman was most likely Lowara, a tribe the Tshurara looked down on as weak. At the time it hadn't mattered. She had considered him closely as a young girl, maybe fifteen, brought tea.

"*Sarishan*," he'd said, using Romany to someone else who spoke it for the first time in nearly a year.

Both women were taken aback. They knew, and knew that he knew, exactly what their business was. And then he had looked at the young girl again and for a moment she reminded him of Sonfranka.

She was not glorious as Sonfranka had been. This girl lacked the flash, the arrogance, the fire of a true Tshurara beauty. But he was certain from the way she moved around the *boojo* woman that she was a daughter-in-law being trained in the business. Like Sonfranka had been to his mother. Only Sonfranka hadn't really had to be trained. She was a natural, gifted, a real jewel of a girl. And then she was dead because she couldn't face the *Gaje* world.

His marriage and Sonfranka's death had simply ceased to exist for him, at least until that day that he wandered into the palm reader's shop in the Midcenter. Seeing the Lowara girl brought it all back, all the images he had blocked off for so long.

Cargo didn't know then that Ghoster had followed him to the *ofisa*. Already, even though they had been working together for only a few months, there was that almost telepathy developing that was rumored to be the foundation of the great teams. Ghoster had come in uninvited just at the moment Cargo was ready to break under the weight of it all, had hauled him to his feet and half dragged, half pushed him into the street. Then Ghoster had listened to it all pour out in some kind of cosmic core dump.

"It was a difficult Walk," he could still recall Ghoster saying seriously. "No wonder you chose war."

And the Ghost had been right. It had crystallized for him later that night after too many annies, reds and a few greens, washed down with a pitcher or two of beer. The Bishop had arranged a very nice political position for him after graduation. And it would have served the Collegium and the Bishop if he had taken it, too.

No, in the mind-distorting haze that was obligatory on liberty, the insight was perfect and vast and awe-inspiring. Ghoster, Akhaid alien that he was who had only known Cargo for a few months, had understood what the Bishop had not. And had used up his good liberty time to take care of Cargo. Then, he hadn't realized that it would become a habit for both of them.

Much later, clearing the psych board to qualify for the batwing, the resident shrink had spent an exceptionally long time on that incident. That one and all the others, and with Ghoster as well. The shrink had told Cargo that it was the damnedest thing he'd ever come across in his whole career, an Akhaid who had most likely saved a human from a nervous breakdown. Privately, Cargo wasn't really sure he was willing to go that far. He had remembered, that was all, and Ghoster had helped him understand. No way he could believe that he might have become really dysfunctional like the walking zombies in Ward Six. But the shrink was supposed to know something about the business.

Ghoster had been the only Eyes Cargo had ever had. Down on Marcanter no one had ever mentioned anything about his new Akhaid partner on the *Younger*, which worried Cargo. He only hoped that his new partner hadn't been in the maze while the pilot died or something melodramatic like that. Not that Cargo had ever heard of any incidents like that ever happening—fighters were built so that if one survived it was likely that both would—but it was a recurrent theme on too many entertainment programs for him to ignore. Besides, what in hell was half a team doing all by his lonesome on a carrier?

The whole situation had Cargo keyed up. The Akhaid factor only made things worse.

After he had stowed his gear in his stateroom, he tapped out the message code on the stripped down ship system. The time spent on Marcanter base had been productive in that much; he had learned enough of the Cardia systems to use them, at least for routine functions. Which was fortunate. Three-B's were rated combat only in the Cardia. It never occurred to Cargo that they might be expensive, but Mike Allen had made him understand that using mode for routine computer work was considered somewhere between waste and sin.

If anyone had asked him to manually "find" a newly repaired fighter for his own group, an "extra" that another group "didn't need," and assign it to himself, he would be hard-pressed. Which was a disadvantage, since he and every other group leader he'd ever known in the Collegium played games like that constantly. There wasn't any choice. Too many of the craft they flew were patched together with more spare parts than originals. He never could figure out how the techs decided which one would become the "hangar queen" to be pilfered and stripped at will when ordered replacements didn't arrive. On the *Torque* there had been maybe thirty decent fighters in a hundred and fifty. Maybe forty more could be nursed along this one time, and the time after. The rest were horrors. Dancing vac in those, the greatest enemies were stress and yield, a possible maze leak, or any one of ten million other things. Cardia fighters rated way down the list.

He hoped that he'd have time to learn that before it was necessary to use, because if anyone found out that his knowledge of the system was so sketchy as to be merely civ, well, that would blow his cover forever. Or if he screwed up

any one of the million and one little things that could be
screwed up. He hadn't thought of that, which was perhaps
lucky. If he had he would have decided not to go in in the first
place.

Besides, hadn't Old Pulika taught him to improvise? And
wasn't Old Pulika the master of the art of deception among the
Tshurara, who were the greatest liars of all humankind? He
could hear the old man's alcohol-thickened voice in his head,
chuckling sadly. *So now you are so* Gaje *that you will kill and
you forget how to lie? That is a sad thing to say about any* chal,
*but to say it about a Tshurara will make the Black Virgin
herself weep blood.*

A nasty, arrogent smile slid over his face. Yes. He could
outlie the best of them here on this ship. And they'd believe
every word. He was a pilot and he was Rom, half Tshurara and
half Gitano and without a scruple in the universe where the
Gaje were concerned. At least for the moment, until he
remembered Rafael again. Kore Verdun was a Romany name,
and he was damned sure going to live up to it.

The message light turned from yellow to pink and Cargo
shook his head. He'd been thinking too long. He accessed the
queue immediately, before the system decided that he'd lost
interest or fallen asleep. Or had gotten involved in paperwork,
which was much worse.

The first message was the official wording to his "transfer"
to the *Younger* and his position and duties aboard. The next
was a slightly sarcastic inquiry as to when he was going to start
filling out work orders for the group. Cargo groaned when he
read that one. They only invented the jobs to keep pilots busy
when they weren't immediately involved in flying missions,
and work orders were the worst. Especially since, if the
Younger was anything at all like any carrier he had ever been
assigned to, fouling up whatever hapless flier drew the
requisitions was the chief occupation and amusement of the
bosun's office.

Well, he couldn't exactly blame the wing skipper for that.
He was the newest one aboard. And there was the matter of his
being the hero. The group would have to cut him down to size
a little, if only to accept him. On a rational level he understood
it all very well. On an emotional level he was ready to go down

to the bosun's office screaming. Which wouldn't earn him any points with anyone.

The third message was what he had been waiting for and wondering about. It was from the wing skipper, a formal request for him to present himself at the wing wardroom at eighteen hundred to meet his new Eyes.

He wondered briefly if his Eyes had gotten the same message. It would make perfect sense. And the coldness of it bothered him.

He swore softly at the board, which blinked politely and failed to respond. At least that much was perfectly familiar. Then he gave it up. It was almost time for dinner anyway.

It being his first meal in the wing wardroom, Cargo managed to get in a little early. He stood and greeted each officer, trying to match names and signs and faces without relying on the uniform pins. One by one they filed in, his own new group careful to identify themselves and making sure the steward assigned him a place with them. The wing skipper came in last and took the head seat at the head table.

Only then did Cargo realize what was bothering him. As he scanned the faces around him there was not one single Akhaid among them.

Chapter

6

Amayut Tzii MM was nothing like Ghoster, Cargo thought despairingly. *How the hell are we ever going to make it in the maze?* he wondered as he looked at the tall icy Akhaid. The being would have been beautiful, its quasi-scaled skin glittering a rich copper ruby and its whiteless eyes titanium bright yellow, if only it had seemed just a little willing to view him as a partner and not a specimen ready for dissection.

"I greet you in the dancing stars," Cargo greeted Tzii in passable Atrash.

"Ne parlez pas cette langue, s'il vous plaît," the Akhaid's voice dripped contempt in a perfect Orleanais accent. *"Je m'appel Dancer. Mon nom est trop difficile pour vous. D'accord?"*

Cargo smiled wickedly. Dancer, was it? According to Ghoster that meant something very specific among the Akhaid who Walked. The Dancer was one who had achieved perfect freedom.

Most Akhaid Walkers Walked because it was necessary for their physical maturation. A series of extremely high stress situations forced the biochemical changes required before they were capable of reproduction. Cargo had been delicate enough not to inquire further. He was not particularly interested in Akhaid sexual practices, and furthermore, his Rom upbring-

73

ing had inculcated a certain verbal modesty. But the Walking was essential to understand the Akhaid.

He regarded his new Akhaid partner again. "Dancer?" he inquired too gently. "And are you?"

The other's ears went stiff with what Cargo assumed was anger. At least it always had been in Ghoster. He was strangely pleased. Dislike was at least something between them, although it was not exactly what he would have called an optimal program.

"*Ce n'est pas important a savoir. Pour vous.*" Dancer hissed.

And then Cargo couldn't contain himself anymore. The smile forced its way from inside him, aware of just how crazy the whole universe was at the moment. And this Akhaid, who couldn't be more different from Ghoster, was simply playing a role in Cargo's perceptions, being perfectly defined and defining the universe as the powers that be would have it.

So Tzii's call sign was Dancer. There was never a being, human or Akhaid, who at that moment Cargo would have considered being further from that state of being.

"Well," Cargo said merrily, "at least you're arrogant enough to keep up with me in here. We'll see how it goes in the maze."

The Akhaid's ears flattened slightly and the thin-lipped mouth relaxed. If Ghoster was any guide, this being was somewhere between fascination and disgust. That suited Cargo just fine.

"We shall see," Dancer said very formally. "But I expect that it will be you who can't keep up with me." The Akhaid turned to go.

"Just one thing," Cargo said to its back. "Curiosity, nothing more. What happened to your previous partner?"

The Akhaid turned and shimmering yellow eyes met obsidian black. "Lost his nerve," Dancer said coldly, and left.

"I'll bet," Cargo muttered under his breath when the door had closed after Dancer's exit.

He had barely time to collapse on the banquette when the room was suddenly full of people, most of them human and most of them recognizable. Seniz Ayhan, Richard Dee, Gen Takura, Devi Deseka—he was proud that he managed both names for each and could match them with the faces. In the Cardia service, he had learned, call signs were not used the way he had always used them as a Krait jockey and later a batwing. Here they weren't permanent nor were they substitutes for names, more revealing and more careful than the names listed on the official register. No, it was the official names that were used on assignments and listings, lightly burned into the door tags and used by friends, colleagues, and near strangers. Maybe that was the most uncomfortable thing of all, he thought, being Kore Verdun all the time. No one in this group, which was his group, called him Cargo. And none of them would.

Only the three Akhaid who accompanied them did he think of by their—nicknames, he reminded himself—names that would not be used officially any more than anyone here would address him as Cargo. The shorter, stout one was called Rugby, and he wasn't sure which of the two others were Mick and Cacciatore.

"So, what do you think of our resident killjoy, boss?" Rugby asked.

"Does anyone know what's with him?" Cargo asked, half curious and half from pure self-defense.

Devi rolled her eyes and Richard staggered across the floor pantomiming a stomachache, or perhaps the aftermath of a night at the MidCenter.

"Someone doesn't like you, boss," Seniz said cheerfully. "Or else it's one of Dancer's kin. Like, they're hoping you'll have more guts than the last guy did and evaporate him for them."

Cargo shook his head and tried to smile, to catch back the feeling of just how crazy the whole universe had all at once become. It didn't work. He shrugged instead. "I guess I'll find out Sunday." Due back in manifold Saturday, and his group had drawn the dirty watch on Sunday. Which was really something of a relief on the *Younger*. The dirty watch meant that they ate at the reverse mess where the carrier's infamous chef did not hold sway over the dining room.

At least, it had seemed good luck at the time. He wondered now if he had any luck left at all, or if he'd used it all up. Going into mode with someone like Dancer seemed to be the worst luck possible.

Surreptitiously, Cargo rubbed the holy medal at his neck. And as much as he knew that there as no luck in the manifold,

only hard work and skill and probabilities, he needed that
medal to reassure himself.

Then he stopped. He may as well believe in luck, if he could
be the leader of a Cardia fighter group now, who had once been
a very good thief and a very bad prisoner and Mirabeau's son
and Cargo of the batwing. He had been all of them for a time.
And all of them had been lucky in the end. Maybe Niels Bohr
was right when he said, "Albert, don't tell God what to do."

"You going to sit there all day, or you planning to come with
us down to the rec five and play Smash?" Gen asked,
frowning.

Then Cargo did smile, calculating. "Smash? Who needs
Smash? Anyone here up for a friendly round of khandinar?"

Four tiny red pills lay in his palm. That much was exactly
the same, right down to the color. Well, not exactly the same.
As a Krait jockey, and as a batwing, Cargo would have
normally taken six or even eight. Four Three-B's were supposed to be enough for a routine three-hour stint on patrol, but
Cargo hadn't had a routine three-hour patrol in his life. Once
things got exciting, having to bother with something like the
Three-B's only made the situation more difficult. Still, this was
the Cardia and Three-B's were expensive. Pilots were trained
rigorously here not to waste them.

He hesitated for a moment before swallowing them, knowing that it was Dancer in the back seat who was downing the
Akhaid equivalent and would meet him in the maze. He winced
slightly at the thought and waited for the drug to take effect and
open the microwave circuit in the DNA chip in his head. In the
meantime he did one last quick preflight and readjusted his
gloves for at least the seventh time. They just didn't fit right.
Typical military. He wondered idly if anyone back on the base
ever had gone to the tailor he had recommended.

Supposedly all the drug did when it crossed the blood brain
barrier was open the circuit, but as it began to work Cargo felt
again the easy strength and illusion of power it almost always
brought. He didn't care how many psychiatrists said that that
was completely ridiculous. They didn't take the stuff, didn't
lean back into the microwave communications on a neural level
and slip into the maze.

Every maze was different. The craft's Akhaid computer soul

and hard gear and the two beings who flew in it all merged together into one single entity called the maze only because no one had thought of a better word. Always creating it before with Ghoster, there had been at least a certain familiarity about each maze, although he and Ghoster had been carefully separated by the species membrane. Without that insulation from each other, their essential alienness would drive the other insane. That much had been proven somewhere in the murk of history when the things had been invented, at least a good thirty years before he had been born.

This time he didn't slip easily into the twilight consciousness of cybermode. Instead the maze practically grabbed him and created itself around him. Carefully he felt for the emanation that had to be Dancer, investigating to find the shimmering surface of the membrane that neither of them could cross.

There was nothing. Only darkness in darkness. The membrane was neither brilliant and glittering with presence nor was it hard and unyielding as it was when he was alone. Instead Cargo felt a kind of nonpresence, as if Dancer were not actually a living being at all, but a third mechanical component of the interface. He couldn't *touch* Dancer in the maze at all.

For a moment he panicked before he remembered that fear was more dangerous than any living enemy. Slowly he forced himself to breath deeply and control the terror. And work through the maze, feeling inside it and shaping it with his mind.

It was like most training and table mazes, he decided. It slipped over him and drew him deeper into itself, leeching his thought faster as he sank into the depth. Then came the shift when he no longer thought words at all, but barely half-finished images that the maze completed avidly and rushed to create in reality. If he didn't look for Dancer it was comfortable enough.

Then Dancer is not here, or dead, he decided finally. That was not quite enough; awareness of the other's consciousness, or lack of being, drifted dangerously close to his field of perception, but he shoved it firmly back. He had to fly. Dancer either was or was not there. At this moment he had no choice. Already the maze was connecting him to Control, through the Master Maze, and he was aware of the magtracks polarizing, the force rippling through them, trembling, bringing the fighter craft to life.

And then the tracks themselves hurtled the tiny shell out of the carrier into the dark.

Years of inground habit took over. Cargo found himself going through a systems check, then navigation orientation as he automatically took position with the group. He could see the others glittering around him, their titanium hulls burned pinks and yellows that pleased him. It was a good group. The more hits a craft took, the darker it burned. A violet or indigo fighter was bad news.

"Once over lightly," he thought into the maze communications, and felt more than heard the group's assent. They had all been briefed and he had read the *Younger*'s mission profile more than once, but he wanted to see it. Maybe the others already had, but having been out-manifold often changed the exact positioning in a convoy.

They swept back from the carrier, carefully noting the positions of the various merchant ships traveling under their protection. No matter how many times he told himself how important it was, that the outer colonies would starve without supplies, Cargo hated convoy work above all. Mostly because he hated the merchies.

Even now eyeballing them through the undistorted void, they seemed a motley mess rather than an orderly progression. Spacing was uneven, the hulls themselves showed the burn and scrape of long hard use, and he had no illusions about the beings in them. He'd done convoy work before and seriously doubted it was any different in the Cardia. Arrogant merchie civs, all too ready to be critical of their defenders. Cargo only hoped that he wouldn't have to see any of them when they returned from patrol. Even better, never.

A chorus of emotions, assents, chuckles, solid agreement, surrounded him like a cocoon. Cargo nearly laughed at his own stupidity. He hadn't shut down the intergroup communication. And then decided to leave it on just a little longer.

"Seen enough?" he asked through the maze as the miserable spectacle came to a ragged end. "Let's split two-two, with Dee as swing."

"Right, boss." He understood, and watched the formation change. Ayhan stayed on his wing and Takura and Deseka took the opposite tack on blue orientation. Dee faded slightly and adjusted on red axis. A common Cardia form, it was very different from the way Cargo was accustomed to working. Which was fine. Learning was always a good thing, so long as it didn't get him killed.

The patrol route had been marked in the maze. It showed him eagerly exactly the pattern with all the nav info noted with nearly running commentary. Cargo didn't react. So far it was all very routine. He could almost sense the disappointment in the maze when it had to report an all-clear on the sensor search.

"Looks like no joy, boss," Ayhan thought through the maze.

Cargo didn't reply. Ayhan's observation didn't deserve comment. He almost wished there had been something unidentified that could be explored, or a remote hostile that Dancer or Rugby would burn with the Eyes from this far out, and no contact made. A null made him itchy. Nulls shouldn't be there. Nulls were dangerous. Most of all he didn't trust them and didn't trust the equipment that was supposed to tell him exactly everything out there.

The maze was insulted. Good trick in a machine, Cargo thought, half nasty and half amused. The maze didn't seem to find any humor in the situation. It reminded him not very gently that it had the best and newest sensors made, fully tested and well maintained, and that it had gotten a six on its last overhaul. A six, it informed him, meant better than factory virgin.

Cargo slipped up a notch, to where the maze interface worked through words. And he thought to himself in Romany so that it wouldn't understand. *Things are backward. Dancer is like a machine, the maze is almost alive, as if the two are reversed. Or Dancer had undermined this maze . . .*

He didn't want to complete that thought. It was far too logical, too obvious, and too dangerous to contemplate. He'd been in one crazy maze before; that was the worst thing he could imagine happening in a fighter. Only this maze wasn't crazy. Neither was his Akhaid partner. Just that they weren't really right. Unless this was the way the Cardia worked it. Or there was some other reason Dancer was different, that it was deliberate.

Cargo considered this for a moment, then returned to the deeper levels of the maze. Here he could almost feel the systems like his own body, and there was no time lost between the idea and the execution. Here, down where the membrane was dark, was the place where he was truly in command. Unless there was something very, very wrong with this maze and Dancer had control, that was. He was the pilot and the group leader. The maze had to be his.

"Oh, yes it is," the thought came very cold and very distant through the membrane. Cargo wasn't sure it was Dancer, but there was no other strong candidate. He wondered whether to pursue the matter at this level.

"Not a good idea," the being that had to be Dancer answered.

Cargo scanned the void as he turned it over in his mind. The stars were thick here, the colony they were heading to was on the very edge of where humans or Akhaid could live. Closer in to the galactic cluster the radiation was too harsh and the stars and planets all the wrong kind. The darkness moved and flickered around him as he pondered the whole problem of Dancer.

And then intuition exploded, and he wasn't at all concerned about the niceties of partnerships and the maze anymore. There were batwings out there. He knew it, with a complete and firm knowledge as if they had registered on every sensor on the little fighter.

The maze protested. There were no Cardia stealthcraft in the vicinity. Master Maze kept them informed of that. And anything else the maze could sense. There was nothing out there. Human error. Silly thing, hunches. Funny how all pilots believed them.

The maze treated him with some combination of reassurance and contempt. Cargo didn't buy it. He knew. He had seen them, or, more accurately, had barely noted the negative image of the masked craft as it glided between his own position and the brilliant starfield beyond.

Batwings. Of course. Impossible to target. Nothing picked them up except their own movement.

And then he remembered how he had once been hunted down in the Cardia copy of the batwing, the stealthfighter Ghoster had stolen and given wholesale to their enemies. And the Collegium pilots had a scheme worked out for defeating them. He had almost gotten caught in it.

As he thought he opened the maze to the others in his group, trying to be certain that they understood exactly what he was thinking. And he wove a mask with the maze itself so that the batwing out there, if there was only one, wouldn't pick up on the communication. Hard enough to mask that much; he was fortunate that the stealthcraft were on complete passive with no way to reach out and follow a narrow beam directional signal. At least no way without revealing their position. And that was the one thing they would never ever do.

The only way to find the black nonregistering craft was to backlight them. Like the Kraits he had flown most of his career, the Cardia fighters were brightly burned titanium, highly reflective even in the dim starlight. Three fighters, one for each axis, should be able to box one in. The fighter craft themselves would do to track the negative batwing.

Red. Blue and yellow axis. He called in Dee. Deseka and Takura would have to fly out the rest of their pattern, but at least they were aware of the silent threat.

Dee made the first pass, red axis, as he came in. Nothing blotted his craft from either view of detection as he arrived. Then Ayhan made her run on the blue. A narrow band of darkness, so minor that it could have only been imagination, knifed the jaunty hot pink image of her fighter. The maze politely dissuaded him from registering it, but Cargo knew. The batwings were as thin as knife blades, drifting like wisps of silk through the void. He knew them, knew how they would show. Like a crack of eternity, only the barest hint of what was beyond.

He knew it, but he kept the silence of eternal vac. Yellow. His turn. And he knew with the purity of luck and tradition and perfect intuition where the batwing was. He could even direct Dancer where to fire and was certain to the depths of his soul that he could annihilate the stealthcraft.

Instead, he faded. Beginning the yellow axis run, he instructed the maze to change angle slightly, bringing him farther out and at a slightly sharper angle than he had originally intended. He knew perfectly well where the batwing was, and if the pilot had any sense at all, that stealthfighter would play dead. And he would miss it. Just barely, but there would be nothing for the others to see, no shadow drowning out sight of his electric green craft.

The maze half approved. He knew that it had no comprehension at all, only that it thought that he had finally agreed that its superior sensors couldn't be wrong. Thank the Black Virgin and all the saints that it couldn't read emotions the way it could structure images. Then it would know and Dancer would know, maybe know it before he recognized the reaction himself.

Cargo had been a fighter jock most of his admittedly short adult life. The only way he had ever considered combat was a battle between his mind and a machine. He never saw what was behind the controls of the lethal little craft his Eyes had sent to live on the Wall. If the Cardia had a Wall. All a game, it had been, mind and nerves like the dares when he was a boy and the streets were school.

But this time it was different. This was a batwing like the one he had flown. If half the people he had trained with weren't dead he could give pretty good odds that he had gone drinking with the being in the cockpit and maybe even fleeced it good in a game of khandinar. So he faded, changed the angle just the slightest bit, and for the first time in his life avoided a head-on clash.

As he finished the pass, still low and out, he looped out red just a fraction of a degree to end up in the position where the batwing Eyes would have a hard time finding him. If he wasn't going to obliterate someone he might know, he hadn't gotten a deathwish yet.

"Guess I was wrong," he said the words in his head for the maze to communicate. "Nothing out there."

"Well, a hunch is always a gamble, boss," Ayhan answered. "Too bad, no joy this time. We'll get 'em next."

Cargo sighed and allowed himself the luxury of a blink. Something in him had changed radically and there was no going back. But he didn't want to see the difference and face it, not just now, not yet. There was still so much else crowding his head that he could hardly think.

"Ayhan, take lead. Dee, take wing. I'll go on standby," he informed then finally.

"Sure, boss," Dee said. "But don't take it personally. Hell, that's one great way to find a stealthcraft. Now all we need is a real one to practice on."

The deception wrenched at his innards. Cargo left the pattern slowly, disengaging as if from sleep. Fading, trying to avoid and unable to, he directed the maze from a fog, forcing the fighter to drift as if underpowered back to the standby position.

Then he heard the voice as if it were in his own head, a nightmare that shattered into waking reality. "Hey, there, old buddy. You gave little ole Stonewall a mighty scare, you did."

"Jesus," Cargo muttered aloud. He tried very hard not to believe it, but the maze insisted that communication was coming clearly but it could not find the source.

"Yeah, old buddy, bet you didn't expect to find old Stonewall a way out here in this godforsaken twist of the void where they don't even know how to mix a proper mint julep. You got to bruise the mint, not cut it, that's the trick."

Cargo's whole body felt like lead. That was Stonewall, better than if he had given some password. For a moment Cargo wondered about his ability to kill a real being. Killing Stonewall would make life so much simpler.

Chapter
7

It would be very easy to kill Stonewall. Cargo was in an enemy craft with a Cardia partner—although he suspected otherwise—and there would never be any questions asked. Stonewall deserved it, too, he thought. Stonewall had been riding his back ever since the night the two of them had met, was responsible for this perfectly insane position in the first place. Besides, if there were any questions about him, they would be settled by his killing a batwing. They were notoriously impossible to get, and with good reason. And there would be a kind of perfect justice in Dancer firing Eyes and Stonewall going to live on the Wall. Cargo rather liked the image.

"Now, good buddy, I can tell you it is a real relief that it is you out here and not some goddamned gomer ready to fry my behind," Stonewall drawled. "Because this works out better than even I could have planned it. Now you know I don't believe in any supreme being or anything like that, but there has got to be some random luck running around the manifold."

Cargo merely groaned. Maybe it was Stonewall's luck but it was apt to be his own downfall. Without planning to, rough calculations ran through Cargo's mind. The probability of their meeting in this manner was so close to zero that it was almost closer to miraculous than coincidental. Cargo had not ruled out the possibility of miracles completely as Stonewall had, just in case he ever really needed one.

No coincidence. Tracking.

The thought came from the maze and Cargo was hard-pressed to identify it. Then he understood. Cold as the void, it was Dancer, who must have been observing every thought he had let slip into the waiting darkness of the maze membrane. Dancer felt so very much not there that Cargo had just about forgotten his presence. Now there was another factor. He wondered carefully in Romany just how much Dancer had caught.

As usual, the maze registered disapproval at his thinking in a language it had not been programmed to understand.

"How?" Cargo formed the thought and sent it carefully through the membrane.

No answer came, only a cool shadow that turned the membrane slightly shimmering and then receded. Still, Cargo didn't doubt that Dancer was right. Something about the idea of Stonewall tracking him down made hideous sense. It was exactly Stonewall's style. Not that it had been any real secret where he was going, not with it announced by Ki Shodar himself over a live Cardia-wide broadcast.

However Stonewall had found him, Cargo now had to decide what to do with him. It seemed like Stonewall didn't worry much about the possibility of landing on the Wall, and for a moment Cargo had a very strong urge to shoot just to prove Stonewall wrong. And he knew perfectly well that he would never do it. He was going to let Stonewall go, praying only that the Intel operative would leave him alone forever.

"You know what, good buddy? You are going to get some brownie points, you are. How much hurrah you think they'll make if you bring in a captured batwing? Will that make your day or what?"

Cargo froze. He had never considered the possibility, and what was more, he couldn't quite figure what Stonewall had to gain by such an action. That Stonewall had something to gain he never doubted. Stonewall had never done anything, ever, that was not ultimately calculated to his ultimate goals, of that Cargo was dead certain.

"In."

The coolness again. Dancer. And Cargo understood immediately that he was right. Of course. Stonewall couldn't penetrate the Cardia without extreme risk and difficulty. If he could do it at all. But as a captive, that would immediately take him through all the official barriers. No doubt he would want Cargo to help him escape later, once past all the ident checks, when it would be easy to establish a new persona on-planet.

Through the membrane Cargo sensed something akin to pleasure. Dancer agreed and approved.

"Now come on, Cargo, what is taking you so long? I just gave you the best present you ever got. All you do is haul me back to that beach ball of a carrier sitting out there like an overstuffed Christmas turkey and we're back in business."

Cargo did not know what an overstuffed Christmas turkey looked like. His mother always made roast lamb. The whole thing was disorienting. Then he felt Dancer behind him, solid like a wall and just as supporting, already turning the maze to the task of taking the batwing's controls. Then an evil thought came to him.

"Stonewall, I'm going to blast your aux and masking. So that it looks like you got taken in a fair fight, right? Or else there'll be questions."

Cargo could practically see Stonewall cringe and then brace. It was a delicate shot, but he knew the insides of a batwing down practically to the atomic level. With precision he had never shown before, he guided Dancer through the maze to exactly where the shot should be. Then he took the image only two millimeters to the left. Only two millimeters, but it would be enough. That would do exactly what he told Stonewall he would do, but it was not the perfect optimal shot.

Dancer was with him, unobtrusive as always, but he could read the grim agreement under the mask of proper disapproval. Then he watched through the maze as the Eyes opened and fired exactly as he directed.

The batwing shuddered violently. The aux fuel lit in the line and blazed momentarily before the cut-off valve reacted. Now the batwing looked decently disabled.

"Why did you do that?" Stonewall demanded, his thought/voice overwhelmed with amazement. "You shook the brains out of my ears and the stuffing out of this bird. You are crazy, do you know that, Cargo? You are out of your ever-loving head."

Cargo only chuckled softly. Shaking up Stonewall made him feel a lot better about everything.

Through the maze he was again aware of Dancer's approval and a vague, amused pleasure.

"Who are you?" he asked. "Or are you another one, too? Nothing is what it seems?"

The maze was silent. Cargo made images of the trajectory back to the *Younger*, images that included Stonewall's batwing in tow. The maze responded smoothly with none of the indications of personality it had shown earlier. Unless he had read it wrong and the personality had been Dancer all along.

The maze rippled at every level. Cargo could feel it respond and shift even in the aspects where he was absent before it calmed again and everything was exactly the way it had been before. Only not exactly, although Cargo wasn't sure how he would describe the sensation. It reminded him of a particularly recalcitrant Krait he had been assigned once, and how after balking him at every opportunity, it had been given a careful shakedown by the best mechanic on the *Torque*. And when he got it back it was exactly the same Krait, only with all the rattles gone and the rough spots totally eliminated. As if, somehow, the entire maze was now again more perfect and more clear than its makers had ever intended.

And it was cool to the mind and refreshing. He was completely at ease within it, and while it was still dark it sparkled like bright black steel. He knew it was Dancer. There was a glory and a humor to the calm depths that had nothing at all to do with him or the maze or the war or the Akhaid or anything outside of the individual that was his partner.

"Who the hell are you?" he asked through the maze, more in awe than anger.

The whole being that was the point of contact between the four that made up the fighter craft rippled again briefly and then returned to normal. Regular normal, with all the glitches restored to their proper places. Cargo understood that Dancer might tell him later. Or rather that Dancer would attempt to tell him what the Akhaid thought he would understand. Which may not be a whole lot, or might well be more than Dancer assumed. The Bishop had not neglected the spiritual and philosophical side of his instruction. Through the opaque thickness of the maze at normal, Cargo sensed Dancer's relief.

Then the bloated round bulk of the *Younger* filled the view and he had to concentrate on guiding the maze into the hangar locks.

"I'm coming home for Christmas with a present for all good fliers," he said through the Master Maze as the hangar control took over the lock functions and hauled both vehicles up the tracks.

"Well, look at that," a control tech said so loudly it hurt his ears. Which was funny since the transmission was still in full maze mode. "That Verdun is not content to be a hero one time only, oh no. That boy got a taste of glory and had to go back after more. Look at that. A real live full-size Collegium-fucking stealthfighter and he took it all by his lonesome. Well, now, I'm real impressed. I bet there's a party on the deck tonight."

Cargo winced from the condemnation in that banter. Then he powered down and cracked the hatch, and another voice drifted in on the vigorously vented air. "Did he have to? Can't you keep those cowboys in line? What do you think we are, made of money? All that extra fuel and a patrol of five just to bag a single fighter and you all act like it's some kind of victory."

The control tech was downright friendly compared with the merchies down there. More than anything in his life Cargo didn't want to see them. Most of all he had to get to the head. He gulped the air and started to climb down on the side away from the gathering. Grateful to the tech behind him who steadied him on the rungs, he whispered a quick thanks. The blood was only just starting to come back into his feet.

He leaned against the bright burned hull of the little fighter and made his way back to the bulkhead, careful to keep some screen between himself and the unpleasant voices.

"What I don't know is why they were so far away," another of their convoy merchants whined. "If this stealthfighter attacked us they would have been too far away to help. All our goods . . ."

"Shut up, Rashtaheldd. What I'm worried about is, there was one of these things found out there. What about any more, that's what I want to know. Why didn't they go look for another?"

By the time he had traversed the three meters to the head, Cargo wasn't sure whether he wanted to piss or puke.

•   •   •

"That's not exactly a routine request," the Commander said, tapping her fingers gently against the edge of the metal desk. "And there are the interrogation teams."

Cargo sighed and waited. Already things were going better than he could have assumed. She was at least willing to consider the possibility. That was about what he had expected.

"I was a prisoner myself, ma'am," he replied softly. "I know a little about it. And I'm curious."

A smile curled on her lips. "Yes. Curious. I would be too. I'm glad you admitted it. Well, I don't think it can do any harm, but I'll check with interrogation. They may want to update you, or even brief you on something or other. Anyway, I'll recommend it, but the Security Office has the final say."

He thanked her and stepped out before he could become a nuisance. That was one thing he had learned very early. The rest of the group was waiting for him in the hot room anyway, which by rights was where he belonged. He followed the dull-colored corridors without noticing them the few meters between the watch office and the hot room.

Room was really a misnomer. It was a hangar bay, just as large as any of the others, but with only five fighters tracked and ready and an assignment board overhead with their names all in red, indicating hot-room duty. One corner of the overlarge bay had been made up as a lounge, with three large sofas, a game table surrounded by six uncomfortable portable grid chairs, a coffee table, and a reading rack with adjustable lights. The coffee table was full of white paper, some of it wrapped around what Cargo assumed were sandwiches and the rest discards sprinkled with the debris of lunch. Two boxes were precariously balanced on the reading rack, one of them a popular brand of cookies that Cargo remembered eating in great quantities his third year of university. The other box was covered with writing in Atrash, and although he couldn't read the language he assumed that it contained something comparable.

"Come on, we're lucky today," Rick Dee said brightly, looking up from the last bites of a pickle. "Good stuff, out of the dirty watch. Nothing but the best here. Take a look. Corned beef on rye, tuna and tomato on hard roll, and fried chicken pieces. None of it touched by the hands of you-know-who."

Cargo chuckled appreciatively.

Rugby looked up from what appeared to be a hard-fought game of Conquest. "How did it go?" he asked.

Cargo shrugged. "I'll know when I know. You know. Who's winning?"

Rugby's ears curled slightly at the tip. "Seniz. She always does. Unless Gen and I devise a brilliant plan in the next fifteen minutes, which is not completely out of the question."

"Right," Seniz broke in. "When you're not praying for the hot bell so you can jump up and overturn the table and we have to start all over again like last time."

Rugby looked straight at Cargo and put on an expression that on Ghoster he would have called false innocence. "Effective tactics."

"Only in a target-rich environment," Gen grumbled, never taking his eyes off the board. "Given the current situation we could be dead and the Watch Office wouldn't know it."

A general grumble of assent confirmed it. Cargo remained silent. Usually he preferred hot duty to be quiet. They were there as the immediate reinforcements in case a routine patrol turned out not to be so routine. But with the exception of the one batwing he had brought in there hadn't been an enemy vessel sensed since they had returned to the manifold. And it didn't look like there were going to be any, either. The Collegium had better targets than a struggling colony out on the fringe. This wasn't anyplace they were likely to show up; the rest of the group knew it as well as Cargo who had flown the other side.

Seniz smiled in a predatory manner. "Would you like the next game, Verdun? Winner take all?"

Cargo matched her smile. "How about a few rounds of khandinar? I wouldn't give you much of a game of Conquest."

"Sure," she said, and Cargo was pleased to note what he thought was amusement on Rugby's face.

Cargo glanced over the group. Something was wrong, someone was missing. It took him a moment to connect. Dancer. He asked quickly if anyone had seen his partner.

"He was in here, boss," Rick said. "Maybe he went down for a refill of whatever he was eating. I didn't look."

Cargo tried very hard not to lose his temper. He'd been out, too. But at least everyone knew where he was and the watch office was wired to the hot room, and if there was a bell call he would have been ready and in the cockpit before anyone had ever noticed he wasn't there. That was the whole point.

But he had to stop getting so angry at Dancer. Maybe the Akhaid had told someone where he'd be. Maybe he was even in another corner doing something quiet, who knew? Only Cargo was perfectly aware that while everything looked fine on the surface, another thing was happening that he couldn't see. And it was all happening around Dancer, and, Cargo suspected, Ki Shodar.

He forced himself to take a deep breath and sit down on one of the sofas, the turquoise one with a black and yellow abstract pattern that had been popular long before anyone in the group had been born. Breathe. Relax.

Breathing gives you distance from your emotions, he remembered the shrink in the stress management seminar at the university saying. *Emotions come and go, like the wind. You can let them rule you or you can let them pass. Let them pass and remain calm, detached. In the calm place you can decide what you will do. Action, not emotion, is the only final scale.*

The memory startled him. Cargo had forgotten it all. He closed his eyes and tried to remember the calm that he had experienced so long ago. It was that meditation that had helped him decide to follow his own path as a pilot rather than the political appointment the Bishop had secured. Now it came over him again, rusty and unsure, but real.

He had always hated hot duty. The waiting, the quiet, wore on his nerves. Always, no matter what he was doing, he was tensed, listening for the bell. Even sleeping in the hot dorm he was coiled, waiting to spring out of bed at the first call. But the alarm was the only relief. The sitting, the waiting, the long hours of boredom cooped up with the members of his own group without the distractions of even paperwork to take up their time, all of it made Cargo jumpy and ate away at his strength.

Ghoster had known that, and Two Bits had too. They had kept him distracted, the two of them, kept him out of trouble until he had become a batwing and was off hot duty forever. Or so he thought.

And then through the calm he saw just how funny the situation was and he began to laugh. Here he was worried about hot duty when technically he was a civilian, and here under cover. Only they knew who he was, his cover was blown, and he was still playing the same old games.

For that moment through the laughter he broke into a new place in the calm, a place where he could see himself as part of a larger pattern. And he knew that it was time to change, to try something different. It was like the moment at the river when he understood that turning in his wings was the only thing he could do. It was time to move on. It was time to Walk.

Then the moment was gone and he was only Cargo again sitting on the ugly turquoise sofa in the hot hangar. But some of the cooling understanding had remained, enough so that the edge of tension was gone. He had made a decision. Even if the situation was the same, he could be different. He didn't have to be part of it.

As he opened his eyes and they found focus in the dark recesses of the opposite corner of the bay he saw a bit of white movement. Detached, he studied it carefully. A flutter of white rose and descended, then shifted so that he could see clearly. Dancer was getting in some rack time. Not a bad idea at all.

"Hey." Seniz had risen from the table and was now standing over him. "You ready for that game of khandinar now, or you gonna join you partner in the kiddies' nap corner?"

Cargo stood up to join her. Cacciatore and Rugby were still at the table, Rugby shuffling the eight decks of cards used in professional play in his long-fingered Akhaid hands. Cargo took a place at the table and waited for Rugby to deal. It was going to be a very long rotation.

There had once been a brig on the *Younger*, but it had been in disuse so long that the chief quartermaster, hating to see perfectly good space go to waste, had quietly turned the three small cells into additional storage for the fighter techs. Stonewall's capture had caused dismay among them. No one wanted to give up the space, especially not when Security had one use in umpteen zillion years and Repairs was strapped as it was. Even on a carrier the size of the *Younger*, turf was physical and real and something to fight over. Sometimes, Cargo suspected, there were more turf battles between the departments than engagements with the enemy. At least it seemed to be going that way on this cruise.

"You know, you've caused us a lot of trouble," the security chief had said in the same tone of voice he might have used had Cargo been arrested for violation of some local colony code. "You bring us a goddamned prisoner and we don't have any place to put him. And now you want to visit him, no less. Next time you get any bright ideas, check them out with the skipper first, right? Before you go and get us in trouble with the quartermasters."

Cargo didn't dare breathe. He had to talk to Stonewall. Not that he was entirely ready to go along with the other's plans, not without a hearing, but he had a couple of very good guesses as to what Stonewall might be after. And the decision was his, finally and irrevocably. That made it a little more bearable. He couldn't stand the idea of Stonewall standing his back up against the Wall one more time, and he couldn't discount the possibility either. All of it crammed his head and threatened to burst out right here in the security office.

"Well, what the hell are you waiting for?" the chief growled at him. "You maybe want an engraved invitation? Haul your leaden ass out of here."

Cargo didn't wait to be told again. He pivoted precisely and marched through the door before the chief could have any second thoughts.

There was a good bit of corridor to traverse between the office and the brig. In the original design that hadn't been the case, but it just made a whole lot more sense to locate Security near the bridge and shift Repairs from a cubicle near Mechanics down to the old security office. Which, for the twelve previous years of the *Younger*'s commissioned life, had been perfectly adequate. Unfortunately, only the three cells originally designated as the brig by the designers had been equipped with Eye locks. So Cargo found himself wandering through sections he had never seen before, not on any ship on which he had served. He managed to pass a galley full of baking smells that had to be investigated, and turned out to be fresh cinnamon buns. Two were forced upon him then and there, which better equipped him to endure questing through the bowels of the Maintenance and Repair departments, and four others wrapped in a napkin he counted as materials of interrogation.

Cargo didn't even have to talk to the petty officer on duty to know that Repairs was not only miserable, but defiant about being put out for a mere prisoner. Pieces of machinery that probably had been stored in Stonewall's cell were stacked in magboxes out in the hallway. The remaining passage was so narrow that Cargo had to squeeze up against the bulkhead and twist his shoulders away from the cages.

Probably, he thought, one of the interrogators was over-weight. It tended to run in Security, and the techs weren't above rubbing their noses in it. Good thing, too, he added with grim pleasure. Security was no different here than it had been at home, which meant they could use a few lessons in humility. Even more than the spook squad, Security offended honest pilots. A bunch of police who sat on their fat asses all day and never risked their necks looking for something to pin on the people who went out on the front line. Cargo only hoped the fat interrogator was more miserable negotiating that stretch of corridor than he had been.

The Eye lock opened to the security code and Cargo stepped inside. In spite of the glaring lighting Stonewall was curled up on the cot as if he were sleeping. Barren but clean, the cell was very little different from his own quarters, Cargo noted. The head wasn't decently obscured and there was no color at all but white, and the place lacked a terminal and a chair, but otherwise the arrangements seemed more Spartan than unpleasant. Of course. The brig had been designed only for the common run of prisoners, EW's coming back from liberty more than a little soused, a repair chief second who got into a minor skirmish in a planetary bar over some imagined insult, or the new kid who went AWOL out of homesickness.

The designers had never considered the possibility of enemy prisoners of war. In the kinds of battles the *Younger* fought there were no prisoners. Not because of any ideology, but because vac was a harder master than any living one. Cargo remembered an instructor in flight school saying not so long ago that if you could limp back to a carrier you weren't really damaged, and if you were really damaged you wouldn't have time to say more than one Our Father before the coffin blew. One night he had even worked out the probabilities.

And, he recognized wryly, if anyone else on the *Younger*

had, there would be a whole lot more explaining to do than just luck. Even a hero's luck.

"Stonewall?" Cargo asked softly.

"My name is Greydon Beauregaurd . . ." Stonewall mumbled, not turning.

"Stonewall," Cargo said more firmly, demanding attention.

This time Stonewall rolled over and squinted at Cargo. "Oh. It's you. You one of them, now? I was just getting a little sleep . . ."

"Sorry," Cargo interrupted. "This was when I was sent down. I don't exactly have the hourly access code to this place, you know. And you had better remember that this was your idea in the first place. Which brings me to the point. You've got a little explaining to do."

Stonewall groaned. "Not now. Is that what you were sent for, anyway? Get me talking and this place is bugged and Security gets everything. Might be better than sitting with the fat guy again. I swear, he sweats just looking at me. I mean, I am certain that he finds this cell even less bearable than I do, and I do not find the accommodations exactly on par with the Luxor InterZone."

"You never stayed at the Luxor InterZone," Cargo muttered crossly.

Stonewall grinned in that familiar, maddening way of his. "I most certainly did. My great-granddaddy never ever would have stayed anywhere else. When I went out to recruit you I had a stipend to stay on Luxor for a week, but since I knew damned well that you couldn't resist my invitation, I blew the whole thing on one night at the InterZone. And let me tell you, it was worth it. The place is not overrated."

"Goddamn you, Stonewall, I didn't come here to have you talk about hotels," Cargo sputtered. "And the place isn't bugged."

"That's stupid."

Cargo snorted. "Whatever. Even if it was, it isn't anymore. In case you didn't know, you are responsible for a major turf war between Repairs and Security. This cell has been a storage shed since the ship was commissioned. Believe me, they'd make damned sure that whatever leftover bugs still down here aren't working out of pure spite."

Stonewall grinned evilly. "Ah, yes, spite. An emotion that I can always rely on. Nothing lame and unreinforced like love and propriety. Spite is part honor and part duty. You know, old buddy, I could like this place."

For a moment Cargo seriously regretted not having killed Stonewall when he had the chance. The only choice was to leave. He couldn't listen to the Charlestonian's cruelly twisted logic any longer. If he had remembered that in the first place he wouldn't have even been here, back in the military he had already renounced once. A second time was simply insanity.

But then Stonewall's voice became lower and serious again. "But that still leaves duty and honor. Cargo, for all you are a Gypsy, you understand those things better than most people who would call themselves gentlemen. To the manner, if not the manor, born. And it may be my duty to track down an informer. But my honor demands that I get Gantor in the bargain. Who do you think planted that rumor about genetic engineering experiments? At least Ghoster thought he had a morally defensible reason to keep us killing each other off. Gantor only cares about his own hide, and I mean to have it off him and hang it over the ancestral mantel along with my great-great-granddaddy's sword."

Cargo blinked and tried to track. He was lost. Gantor? The name was familiar but he couldn't place it immediately. The whole thing swam like boiling stew, where the only way to discover what was in the pot was to taste it. Only in this case the mixture smelled noxious.

"Can you be more specific?" he asked Stonewall, stalling for time.

The evil grin became wider and more set. "It's really very easy, Cargo. All you have to do is wake up and open your eyes. Having Bishop Mirabeau for a father can be as much a disadvantage as a blessing. You're as innocent as he is. Think. Gantor is the Prefect in charge of Operations and in line for Vice Minister. Functionally he is the commander of the Second Directorate. You haven't forgotten the good old Second Directorate, have you? Anyway, that's Gantor. I had a meeting with him before I tasked you, actually, and a very interesting talk we had, him and me. Indeed it was. You see, Cargo, our former boss Mr. Gantor doesn't dare let your Bishop succeed in his negotiations because that would mean that Mr. Gantor had served his usefulness. And Prefect Gantor has ambitions to become Minister Gantor. Even Trustee Gantor, if he is very careful. Only the record of the Second Directorate won't look very good under open inquiry if he rises to the appointment. On the other hand, if we're still at war, there is every reason to keep the books closed. Security and all that. You understand. And they'll buy it. I'd even buy it, only I met with that slime worm myself and believe me I know how to smell a stinking sewer when I climb into one. He had the nerve, the unmitigated gall, to request that I make you, well, unavailable for future employment. Because of the Bishop, you understand. What that pig thing that doesn't deserve the name sentient didn't understand is that a gentleman does not kill his friends just because some greedy, gibbering, cross-eyed, no-account ass-hole wants to get ahead."

"So what does this have to do with you being here and Ghoster?" Cargo asked, his head spinning. It was too much all at once, too much that he had never suspected.

Stonewall hissed through his teeth. "I think you must be eating annies mixed in your potatoes," he said. "Or you got mush for brains. I've got to get to Ghoster and get whatever faction of his to understand that we've got to stop this squabbling *right now*. Then leak it out through him, through the Akhaid side, that the genetic engineering thing was all third-party disinformation. Or something like that."

"You mean you don't have a plan." Cargo had no need to make it a question.

Stonewall shook his head in mock despair. "Old buddy, I have something better than a plan. I have experience. All I need for you to do is spring me free and clear once we get to wherever it is we're going to. By the way, where is it? Once I'm clear, I will resolve matters in a month. If I were a gambling man I'd say we could let, say, five hundred big ones ride on it."

Cargo sat down on the disheveled cot and rested his head in his hands. Stonewall was getting to be a habit. Worse, he had misjudged the *Gaje*, or was misjudging him now. Whichever, he was dazed and hated it. Like everything was reversed all at once.

"Don't tell me," he muttered to himself. "Next thing he's going to say is that Plato's alive and that Fourways is really the Trustee Jong Tu in disguise."

The words only made it worse. He hadn't known the legendary Jong Tu, but thinking about Plato only hit that much closer to home. He had managed to avoid remembering much, buried in paperwork or playing khandinar until he collapsed. At least counting cards focused his full mind so that he was unable to let his attention drift to the memories that still haunted him. Plato alive, the clean smell of her skin, the way her curls tickled his neck. And if Stonewall knew that Plato was alive he would kill Stonewall with his bare hands, and prayed for the opportunity. After all, when they were in training on Vanity he had pulled something similar, reporting Bugs dead when she was only under cover.

This time, though, Stonewall's face was a mask of sorrow when he looked up. "Sorry, good buddy. I'm a pretty mean magician, but when the luck's all gone I can't pull anyone back from the dead. We're the only ones that are left among the living, buddy. You and me and Ghoster. We're the only ones who know."

"Sometimes I hate you," Cargo said, and watched with amazement as Stonewall seemed to grow older before him. There was something with the expression, with the skin. Something in the very quality of the gaze that reminded Cargo of Mirabeau.

"It's even worse than that," Stonewall said as if he hadn't heard. "I don't know how to say it because I don't know what it is. I hate Gantor and that's enough for me. I can stop him and that is where it ends. Only it doesn't end there, Cargo. There's something else that I can't see at all, something to do with Ki Shodar and Bishop Mirabeau when he was still a Trustee. Something that's been buried so deep and left to rot that everyone knows it's all gone. I've got to get there, Cargo. The rest I could probably do on my own. But you're close to Shodar and closer to Mirabeau. I don't care if you hate me, not really. We're friends no matter what you think you think. And I just can't believe that you can sit here and listen to me tell you that you've got the power to topple this whole damned tower down, and you're just going to sit there and do nothing. I wouldn't lay one penny on that."

Cargo heaved himself up from the cot and walked three steps to the glaring white wall. The bulkhead was painted, but the metal still conducted the cold. He leaned his forehead against the chill surface and tried to let everything disappear. Like the calm place he had found looking for Dancer, he sought and quested for the place where he could laugh at Stonewall and what Stonewall was saying.

Only it didn't come. Panic encroached on all sides and he wanted to run and hide. Anywhere would be fine. He should have stayed on Luxor. He should have followed that Walker into the river that day when he said good-by to Plato, followed that frail and shining rag of humanity into the deep currents and muddy tides and drowned. For the first time he understood Sonfranka, why she had lacked the courage to face something new. Essential newness was not the problem, just the kind of newness it was. The whole manifold had twisted itself into an improbable shape, a form that denied God and mathematics and his own existence.

Then, crystalline and distant, he heard an echo from the maze. No longer in it, it surrounded his mind and buffered him with itself. Only it wasn't just any maze. It was the maze that held the matrix of Dancer, cool and subtle flowing through the familiar and malleable patterns. And Cargo heard a soft clear laughter from the place he had touched once and he knew it was Dancer.

"I'll do it," he heard himself say through the thick barrier of the maze. "Goddamn you, Stonewall, this is getting to be a habit, but I'll do it."

Only it was like he wasn't really there and hadn't really said the words, had only listened to them said by some other entity. And in the background Dancer permeated his being and laughed.

Stonewall's voice pierced the maze's distance. "I knew you'd come through, old buddy. I knew I could count on you."

Chapter
8

Spin Street on Tel Hala wasn't any different from Spin Street on any other world or in any colony. Without the appeal of a true city MidCenter, Spin Street catered to the port business, which usually demanded only the basics. Like in the Collegium, it was called Spin Street in the Cardia as well. And like in the Collegium it was gaudy and loud and cheap. So far as Cargo was concerned, after the *Younger* it promised to be paradise. That is, after a certain duty had been discharged. He still couldn't figure out how Stonewall managed to get him to agree so readily to such stupidity. Tel Hala. At the very least he could have picked a proper planetary society to get lost in.

"So, boss, we reported all stowed," Seniz told him happily as they waited for the liberty rotation schedule to appear on the "big board" in the wardroom. "So you think we'll make it down before dinner?"

Cargo half smiled and shrugged. Before he had considered Stonewall, his top priority had been no different than his second's—a decent meal. Any kind of meal would do, just so long as it was fresh and not made by their own infamous chef.

Now he could hardly focus on even the temptation of edible food. Stonewall, as usual, had come along and screwed everything to the Wall. Cargo cursed under his breath in Romany, wondering why he had ever agreed to help good old Greydon Randolph again. This was getting to be a habit, and a bad one at that. Every time he had seen Stonewall his life had gotten worse.

"I'll second that, boss," Gen said.

Cargo blinked. He hadn't realized he had said anything aloud. Then he glanced up to cover, and quickly muttered thanks to whatever deity of luck had guarded him. The schedule had appeared just as he had muttered, and his group wasn't listed until halfway down.

Relief flooded him. Much as Cargo knew that his group really were hoping to move up the priority list due to Stonewall's capture, he was just as glad they were slated to remain aboard until the next morning. Technically that meant they could leave at what some people called "oh-dark-thirty," but given this group Cargo was sure most of them would prefer the sleep. Which meant that they weren't going to have much time for the distractions Tel Hala cautiously provided.

"Well, it isn't like this is prime liberty country," he said, trying to be encouraging. "We'll be at the top of the list next time and that's supposed to be Paese. I don't know about you, but I'd rather spend my time on a real planet rather than in a habitat. And Paese is famous for its food, and it's supposed to be a great place for just about everything. I never even heard about Tel Hala before now."

"Yeah, well, I'll starve to death before we get there," Seniz replied quickly. Then she bit her lip and relented. "Sorry, boss. We know you did your best. And what the hell, you may be right. Only you're buying on Paese, right?"

Cargo nodded solemnly. "Best restaurant in town." He took two steps to the left, preparatory to leaving the room altogether, when he heard Richard's lowered voice behind him. "Great, Seniz. Guess whose money is going to pay anyway? How many times have you lost to him in khandinar?"

Cargo slipped through the door before he could hear any more. Seniz had stopped playing after the first game. Not that she was a real spotter, but Rugby was and had probably tipped her off. Seniz Ayhan and Rugby were a team he could understand, the way he had been with Ghoster. Not whatever strangeness he had felt through the maze with Dancer. Not the cold silence that greeted him every time they climbed into the twin cockpits and swallowed Three-B's.

Shodar had done this, Cargo thought. The whole thing, start

to finish, was a set-up. The Cardia leader had to know about Stonewall. Unless the Bishop was involved. The whole thing turned cartwheels in his head, threatened to make him dizzy.

Maybe Shodar knew, but there hadn't been time for a message to go out and come back, for all the command codes to go through. At least Cargo hoped not. It all came down to luck, that fickle, useless stuff that didn't exist except in a fighter-jock's dreams.

The rotation had been sheer luck, and undeserved at that. A fifteen-hour interval would be a big help, and having half the ship's complement gone would be even better. Cargo chewed his lower lip as he made his way through the dull single burn corridors to his own quarters. So long as his roommates weren't there he would be fine, because the last thing in the world he needed was to try and fake conversation.

Two of them, Yoshun and Mac, were there but in the process of heading out. Both alluded perfunctorily to his rotten luck before they left as quickly as possible. As if luck could rub off, as if they didn't catch the first shuttle down they would be left stranded on the *Younger*. And then the tiny stateroom was quiet. Which was good because Cargo needed to think.

The biggest problem was the Eye beams. Once that was past, getting Stonewall down as a member of the crew wouldn't be any trouble at all. But Eye beams weren't anything Cargo had been taught how to deal with.

Deception he knew, and picking traditional locks. In fact, his uncle had made them all pick locks until they were as fast as using a key. But the Eyes didn't work that way, at least not doorguard Eyes. It was almost impossible to break the circuit once it was established. And Cargo had gone over all the specs yet again to try and make out some flaw. That was the problem with Eyes. They were made so there weren't any, not that any humans could break.

Which meant it had to be human error. The Eyes were controlled somewhere, and Cargo was certain that the original link had to run through the old security office. The fact that the department had moved didn't deter him. No one would bother reconnecting the whole show. At best the control panel would still be functional in what was now the repair office, but Cargo didn't think his luck would hold that far. What did make sense was a patch through to the new security office. And a patch was even easier than a pick lock, Cargo told himself happily. Temporary and put in over protest by the Repairs department, the very people who weren't happy over their space being commandeered in the first place, it was probably a grossly makeshift affair.

A slow smile spread over Cargo's face. God bless interdepartmental politics. May the Virgin guard turf battles forever. Yes, certainly this operation was divinely inspired. If only it wasn't Stonewall he was rescuing Cargo would have been insufferably pleased with himself. What had Old Pulika said about the Rom and luck? He cast back again but all that was left was a shadow. No matter. The way things were going now he was golden. He could do no wrong. Like the time he had stolen C. L. Wong's yacht.

He was so pleased that he was able to do the only reasonable thing for a person in his position. He rolled over to get some good rack time before he was ready to act. After all, the *Younger* had to eliminate half its crew to make matters even more perfect.

When he woke in the darkness shreds of dream images floated on the edge of consciousness. Ghoster had been there and that had been important. And C. L. Wong's yacht and how everything had finally gone wrong and they had been caught and put in juvie, and his cousin Angel with the knife and his father stabbed to death in a card game. All of it twisted crazily and he tried to follow it, remember. Because there was something important there, he was certain of it. But the images just drifted away, after-dreams that left only a faint unease before they dissolved.

The dreams faded but the fear didn't. It was only springing Stonewall, Cargo told himself firmly and knew he was lying. Not that he wasn't worried about Stonewall, but he hadn't committed to the action yet. If things didn't go well in the next half hour there was always Paese, which would be a better choice for Stonewall than Tel Hala anyway.

He glanced at the hard blue chrono display. It was oh-dark-thirty, all right. Four twenty-seven in the morning. He'd overslept by forty-five minutes. Losing the touch, away too long, that must be why. In the back of his head he could hear Old Pulika say, *Between two and four in the morning is always the best time. The body is low and tired, the metabolism is down, it is the time most favored for disease and for sleep. Judgment is distorted. So if you want to work the street, always remember two to four.*

He had pondered that advice at the time, and had continued to think about it through the years. Mostly he wondered how Old Pulika, who was illiterate, could possibly know standard long-haul material like established facts about Circadian rhythms. Long-haul? He almost laughed aloud at his own oversight. Old Pulika covered more territory in any three years than a merchie would in a lifetime. Just because the old man was unlettered didn't mean he was stupid as well. In fact, Cargo figured that next to the Bishop, Old Pulika had been the most astute person he had ever known.

So he had overslept. At least he knew what he was about. Good chance that anyone on duty now would be seriously lax in judgment. Wariness always went down when they were near a colony or a planet, especially with a convoy. The Collegium wouldn't bother attacking now, not when the point and the goods were all delivered. On top of that, there was the promise of liberty and the fact that most of the crew had been a very long time without. Not that the *Younger* appeared negligent in duty, but that the details that perhaps several weeks ago would have alerted someone to a potential situation were now likely to be overlooked. Circadian rhythms, Cargo thought, and overwork, while his mind was fresh and focused on the task.

He dressed quickly and grabbed his ready-packed kit, the one with extra civvies for Stonewall. Then, before he could consider anything more seriously, he wandered down the empty hall deep into the mysterious precinct controlled by Repairs.

Deserted and unlit except where he passed, Cargo thought that this area of the *Younger* could be one of the infamous "ghost ships" that were rumored to haunt the Cygna sector. In his student days people claimed to run into them all the time on yachting trips, a great ship that once was home to perhaps a thousand, all fully decked out and deserted. No hint of where the people had gone or why, only remnants of what was once a place alive, and now only waited.

Stupid, stupid stories, like the stories his mother had told him of the *mule,* the ghosts, who protected their people. And some who cursed. She had even given him *mule* string to unknot and call on someone on the other side for protection. Suddenly he wished he still had some of that string, to talk to Plato and Two Bits only just for a minute.

Then he blinked and looked around. He was only spooking himself, and he didn't believe in *mule* or ghosts or ghost ships. It was only the repairs section of the *Younger* when half the crew was gone and all but the very few on the dog watch were asleep.

Past two more bends in the hallway and he was outside the former security section. He hesitated, considering two options. One, he could go, disconnect the patch-through, and then either trust Stonewall to notice and leave or go down and get him. Cargo discarded that as unnecessarily risky. Easier to go past the cell and alert Stonewall to what was going to happen. Only that posed another problem. The Eye beams were for security, but there was the small matter of a titanium door. It was one thing to turn off the Eyes and pick the absolutely ordinary lock on the door. It was another to communicate through it.

No questions, then. Cargo winced, knowing that he had been forced by circumstance to choose the worst plan possible. Not that there was any other choice, only that he didn't like to play so close to the odds. Unconsciously his hand reached the chain at his neck and stroked the St. Maries-de-la-Mer medal. For luck, his *draba*, even though he didn't believe in *draba*. It never hurt to respect it, just in case. If there was ever a time he would need luck it was now breaking Stonewall out of the brig.

He approached from the brig side so he could recce the situation before trying the office. The cages filled with machine parts that Repairs had sullenly stored in the corridor created excellent cover. With luck, with the *mule*, there was some chance that they wouldn't be found too quickly. Good enough.

Cargo dropped his kit casually by Stonewall's cell and kicked it just far enough that it was hidden by what looked to be a burned-out aux converter. Then he went to the office that had once been assigned to Security and was now staffed by Repairs. Wondering how many people they had on duty now, he opened the door and sailed in as if it were the most natural thing in the manifold.

"Hello?" he asked, testing.

Only silence. He glanced around quickly. Nobody. Not even a half-filled coffee cup, a game up on the screen, a crossword book and pencil jammed into the chair clip. Not a single sign of habitation.

Cargo thanked all his *mule* and all his *draba* for this piece of luck, knowing that it was inevitable and he had simply overlooked things. Repairs had no reason to keep a night shift on, not now. They'd had a rather quiet run and the department had managed to keep pretty much ahead of schedule. Just because he had been thinking like a pilot or a batwing who was never really off didn't mean that the rest of the universe worked that way.

It was great luck that Repairs didn't have anyone on watch, but Cargo knew that he wouldn't be quite so fortunate with Security. And if he didn't know that any tampering with the patch-through would set off more alarms in the Security Office than in a bank vault he wasn't Old Pulika's nephew.

If only Two Bits were here. Then one of them would go up to the Security Office and start a conversation, distract whoever was there. Two Bits had had a special talent for that kind of thing. Then, when the alarms went off, Two Bits would outrun anyone and get down here first and find a faulty connection. Maybe the chair hadn't been properly clipped to the stand and had overbalanced, pulling the connectors with it. Nothing to worry about at all, five minutes to fix up everything and maybe they shouldn't report it. After all, Security was already in the deep one with Repairs for starters. A report would only add insult to injury.

It was a perfect plan. Too bad there wasn't anyone to help him carry it out.

Then, very slowly, Cargo grinned.

Quickly he flipped through the duty roster and found a name, a good common one that with any more luck would be duplicated so many times through the ship that it would be impossible to figure out who it was. Besides, the name carried a poetic justice to it that Cargo felt sure indicated that it had been a gift from the *mule*.

The next order of business was to look up the intercom code

for Security. Old Pulika always said that the best plans were a gift from the saints and came only when they were needed, never before. Fair enough.

Not until he had those details ready did he begin to search the cluttered office for what had once been the Eye Board, with a makeshift through-unit. It didn't even occur to Cargo to wonder how he'd recognize it. *Draba* and the saints were with him, he was riding luck like a game of khandinar when he had seven thousand up and broke the bank. There was a clarity in the air that matched the clarity and perfect focus of his mind. Everything was of a piece. Even the dregs left in the bottom of the coffee pot had a shining, perfect presence.

The office was not small, but there was no reason to search the whole thing. The Eye Board had to be installed in the control bank, a control bank that Repairs really didn't need but probably used for scheduling and inventory control. There was only one console in the middle of the room with four stations around a central core. Cargo walked around the console twice before he found the Eye Board. It wasn't large and was set under three screens that must have been placed there to watch prisoners. And the setup was just about what he had expected, a jury-rig held together with spit balls and threats and threaded up through a ventilation shaft.

He sat at the station and ran his hands over the smooth, cool aluminum. Then he encountered something sticky that drew his attention. A splotch of coffee that hadn't been completely cleaned up still clung to the shining surface. Cargo was furious. This was not the way to keep a ship. No chief worth the rank would permit this kind of slovenly upkeep, not ever in his experience. Then, slowly, the anger turned to a silent muttering of gratitude. Indeed, the Black Virgin was guiding his every step. This was much, much better.

All the pieces now perfectly aligned, Cargo went to the corner and poured himself a disposable cup of what had once, a very long time ago, passed as coffee. He returned to the station and sat down for a moment, placing the cup on the ridge over the screens, checking the position and the distance. Then he took the cup in his hand again and poured it over the transfer box.

Nothing happened.

Cargo sighed and prepared to go to plan B when the

intercom started beeping furiously. As Cargo switched to audio his ear was blasted by the explosion coming from the security officer on watch.

"What the hell is going on there?" an enraged voice demanded. "If you're turned off those . . ."

Cargo smiled angelically. "Sorry, sir," he said, trying to keep his tone contrite. "Just a little spill messing up the patch to your office. Everything down here shows the cell secure. I'll get it cleaned up right away."

"What's your name?" the security officer asked. "I'm going to report this to the head of your department. To the Captain if I have to. That prisoner is important, do you understand that, important. And don't think I don't know that you people aren't pulling everything you can just to stuff a few cubic meters full of broken down shit."

"Wong, sir, R Tech Three. Clinton LeRoy Wong."

He heard a mad scrabble on the other end, and then opacity. He switched off the audio on the unit and was into the Eye control without pausing to even consider the pleasant ironies of life. Not yet. He pulled the patch out of the board and studied the panel in front of him with professional concentration. He had never been Eyes and had never trained with them, but there was a certain level of familiarity all pilots acquired. He should be able to turn the damned thing off, only the configuration was different and commands probably were too. And there wasn't time to call up a manual on the system, even it he had the authorization code to do so.

Instead he took a deep breath and tried to become calm. Then he pushed the first button to the left.

All three screens flickered to life. *Ready/Start* appeared in hard chrome yellow across all three. He hesitated for a second and tried to remember the commands for Eyes. Then it struck him. On board a Krait there was no stop signal. A sigh escaped through his teeth. Great.

Cargo thought about Old Pulika who had taught him to lie and steal like a proper Gypsy _chal_. Pulika used computers all the time, strange ones, and the old man could hardly read his own name. "It's easy," he had told Cargo, smiling with his missing incisor. "Most of them have an audio button. You find that. Then you ask help. And it will tell you enough to start. Once you start you can lie to a computer just the same as a

person, only easier. A computer doesn't have any trouble
believing you. They don't know never trust a Gypsy. Eh,
boy?"

Cargo didn't want the audio, just in case anyone should
wander down into this godforsaken part of the ship. He turned
it off and used the keyboard. Otherwise, Old Pulika's advice
was perfectly good. *_Help_*

And just like magic all the commands he needed scrolled by.
Truly, he vowed he would change his ways. He would light a
candle to Ste. Anne and thank her, and all the saints who
looked over and protected the Rom. And he would never ever
say that the *draba* didn't exist. Surely luck walked the
manifold, and for this one night luck walked with him.
Profound gratitude that no one had bothered to secure the
system flowed through him along with the knowledge that to
aid him was the only reason this was so. His fingers flew over
the command keys, touching the multicolored buttons on the
control board as if he had used the system all his life. Finally
the screens came back with *Eyes Closed//temp test//temp
test//ten-minute cycle//test//test*

Cargo was in the corridor and picking the lock on Stonewall's cell before the message could go into automatic repeat.
It took less than a minute to get through the lock. Standard,
Cargo noted, nothing that would hold any decently trained *chal*
at all. The *Gaje* relied too much on their Eye beams and their
technology, and they themselves might not think to pick a lock,
not if the door itself looked thick and sturdy.

Stonewall was lying on the cot. Cargo half shook him and
half hauled him up. "Come on. Now," he whispered harshly,
and pulled him up. Stonewall was barely done rubbing his eyes
when Cargo relocked the door before hooking his kit from
under a pile of machinery. The top layer contained a repair
overall, R Tech rating four, which Cargo threw at Stonewall.

"Put it on. Fast," Cargo hissed.

Stonewall stepped into the oversized work suit and began to
smile. "Now, did the cavalry just come over the hill?"

Cargo blinked and shook his head. He hadn't considered
what he would do if Stonewall was seriously disoriented after
being interrogated for so long. There was no time for that now.

"Look like you're working," Cargo ordered brusquely.

Stonewall shook his head and then opened a cage that held a double power amp, badly cannibalized from the looks of it.

"You know, ole Joe down at the filling station when I was a kid, he used to bring me into the garage and show me all the parts and how they all fit together. He was one of the old-fashioned kind, could just look and see what was wrong. No matter how complex or simple, he just knew. 'Engines talk to me,' he used to say. Can you imagine that? Engines telling him what was wrong."

Cargo stepped away. He didn't want to hear Stonewall's recollections and he didn't have much time. He glanced back once at the tall agent bent nearly double in the stacking cage and wished that Stonewall wasn't so blond and tall and noticeable. Nothing he could do about that, though, and right now he couldn't forget the Security Office monitoring how long the patch was down.

At least it took very little time to relock the Eyes exactly in pattern, and the transfer box slipped into place easily. Only then did Cargo remember to breathe.

"Took you forever. What were you doing down there? Your laundry?" the security officer complained over the intercom. "You gonna run a test for me, or do I have to come down there and do it myself?"

"Starting right now, sir," Cargo answered smoothly, pretending not to have heard the insults. "I took some time to double-check all the connections. Everything is copacetic."

He cut communications and keyed the test to run. Lights flickered over the three screens and never quite resolved as the patch kicked in. Then, as the tension drained, he was aware that he was very tired. There was still more to be done and every minute he waited was added danger, but he was through the worst of it.

The intercom buzzed. Cargo opened the line without thinking.

"That you, Wong?" the security officer asked.

"Yes, sir."

"Test checks out. Funny thing, though. I've got you listed as having taken the eighteen-hundred shuttle. Last night. And where in the holy Deckmejian's hell did you start saying copacetic?"

Cargo didn't even wait to turn off the intercom. He was out

of the repairs office before the security officer spoke again. He practically flew into the corridor and grabbed Stonewall en route.

"Move!" he commanded sharply. "If we're not down at the shuttle bay in less than five minutes you can kiss your life good-by."

Stonewall barely grunted acknowledgment.

They ran. Cargo led through the empty early morning labyrinth of the ship, cutting the route short where he could and still avoid population. It was nearing oh-six, when the ship came fully awake and the covering isolation would be gone.

The carrier seemed to go on forever. And then he was at the shuttle bay, two sleepy techs serving the last minutes of their late-night duty.

"Next one down leaves at oh-six-thirty," one said groggily.

Cargo took a deep breath. With an effort of will he relaxed and smiled. "You got a twofer loaded for down?" he asked in his most charming manner.

"Don't know. You authorized?" the young woman replied.

"Verdun. Kore Verdun. I've got the hours, if that's what they want to know."

The tech's face changed from indifference to respect bordering on awe. "Kore Verdun? No problem, sir. No problem at all. Twofer slip AA18. May I ask who's with you?"

Stonewall stepped up. Even tired and disoriented there was a twinkle in his eye. Cargo shot him a hard glance. Please don't fuck it up, he thought desperately, sure that the security officer would have already called and alerted the shuttle team. Only the fact that he was famous had brought him through, and they were so close.

"I am hurt that you don't recognize Rally Johnston," Stonewall drawled. "After all the work I did souping up those specials, and I know a smart little thing like you would be up on those specs. And I promised my old buddy Kore here that I would fix him up special for the Tel Hala races. You heard about the races, right? And I know in my bones that we have got to show those cylinder living rubes what a race is about. Got to win us some respect, we do . . ."

"Come on," Cargo interrupted. "Sorry," he said to the tech, "but if we don't get going now, he's going to be here all day and tell you about every racer he ever built . . ."

"Since my uncle Joe down at the filling station got me fixed up with my first go-cart," Stonewall finished.

As the young tech rolled her eyes, Cargo dragged Stonewall to the twofer slips. "Damn," he muttered when they had sealed the hatch and the tack sequence had locked in. "Did you have to take it that far?"

"You know, Cargo, that's the problem with you. You think that you are the only decent liar in the known manifold. Well, even I know that if you're going to tell a lie, you'd better tell a whopper. Sometimes I just don't know what I'm going to do with you, buddy."

Cargo sighed just as the tiny shuttle began to shudder with the track activated. Then they were free and clear of the *Younger.* Done it, he thought. He had managed, surely, but what had he done? The question circled in his mind until he knew that he had been manipulated by Stonewall. Again. But this was the very last time, he swore to himself. Stonewall had all the lives of a cat, but he had used up three of them on Cargo, and that was enough. The next time he was on his own.

The Tel Hala maze brought them in. It wasn't real flying, not the way Cargo counted it. He had little control over the craft and that made him fidgety. Besides, he wondered when Security would come after them, if they had gotten away quickly enough.

Ahead of them the great circular doors of the habitat opened and they were towed from the dark void to a loading dock. Out of the twofer Cargo felt better, more able to lose himself in the pleasures offered on Spin Street. It was over. Never again, he promised himself. Truly never again. Stonewall had asked enough favors for three lifetimes.

The Tel Hala chute was reminiscent of the one on Mawbry's. Stonewall sat silent four seats away as Cargo gazed out the window as the various sectors of the habitat went by. All of a sudden he had the urge to find a chute board and ride it the way he had when he was a boy.

The impossibility of that made him feel sad. In fact, Tel Hala itself made him melancholy. All habitats were somewhat alike due to necessity, but this one was just close enough to Mawbry's that he half expected to see the Cathedral when the chute entered the other side. Instead there were only the stops, one after the other. The names were different, that was all.

Cargo didn't need to know which neighborhoods were which, he could read it in the colors of burned graffiti on the station mesh. These were the "nice" places, the places he had never been. Not the one or two really wealthy sections where the original burn murals were not only intact but still gleaming, the sections he had called home when his name was Mirabeau. Nor were they the places where kids ran the chute and gangs had burned the mesh so many times that all the slogans had melted together into an indigo blur, like the places he had grown up. These in-betweens were a mystery to him.

As he sat and stared out the window he ignored the other occupants of the car. No great surprise, then, when the chute made its final loop back to the port side, that Stonewall was gone. Just as well. He had ridden the chute nearly full circle, and now it was over. There was just another Spin Street and the morning on Tel Hala was already old.

Weary and worn, Cargo got off at the Spin Street station. He slipped his credit tab into the changer, hoping there'd be enough pay accumulated for a good meal, a place to sleep for a few hours, and maybe some reds that would take away all the pain and all the frustration. He only wanted to blend into the street, just another fighter jock with a night's liberty in town. The read-out was light blue and too long. Cargo blinked and hit the box twice. The reading never wavered.

There, officially and in record, was a figure about twice as high as the one he had once had in savings. Shodar had finished what Stonewall's Directorate had only started. Kore Verdun now had a credit history, a civ past, all held in the electronic memories of the Cardia.

At least he was too tired to be scared; he knew he should be. Ki Shodar knew too much, was too close. But Cargo had spent a long and boring assignment and his mind was numb. He headed for the chute elevator, and not even the knowledge of Shodar's scrutiny could keep his eyes open during the long descent. It was with real effort that he made himself wake up enough to walk when the cage hit the street.

As he stumbled out of the station entrance a tall, fluid figure detached itself from a wall and ambled over to him. Cargo didn't notice. All he could think about was bed and oblivion.

He didn't see the being until they were practically nose to nose. And he knew it was over. And he didn't care anymore. Gone. Done. Only a vague sorrow and weariness were left.

Cargo, Rafael Mirabeau, Kore Verdun, looked into the eyes of fate and surrendered. "You were waiting," he said.

Dancer nodded.

Chapter

9

When the unaffiliated Akhaid dayboat was spotted, Andre Michel Mirabeau hadn't felt so forceful, so excited, so alive in more years than most of his staff had lived. After all, what could Shodar do to him? Not that he wanted to die, but he was ninety-eight and a Bishop and the prospect did not frighten him. Punish him, send him back in disgrace? He had lived through more public disgrace than any ten people he knew, and it had not touched him. What was made public was often far more mild than the shame he carried in his heart. Someone else might fear prison, but the Bishop was long past that. He knew he would miss the beauty that helped him find the calm clarity he needed, but then in prison he wouldn't be constantly worried about his next move and what it would bring. And being without would be something new, a thing he had not experienced in his life. Perhaps he shouldn't discount torture, but Ki Shodar, for all he had done, would not stoop to torturing an old, old man. Besides, he had already done his worst to Mirabeau years ago, and if the scars did not show on his body they were still fresh in his mind.

Ki Shodar had already done his worst, and this gave Mirabeau the power to say no. It was a heady freedom, a defiance generally reserved only for the young who are heedless of the consequences as opposed to unafraid of them. So he was much more willing to listen to the Akhaid who had sought them out when his official transport crossed into the Disputed Territory.

"What I can't make out is whether I should shoot or call for help or tell 'em, hell, come on aboard," the transport pilot had told Mirabeau when the Akhaid dayboat appeared and hailed them.

The Bishop shook his head. "We are not going to shoot. We are on a diplomatic mission, and besides we can't. I took the liberty of having all our Eyes closed. To increase trust. What do they want?"

"Damned if I know. To talk to you, they said," the pilot answered, making Mirabeau miss Cargo all the more. Rafael would have gathered much more information and known how to report it in a useful manner. This being, assigned by the Collegium staff, was no more than a chauffeur.

"Well, then, we are here to talk. That is our job. By all means, invite them in immediately."

The pilot looked toward the overhead and muttered some incomprehensible string of syllables that Mirabeau was certain was a curse down ten generations in some obscure tongue. He didn't let it bother him. Even Rafael had acquired that habit. Instead, he leaned back in the soft white leather desk chair as if he had all the time in the universe.

The pilot left, and the Bishop surveyed his environment carefully. The soft blue of the bulkheads and carpet, the white leather wing chairs and camel-back sofas and the elegant inlaid wooden desk and end tables were all of his own choosing. The antique desk was from the family estate, and while it was a little unorthodox the political imagists at the Collegium Center had had to agree that the effect was subtle and inviting, luring a visitor into a sense of security while backing up the Collegium's claim to history, tradition, and refinement. In short, the whole reflected a perfect specimen of the best the Collegium had nurtured as represented by Bishop Andre Michel Mirabeau.

The Akhaid his secretary ushered in was, to Mirabeau's experienced eye, old enough to be fully mature and female. After five years as Legate to Kzhea-Llyl he had learned to distinguish that much. The being's dark copper skin was overlaid with the deep sheen of age and the unrelieved black eyes met his steadily and with assurance.

"It is a pleasure to welcome you from the water," Mirabeau spoke the polite welcoming phrase in excellent Atrash.

"And an honor to be under your protection," the Akhaid replied. Mirabeau's eyes widened only slightly. This was not the usual formula but one used to honor individuals who stood as Guardians of the Walk, the most powerful individuals in Akhaid society. He had never been treated this way when he was in residence among them.

He glanced down and noticed that this being had opaque black rings tattooed on two fingers. One who was attempting to Dance, then, a being who had not only survived the Walk but had found meaning and sought to enhance it. Two more rings and she would be an Elder of the Walk. Three on each finger was a Guardian.

"Please," he said, gesturing to the elegant wing chair on the other side of the inlaid desk. "I prefer not to stand. I am called Mirabeau," he began carefully. His Atrash was rusty, and there was no guarantee that this individual was particularly fluent in that language either.

"For now I am the Mouth of the Dance," the Akhaid stated. "And the Guardians of the Dance wish to clarify certain things. I have been asked to guide you to their place."

"Guardians of the Dance?" Mirabeau responded, genuinely confused. "I know the Guardians of the Walk, but have never heard of Guardians of the Dance."

The Akhaid's ears came slightly forward in what the Bishop remembered was mild amusement. "I should hope not," the Akhaid said, meeting his eyes with a touch of humor. "Most beings never do. But common knowledge doesn't invariably preclude those things that are not, shall we say, in the public domain. And that is precisely why I am here. To invite you to join us in Tzeryde for a short time."

Andre Michel Mirabeau closed his eyes as his long fingers formed a steeple against the polished wood of the desk. Invite had so very many meanings, and he dared not make a mistake. Not now. In over half a century of political life, the one thing he had developed was a sense of importance. It was the only thing he or any other in his position needed and the only thing they really had. Like the doctor once said, all she could do was tell who was really sick and who would get better, and that was the true basis of diagnosis. His own diagnosis was that there was more going on here than he realized, and if he walked the line very carefully the whole would be revealed to him. But only, as Cargo would say, if he didn't "screw it to the Wall."

He opened his eyes. The Akhaid had not moved. He couldn't read her face, and in that inability he knew that the next move had to be definitive. He cast up a quick, wordless prayer that what he was about to do was not stupid, and then he smiled.

"I would be honored to accept your kind invitation," he said. "If you will give our pilot the coordinates to Tzeryde, we will be under way immediately."

The whiteless Akhaid eyes narrowed slightly and the Bishop had to remind himself that it meant something different than the same expression in a human. "I invite you to be my guest," she said carefully, emphasizing the word "guest." "The dayboat is small, but adequate for two for the journey."

"And my staff?" Mirabeau asked almost innocently. "What are they supposed to say when they return to my superiors without me?"

"You do not have superiors. You are on an independent mission, so our informant tells us," the Akhaid said with a tinge of surprise.

The Bishop nodded. "True. But if this is a continuation of that diplomatic mission, I need the full authority of that status. Which includes this base, this staff, and my own direct communications with the Trustees of the Collegium. Without these I am really just a private person."

Impasse. For a time the Bishop could count in heartbeats they were suspended, perfectly balanced on each side of the equation.

Or perhaps not quite so perfectly balanced, Mirabeau reflected. He had been in this situation more than once before, and there were various possibilities. And the one thing he knew was that on this point he could not budge. Once he permitted anyone to isolate him from his power base he was as good as kidnapped, and may well have to be treated like it. "Invite" was such an inexact word in political circles.

"With your staff, then," the Akhaid said as she rose and gestured with one tattooed finger, a movement that was so subtle the Bishop would have missed it had he not been fascinated by the Dancer's rings. He thought he read something of approval in that small signal.

"It has been an honor to meet you," the visitor concluded formally. "I shall see you in Tzeryde."

"I await our meeting there with pleasure," Mirabeau replied, wondering exactly what sort of pleasure Tzeryde was and if he had in fact made the worst mistake of his career. Or perhaps his very best move.

Only after the Akhaid left and his official pilot returned to verify his orders did the Bishop feel fear. "What the hell did you mean, we're going to something called Tzeryde. I don't have any such place, not planet, not colony, not anything, listed in navigation, and I'm not so sure we can trust that being. Besides which, I don't think that Mr. Shodar is all that happy about us being in his territory at all, and he wants us out soonest. As you could tell if you were monitoring the number of fighters trailing us. If we're not out of his jurisdiction within the next day we're going to be history, and not exactly the sort you'd hoped for, either."

Mirabeau sighed. "So far as the Collegium is concerned, I am in charge of this mission. It is my decision that we accept the Akhaid offer. That is final, and I am not willing to discuss it."

The pilot left, stomping angrily. Mirabeau ignored it. He was not proud of how he had dealt with the being, but there were too many other things to concern him that were more pressing. The most important of which was what was Tzeryde and which side was it on?

The majority of the Akhaid population, so far as the Bishop knew, lived in areas claimed by both the Collegium and the Cardia, and were citizens of each. There were two very traditional Akhaid worlds well out of the normal line of trade that had elected to remain out of the conflict, as there were several human worlds that had taken the same option. So long as they were very few and scattered their neutrality was respected. After all, neutrals served important functions on their own, laundering infiltrators and evidence, moving arms and supplies and keeping communications open between combatants. Indeed, it was through one of the neutrals that his invitation to Marcanter had first come. But the five neutrals were well known and none of them was Tzeryde. Unless Tzeryde wasn't a world at all.

Then he let go and let himself experience the joy, the terror, of the gamble. For good or bad, he had acted and that action would determine a course of events from which history would eventually be written. Already Mirabeau had done that without understanding, and his one mistake stared at him from the news, from his desk, every day. This little dimple of history that was his own doing, his and Shodar's and Aliadro's and those innocent experimenters, all of theirs, this was his to rectify. And if he could do that he would die more than happy.

That night he had dreamed in Greek about Aliadro, but he couldn't remember what it had been about. Only that he had seen Ali, not as the guerrilla leader and apostle of anarchy, but as a serious-looking ten-year-old. Though Mirabeau had only known the Akhaid for a short time, he could sense the questioning reserved behind those opaque pale lavender eyes. Aliadro had never been a little boy, human or Akhaid, and that was what had drawn the Bishop to him.

It was at the height of his career, a Trustee finally, and in residence at the University of Roshan just outside the City of Sides. He could still feel the almost sensual pleasure he had felt the first time he had arrived at the university and been shown to the Trustee's Hall, chosen for this station because he was as scholarly as he was powerful and this was important at Roshan, the traditional seat of his jurisdiction.

He remembered arriving at the Ports of Dawn, as the main twin ports were called, and thinking it a poetic affectation. Coming down just as the twin suns rose over the glittering water and drenched the white stone structures that rose apricot and pink gold, he changed his mind. The Ports of Dawn held their glory only during the brief moments of the sunrise, but those few fleeting minutes were worth the whole trip alone.

That was so like Roshan, heartbreaking beauty that was dying at its height. And so Mirabeau had seen the Ports of Dawn and was able to understand about the experiments, about Aliadro and Ki. They, too, were perfectly beautiful and ephemeral, the splice-life that was abhorred in every other corner of the known universe.

Naturally he had been fascinated. There was no one in the manifold who didn't know about the two splice-life beings who had lived. Aliadro lived on the university campus, raised among the white rats and an ever-changing bevy of graduate students. The Bishop remembered being introduced to the child much as if he were simply one more experiment. It had made him terribly sad.

The next day he had returned to the lab with a packet of some popular Akhaid candy, which Aliadro had accepted without enthusiasm. Mirabeau, feeling awkward, had begun to tell stories, his favorite stories from Homer about Odysseus' fantastic adventures homeward-bound. At the time he thought it was silly; this child who was no child wouldn't understand the implications and would only hear "baby-magic" to be discounted along with Santa Claus.

And that was when Mirabeau knew that Aliadro was no child. The youngster had listened as if he had never heard a story before, had never been exposed to flights of the imagination and tales of heroes and devils and all the things young children thrive on.

Within a week Aliadro was learning Greek, absorbing it whole at a rate that frightened his mentor. Before the year was out Mirabeau had adopted him, simply because no one had ever considered doing so before. Aliadro had been the first of his boys and the most brilliant, and in some ways the best.

Now he felt simply lonely and old and wondered what had dredged up Roshan from his catalogue of memory. Then, in a single image, he understood and shuddered slightly. They had entered Tzeryde late the evening before, and the interior of the great open ship/habitat had been drenched in a golden rose light. He had seen that color only once before—at the Ports of Dawn.

Then the Bishop forced himself to focus on the present, to be fully aware on the eternal now and replace memories in the past where they could be found. Here and now was Tzeryde, and it alone and of itself should be sufficient to occupy all his thoughts.

Perhaps he shouldn't be quite so shocked at the idea of a mobile colony. In theory, even Mawbry's could be navigated through the void, although the thought of that made Mirabeau faintly ill. Smaller than a colony, the ship Tzeryde had started life as an Akhaid exploration vessel, retired and refitted by an independent cartel. Now it spent most of its time in the Disputed Territories or en route to the neutrals, and itself had neutral registry and standing. That took care of the legal entity, and his secretary's meager intellectual resources. Mirabeau knew there was something more important behind all the facts and facades. Somehow here he was touching the secret life of the Akhaid, if only he could recognize it.

He sat at his inlaid desk, and wondered again if he had been wrong to refuse the hospitable offer of a stateroom. But he had felt safer about remaining in residence on his official transport, just in case there was something to the idea of kidnapping or poison or truth gas or any one of a million things he knew had happened to various diplomatic missions throughout history. Already he was too vulnerable. Any more would prove his incompetence. As it was, sitting in an oversized transport in what had to be the docking bay of Tzeryde was not exactly what he would term a position of strength.

Now, however, after the quick official tour and a good night's sleep he could emerge and not seem overly curious.

"You're not going out alone?" his secretary demanded.

The Bishop only smiled and ordered the young cleric to stay aboard, wishing again that he hadn't felt so obligated to the family. Taking a deep breath, he released the port controls and stepped into the glowing apricot light. His once-dark skin, now going grey and ashen with age, turned close to the color it had been when he was younger and still full of hope. He rotated his hands in front of him, noting the change in himself with clinical detachment, and then stepped off the stairs and onto the deck.

The silence and lack of activity did not alarm him. That was normal diplomatic procedure, to clear away all unrelated business so that effectively the entire bay became Collegium Trustee Territory. A polite legal fiction, but one that was scrupulously observed on every mission the Bishop had ever carried out. What did surprise him was Jakta.

Seated next to the door that led to the rest of Tzeryde, Jakta's orange robe blended with the light and kept him hidden. His face, when he met Mirabeau's eyes, had not changed in the fifty years since they had last met and clashed, Trustees together and divided.

He and Jakta had disagreed but they had never been adversaries. Mirabeau knew that the monk had left the Trusteeship of his own will to travel in the void. But Jakta could not be here. It was not possible, and more important it was not rational. Yet there was humor and recognition and even still a hint of mischief in the black eyes that met his own grey.

Then Mirabeau looked down at Jakta's hands lying motionless on his thighs. Around every joint of every finger was a black tattooed ring.

Slowly and with immense grace the monk stood. "Father Michel," he said softly, and the rich voice filled the expanse of the docking bay. "Isn't karma strange?"

Mirabeau blinked rapidly. No one had called him Father Michel since Jakta had left humanity behind. Unable to restrain the emotion, he crossed the deck to where Jakta stood, embraced the old man heartily, and kissed him on both cheeks. "Jakta? You're here?" As soon as the words were spoken he knew they were meaningless, stupid, but there was everything to ask and nothing. "Are you responsible for me being here?"

Jakta's expression never changed. "Yes. And no, of course. There is someone else who had this whole idea, one of our wild young First Ring Dancers. I simply saw the perfection of it."

The Bishop suddenly remembered that it had always been impossible to get a straight answer from Jakta. He only said exactly what he wished and only rarely what had been asked. In any case, pursuing the matter was useless until Jakta volunteered.

"Would you like to come in?" Mirabeau asked, indicating the official transport-cum-consulate.

Jakta's smile was broad and dazzling. "Wouldn't you prefer to see Tzeryde?"

Mirabeau nodded and approached the door. Jakta hesitated for a moment before he opened it, and Mirabeau was faced with a spectacle of relentless beauty.

The docking bay overhung a single great shaft, almost as large around as a full colony habitat, but completely empty except for light. And the light itself was amazing. Rainbows arced through the reflected infinities of space, a million spectra of a million stars shifted and danced through the atmosphere, staining hands and faces and clothing and then moving on.

It made him think of the cathedrals of Earth and of how when he arrived in Paris he had gone immediately to Sainte Chapelle and been overwhelmed by the daylight through stained glass. And cathedral was the word that he used to himself and he knew it was right.

Straining as far as he could, the Bishop could barely make out what looked like prisms comprising the hull. And beyond lay the blackness of eternity pierced by a million stars.

The Palace of Light, Mirabeau thought, and sighed in wonder. On Kzhea-Llyl there had been a few mentions of a Palace of Light, but he had discounted the stories since it was obvious that a place made of starlight was metaphorical. Suddenly he understood that the rainbows, the spectra, the very stuff of the place was refracted starlight. The colors that tinted his palms had a name and a location in the void, but here they were revealed in all their livingness.

This, here was the secret heart of the Akhaid, he realized. Of all the time he had spent among them and learning their language, of all the years he had studied their culture and customs, counted various of them as friends and colleagues and enemies and even one as a son, in all that he had never once suspected that this place existed. Most Akhaid probably didn't realize that either, he thought, but that insight gave him little comfort.

As he gradually adjusted to the glory that bathed him, Mirabeau began to notice other things as well. The place was actually well populated, and the beings were moving as though in a formal dance through zero-gee. And all were dressed in white, which was dressed again in rainbows. At first he had estimated there were maybe fifty, maybe seventy beings there, but he realized that he had grossly miscalculated. There were maybe five times that number at least.

"My friend, I see that your heart understands," Jakta murmured at his elbow. "Now it is my duty to see that your intellect also understands."

Mirabeau followed Jakta reluctantly to the cable tow running from the platform on which they stood. As the tow took them out through the center of the cylinder, he could see that what looked to be perhaps twenty doors opened onto that platform. And beyond that ring there was another, and another after that.

"This is the center of the ship called Tzeryde," Jakta said softly. "It is called the katra, which means matter/energy/light. It is only the center. We are going to the living side. Your transport is on the work side, where the engines are. That was what you saw last night."

"What about gravity?" Mirabeau asked. In the center of the

katra he could feel himself weightless, and wondered if the condition was common.

"What of gravity?" Jakta asked back and shrugged.

Mirabeau smiled. He should have known better. He found the answer at the other end as they entered the residential portion of Tzeryde. As they moved deeper he could feel an increase in the effect of the spin; in that aspect Tzeryde was like every colony he had ever lived in. And only in that aspect.

Apart from the katra, the interior of the living section reminded Mirabeau of nothing so much as a carrier, one of the great pregnant beach balls that were practically mini-colonies in themselves without a good portion of the amenities. Only these corridors were polished steel and brass reflecting the soft amber-pink light that infused the interior everywhere except the katra. The Bishop found the shimmering monochrome restful, hypnotic, suggestive of some primordial fluid that constantly nourished and protected its inhabitants.

The room Jakta led him to was small and completely bare, with the exception of a small altar niche opposite the door. The altar was the same the Bishop remembered from the Trustee offices, the same antique white jade Buddha, the same incense burning lazily in the same bronze dish. Only the single flower, which had always reflected the seasons on the Collegium, here was an alien bloom that Mirabeau had once admired in the gardens of Kzhea-Llyl.

They sat on the carpet, Jakta easily and the Bishop with only slightly more reservation. He was surprised to find it comfortable, reassuring, bringing him back through the years to when he had done just this in Jakta's office to consult with his fellow Trustee. And even though they were not of the same faith, Mirabeau had always found it comforting to know that there was at least one other religious among the Trustees.

"I would offer you tea," Jakta began, "but that, unfortunately, is one of the few comforts the Akhaid cannot provide. So we will have to make do with conversation alone, I'm afraid. I suppose you are somewhat surprised and curious as to my presence here."

The Bishop smiled slightly. "You, my friend, are given to understatement. I am shocked, astounded, and fascinated. But I also know that asking you questions is like trying to pull teeth from a horse. You will tell me exactly what you want to in your own time, and there's nothing I can do about it but wait."

"Which, no doubt, has taught you some patience," Jakta replied, smiling merrily. "But you were very young then, and you have become more and less powerful. As have I. But perhaps I should relieve you of some of your frustration. You know that the Akhaid evolved under different circumstances than we did, and because of those conditions are forced to Walk. It took our xenoanthropologists a very long time to understand that without a series of high-risk incidents to trigger various chemical interactions, the Akhaid do not mature physically. I do not know if you are aware that there are beings who choose not to Walk, to remain immature throughout their lives. These beings do not concern us. The majority of Akhaid Walk in one form or another. Unfortunately, one of the most common is to volunteer for military service. But most of these are content to experience the absolute minimum in order to go on to the next stage of life.

"There are a very few who are not. Like everything important in life, a whole philosophy of the Walk has evolved and become a compelling segment of Akhaid life, cutting across cultural and linguistic groups. And, like anything that fires the imagination and ambitions of a sentient being, the Walk has inspired even more complex and advanced philosophical forms. The Dance is perhaps the most highly respected of all of these."

Mirabeau nodded. Jakta had told him nothing new, but had at least confirmed his suspicions. "And how do you fit into this?" he asked softly, knowing that the answer to that question was really the whole point.

Jakta smiled softly. "Yes. Indeed. When I retired from the Trusteeship, it was because I had heard of the Dance. They, in turn, had heard of our monasteries. Essentially, I was invited to Tzeryde to explore the similarities of our two systems. It was exciting to them and to me to find that our thought and our work were so closely parallel. When there is but one Truth in the universe its proof is everywhere. I spent seven years, as we count them, here on this ship before returning to my abbey. What I would count as a month ago I received a message from the Guardians of the Dance, as the elder abbots here are called.

A confusing message about some young probationary Dancer and humans and the whole war."

Jakta didn't move, his face remained completely impassive, but Mirabeau detected an aura of sadness filling the space. A sadness not of loss, but of compassion, and the pain of being too late. It was a feeling that Mirabeau found too disquietingly familiar.

A note of this sadness crept into Jakta's voice as he continued. "I had stayed in my monastery too long, my friend. I had so little to do with the Collegium and all the experiments, the incidents that formed one on the other like mountains of foam. These things were nothing to me at the time, for even if I was old I was still very young in the ways of the universe. This is the way we are taught. I had nothing to do with the universe, I didn't even know the Cardia had seceded and that a war had ensued. Not until I came aboard Tzeryde. And they told me everything.

"You see, Father Michel, they are trying to help us. Our manner of waging war they found to be a perfect form of the Walk, and they interpreted it in the same spirit. Which meant helping us maintain what they considered to be the fiction we used for an excuse."

Mirabeau closed his eyes as weariness overcame him. Four earlier attempts to establish contact with the Cardia peace faction had been destroyed. Quasi-terrorist attacks had come from extremists just when political leaders began to consider rapprochement. All of these the Bishop had always thought were fate and setbacks to be overcome. Now, looking back on fifteen years of constant inability to make contact, he could discern the pattern. Even his own fall from power— He inhaled sharply, suddenly aware of what had been done and why, and the perfect horror of it caught him like a physical blow. What had been done in the name of love and compassion . . . and then he caught himself. The whole history of humanity was no different.

"How did they find out?" Mirabeau asked heavily. "And why now?"

Jakta let the silence gather before he broke it again. "As I said, a young probationer. One who became friends with a human who made him ask questions. Too many questions. I was called to answer some of them."

"And me?" the Bishop asked, already knowing the answer but not knowing why he dreaded it so. In that answer was the culmination of all his hopes and dreams.

"Perhaps for the time there are enough answers. Now it is time for Tzeryde to act. And you are the most logical choice. Only, they, we, fear we might have waited too long. Shodar was never a good choice, not stable and unreliable. But you are the only one in a position to assist the Guardians here as to the best strategy. I have been out of touch for too long."

Mirabeau looked away. Jakta might have been out of touch with the political situation for nearly fifty years, but the ancient monk had gained something far greater. In his expression Mirabeau saw a thousand years of perfect balance, perfect knowledge, as he had always imagined a saint. He remembered his one retreat with the Trappists and his vague envy, realizing what they could achieve and knowing that it was denied to him. Jakta had had both, but Mirabeau didn't envy him any of it. Because from that place where justice and compassion flow in perfect harmony Jakta was bleeding with knowledge of this action which was both a gift of love and evil.

"So I am to advise the Guardians?" Mirabeau said to fill the silent wound.

"First you should meet the probationer who first observed the trouble. The Guardians believe that between the two of you something might develop." Jakta made a single, definitive gesture and touched a low door panel. An Akhaid entered wearing the simple white garment of a Dancer. A garment not unlike Jakta's robe, Mirabeau noted, then brushed the thought away.

There was something familiar about this Akhaid, and the Bishop was certain he had seen the being before but couldn't place him. Or her. This Akhaid was still young enough and dressed too voluminously for him to tell. He glanced at the hands and noted the single ring of one who has just passed the probationary period. The ring was still dark as new ink and Mirabeau was certain that the mark was recently set.

"This is Orh-keru adzchiLo," Jakta made the introduction.

The Akhaid folded himself gracefully down to the carpet a respectful distance from the two elderly humans. "It is a long name for humans," the Akhaid said simply in Indopean. "My human friends have always called me Ghoster."

Andre Michel Mirabeau fought an unfamiliar tightening in his throat. "And you, Ghoster, do you have a plan for us?"

The Akhaid gestured with his empty palms. "You know me, sir. Just tell me how to find Cargo."

Chapter

10

"Shodar wants to see you," Dancer said, never moving from the blue-burned pillar that supported him.

Cargo looked into the Akhaid's whiteless eyes and understood. So Dancer was his jailer. He should have suspected that from the first. It was his own damned fault if he didn't know better. And now Shodar was jerking the strings again. He wondered vaguely how much the leader knew about Stonewall, and then dismissed it. Whatever Shodar didn't know now, he would know soon enough. And he would have no trouble finding Stonewall, either. Something about that satisfied Cargo's sense of honor. Inside the mess he wanted Stonewall to have to pay. That good buddy had walked away too easily too many times.

"So we're headed back to Marcanter?" Cargo asked casually, as if he weren't concerned.

Dancer shook his head in a disconcerting parody of the human gesture. "I have the coordinates. Don't worry. We leave in three hours." The Akhaid disengaged himself from the open-mesh scaffolding of the Spin Street chute station and began to accompany Cargo down the street. "You have time for one quick game."

Cargo didn't bother to answer. Instead, he paid attention to the entertainment center, such as it was. And it wasn't much. Even Vanity's MidCenter had been better, he thought, and the memory brought back a dull sadness that had never quite disappeared. Back on Vanity where the grass had been violet and the wind had never stopped he had learned to be a batwing and had met Plato and Stonewall. One was dead. The other was killing him. And it all rested on something so arbitrary as the toss, the timing, the luck.

He was vaguely aware of the life swirling around them, the brilliant and cheap titanium chains burned into rainbows that were almost the universal adornment of whores and slumming young admin adventurers. In two or three windows he saw something that was, he thought, unique to Tel Hala. Young women dressed in some kind of traditional dress, black and red and blue and glittering with coins and bangles undulated seductively to high-pitched wailing that was most likely music.

The Tel Halans on the street, vendors, streetwalkers, and the curious, all of them picked up on the music and began to clap their hands in complicated rhythms. The rhythms continued even after the music had ended, and various groups moderated their clapping to the others so that the street had its own staccato beat. It was stark and primitive and threatening, something that Cargo remembered from another life. He had been a Gypsy then, visiting his father's family in the caves outside Seville. In that city and in the caves he had heard the same clapping, the complex interwoven beats without words.

The dancing was obscene by Gypsy standards, and so was the entirety of Spin Street. Suddenly Cargo wanted to be home, wanted the reassurance of the familiar. Hated and loved, *marhime* or not, he needed to hear the sound of his first language and be called Django again. He despised that name. It belonged to someone else, someone who had died a long time ago. And, for the very first time, Cargo felt sorry for killing the innocent who answered to it.

"Come on," Dancer urged darkly, indicating a place that reeked from old sandwiches and cheap perfume, punctuated by flickers of light over huddled figures.

A card den, all ready and picked out. Cargo didn't think much of the charity. He ignored Dancer's pinioned ears as he sailed by. "I'll be back here by noon," he said as he merged with the crowd.

Dancer would be behind him. He could feel the Akhaid, as if those inhuman eyes emitted particles like the weapons named for them. And he ignored it, walled off the consciousness of the being who wouldn't leave. That was only to be expected. But Dancer would be surprised, and the thought of it gave Cargo some small satisfaction.

Moving at exactly the same pace as the throng in the street, he made his way cautiously from the almost respectable to the downright tawdry. Somewhere in there—he watched carefully, eyes a meter from the ground. And then he saw them.

Stifling a smile he slowed carefully and put himself directly in range.

A girl, perhaps eleven or so, with thick black braids and a doleful expression, accosted him head-on. She thrust a red flower forward. "Please, sir, buy a flower to help the refugees from Dari. The children, sir, help us . . ."

"Sarishan," Cargo whispered. "Can you tell me where to find any Tshurara in this place?" It was always better to ask for his mother's tribe, wild as they were. The Gitano, his father's, were even worse. The only Rom who would kill a woman, the Gitano were called. But they were also the only Rom who would kill each other. Cargo had once been proud of the reputation. Now it was only one more thing that would make this young *chai* worried.

He looked at her again. Lowara, he decided, from the carefully guarded eyes and the well-molded nose. Traditional and well brought up. The Lowara tribe was the most gentle, the most conservative of the people, but they also had the greatest *phrai duri*. And Cargo idly wondered if this girl was destined to be one of them.

The girl had either the grace or skill to blush perfectly. "I'm sorry. I didn't know there were any *chals* in the military. I didn't think that killing was something we did," she said prettily, glancing at him with what was clearly suspicion.

Cargo shrugged. "I'm half Gitano."

Her beautifully arched eyebrows knit and her voice was cold. "Oh" was all she said, but that single word conveyed all the elegant disdain of a child with the disapproval of an adult.

Cargo's demeanor went cold. "I am not asking to work with your brothers," he hissed. "Only to know where to find someone who knows my family. That shouldn't be too terrible."

The girl hesitated a moment, then snorted delicately. "Take

the chute to Badel. There's an *ofisa* half a block from the station. Mrs. Clare she calls herself, and I think she's Tshurara."

Cargo muttered his thanks and dropped two loose coins in the girl's hand before heading back to the public chute. According to the section of the map that was neither written over or burned entirely away, Badel was only six stops toward the center of town.

Arriving there, he was assaulted by memories. Not of the days with the Bishop, his life of Rafael Mirabeau, none of that. Here, as he descended, it was as if he were sinking into his own past. Badel was a market district for a colony, the kind of market that might have been a thousand years old or more, that stretched back into the wordless prehistory of humanity. Fruit and vegetables lay in open crates on the street, brightening the atmosphere and tempting the passerby. Food smells warred over the displays of hardware and cheap ornaments, and everywhere there was the constant polyglot chatter of a poor neighborhood brought down by refugees.

Before the war, on Mawbry's and on every other habitat, there had been these districts. Low-end service class, the inhabitants had little ambition and less education, but there was a familial organization to the neighborhoods as well. Even the gangs knew where to stay out of trouble and didn't bother the elderly on their own turf. There were rules in the neighborhood and everybody lived by them, and it was safe to walk out at night and to play in the park and young couples seeking privacy in the bushes feared only the security team or a random purse snatcher. But with the war the refugees had come and everything had changed.

The refugees spoke different languages, ate different food, wore different clothes, and worst of all were willing to take any kind of work at any wages. Anything at all to get off relief. The Bishop had talked about it more than once and Cargo remembered it from his own neighborhood on Mawbry's. Collegium or Cardia, it seemed to make no difference. Or where the refugees came from, for that matter. So the ethnic restaurants flourished and hand-lettered signs in windows advertised for bi- or tri-lingual help, and soon almost every shop was owned by the refugees and they dominated either the honor roll or the sports of the local technical school, and frequently both.

Badel was already well beyond that stage. The Bishop had made sure Cargo could read the signs around him, not the respectable decay but the leftovers of violence. Gang-marks were burned into the station supports and into any surface that would hold burn. Layer after layer, each covering over the next in a parody of the wars they fought. Shards of disposable bottles littered the walkway, and a few young people leaned aimlessly against the wall between the cut-rate socks and a bin of mixed shampoo samples.

He knew them all, the memory only fragmentarily personal and overwhelmingly special. This was where he was from; the fourteen-year-old boys trying to look old enough to buy beer and day-glows had been precisely himself half his life ago. The street kids who dared each other and sometimes died. Their lives weren't worth a lot.

Cargo had never turned down a dare. Not even when his cousin Angel, who had always been the bad one, dared him to run the chute.

The city chute on Mawbry's was old and ran exposed through the central cylinder of the colony. Not like the new ones with the slick ceramic casing which made the ride dark and boring but kept kids from getting onto the lines. Two youngsters had been killed running the chute in the past year, but Cargo could not give in to Angel, not even though his cousin was two years older and fifteen millimeters taller.

He had taken his kite board to the inner hub link nearest the Gaberde Park station. It was a good way from the neighborhood, but the hub was close to the line there and the magtracks nearly touched. Besides, it was the traditional place to run the chute on Mawbry's.

He watched while Angel and Yojo took their places in the station before he jumped the kite down and steered it toward the track. It was an old kite and much patched, and while here in the center where there was no gravity it was fine, if he didn't make the tracks exactly balanced in to the station he couldn't be sure it would support him all the way to the hull. That was part of the game. And he was very, very good with the kite, guiding it more skillfully than Angel himself ever could.

His left foot was strapped onto the running board and his right was still mobile as his muscles cramped with the effort to hold the toe stop on. Knees soft and arms outstretched almost the full width of the kite, he brought the board skimming over the track so perfectly that the blade strips never made contact. The tracks caught him and their power lifted the board and thrust it forward with the same force it used for a loaded rush-hour chute, and he ran it down so fast that the support lines blurred and the colors bled crazily into one another and finally washed out to grey.

The track speed under his cheap stolen bladeboard was an intimation of freedom. Flying, truly flying he was, so fast that even the slightest shift in weight sent the board into aerobatic gyrations. He remembered being afraid and relishing the fear as the price of that bright joy. All pleasure had to be paid for, and this was at least one he was willing to give.

In the middle of the Gaberde Park station, right in front of Angel and Yojo, he had flexed his knees and pushed slightly from the back and jumped to the center express track. He ran the chute, out past Gaberde Park and West Cathedral Heights nearly to the Ag Institute, where he jumped track again to the local. The current slowed on the local line enough for him to jump once again, this time onto the platform grating that rattled his teeth as the board slid to a halt on the rough surface. He had skidded so far that the blades had been scraped off.

It was the best chute run anyone had ever done. He knew it then, knew it the way he knew he would find more answers than he wanted. Sister Mary had been a fraud but she had had a gift that she had passed on to her son.

Mrs. Clare's wasn't difficult to find. There was a sandwich sign out front with a picture of a palm and impossibly cheap rates, exactly like his mother's shop. Only there was something about this one that was slightly different, a thin layer of dust in the window, perhaps, or the way the boys hardly noticed him studying the doorway. Or maybe it was the absence of flyers advertising the medium's skills to the general community. Whatever it was, Cargo knew that this Mrs. Clare wasn't a *boojo* woman, not the kind his mother was. Not one of the great con artists who could pull off a major heist and still leave their clients believing that some curse had been lifted. No, Mrs. Clare filled the daily trade, and that lightened Cargo's spirits.

The *ofisa* proper was up a flight of stairs, but there all resemblance to his mother's ended. The single room was light and airy with no hangings to hide holo projectors and sound wraps. Nor was there a crystal ball complete with a deluxe set of tapes cued to the underside of a polished table. Instead there were only a mirror and one religious picture on the wall, the ubiquitous Bleeding Heart rendered in lurid colors that the Bishop had once said was a trick of the Devil to wean people from faith. The oversized blue sofa and faded turquoise chairs stuffed the room to capacity.

This *ofisa* clearly catered to the community, and Cargo relaxed. He had worried about Mrs. Clare trying to take him in the *bouzer*. Much as Cargo knew about the con, and had even helped set up the tapes for his mother, he still knew he was no match for a real *boojo* woman. The best of them, his mother above all, could almost force him to believe simply by the power in their voices, their hypnotic eyes. And he knew perfectly well that there wasn't any such thing as a curse anyway, not unless it was showing up at Sister Mary's looking like a mark.

Still, the women in daily trade he respected. In their own way they served the community as counselors and therapists and cost a whole lot less than the going rate for those with degrees. They sat and they listened, and if the advice they gave came from no place more exotic than experience, it was no less valid.

Mrs. Clare came in though a drapery door. She was young, maybe only a few years older than himself. Around thirty or so, he figured, but given the kind of life in this neighborhood maybe she was even younger. She looked tired, bruised circles around her eyes, her thick black hair hanging in a single tail to her waist. Unlike his mother who dressed the part of a medium in full skirts and shawls, Mrs. Clare wore grey slacks to just below the knee and the embroidered tunic that seemed to be the national dress of Tel Hala. Even the tunic was in subdued burgundy and pale blue with only hints of pink, far more drab than most he had passed in the street.

She stared at him for a long moment, hesitating, studying. "Kore Verdun?" she asked, rolling the words in her mouth.

Cargo shook his head. The broadcast. He should have known that even a medium on Tel Hala would have seen it. Finally he admitted his temporary identity, but that didn't seem to satisfy her.

"You used to be called something else," she said after a long pause. "Ynglesias, I think. Your father was killed. I remember the funeral. You and all that clan. You were wild." A hint of smile played over her features.

"Who?" he asked, startled, knowing he shouldn't be. Families were large and many people traveled, and his mother's clan was particularly widespread. Still, rack his brain, he couldn't place the tired, large-eyed woman.

"Nona Miller. And you're the one they married off to crazy Sonfranka and her crazy brothers. When we heard they had tried to get you declared *marhime* when she committed suicide, well, I am sorry but we all knew it was going to happen sooner or later."

Cargo looked at her again and time peeled back. His mother had trouble deciding between Nona and Sonfranka for his wife. At fifteen he hadn't much cared, and his mother had finally chosen Sonfranka because of her talent in the *bouzer*. No one could understand why her bride-price was the same as Nona's, who after all wasn't considered nearly so talented.

Crazy Sonfranka. The idea made him want to laugh and cry and run away. It made him angry. It was one thing to remember Sonfranka, fey and lovely and threatening until she had jumped from the *ofisa* window. But that all the pain should be nothing, mean nothing after so many years, that made him furious. He wanted to lash out, scream, demand from his mother why she had given him a crazy wife. Everyone else knew. And suddenly, wordlessly, he knew why. He was half Gitano, untrustworthy and criminal by Tshurara reckoning. What did they know about the rhythms of Seville, about the music and his cousin Angel and how they had all been like brothers?

But Nona was already clearing the tiny card table near the sofa and setting out tea things. She ran back and forth between the *ofisa* and the apartment that must lay behind with glasses and a good pewter pot and a plate of sugar cookies.

"Come, sit," she said. "I haven't seen your mother in a very long time. This war. It's so hard to travel, all the restrictions. I haven't been able to leave Cardia territory in more than five years. Not since the last holiday truce. And, to tell the truth, with the attacks on the shipping, well, I haven't really left Tel Hala in almost that long. So you'll have to fill me in on all the news."

Cargo looked at the tea glasses, at the plate of cookies, with trepidation. Sonfranka's brothers had brought the case before the *kris* and he had been declared *marhime*, unclean. He had not eaten with any Gypsy since except for Two Bits, who was the kind of friend who would follow him even to the exclusion of their people. If it hadn't been for Two Bits and Plato and Ghoster, Cargo realized miserably, he could well have been tempted to follow Sonfranka. *Marhime* had created a loneliness around him as dark as the Wall and as final.

And here was Nona Miller inviting him in, treating him like a relative, and saying both in words and action that he had never been an outcast. All the years and all the yearning had been even more meaningless than Sonfranka's death. The only one who had declared a final exile had never been any *kris*, nor any assembly of the tribe, but only his own hopeless pride.

He sat on a turquoise chair and drank the tea stiffly, in a glass for the first time since Sonfranka had died. Somehow he made his mouth work, made the words come out, told untrue stories about his mother and the rest of the family, and true stories about Two Bits and Angel and their little group of friends. He even showed her the Ste. Maries medal and told her about the pilgrimage to Earth.

He did all these things without noticing them. His body belonged to some robot programmed to perform. Inside, his whole mind fought to retain some sense of grounding while his entire universe crumbled.

Nona sat on the sofa and nodded, smiled, made her eyes round as he told her one story after the next. "It's been a long time since I've seen any of that part of the family," she said softly. "I wondered why you left so suddenly after Sonfranka's death. My mother, of course, insisted that her crazy brothers were coming after you. My father said that you wanted to forget everything."

Cargo smiled distantly and shrugged. "I'd been accepted to the university. I'd always planned to go."

Nona's face was blank. Cargo could sense her disinterest with the university, the Bishop, the whole of the *Gaje* universe. For Nona Miller there were only her own people. All the rest had been created as marks to use and live on, *Gaje* who were no concern of theirs. And *Gaje* things, even *Gaje* wars, had nothing to do with the people. In all the known manifold the only thing that mattered was the family and the clan and the tribe. Maybe even in extreme situations all Gypsies. But never *Gaje*, and so Cargo knew that Nona Miller had no interest in his life since leaving on the first shuttle, even before the *kris* had finished their deliberation.

"And what about you?" he asked conversationally. "How have you been, how did you end up in a place like Tel Hala?"

"I got married to Stephan Demontrose a little after you and Sonfranka. He's a Drive mechanic, can fix just about anything. We'd go here and there where he got work. Tel Hala advertised and we came. That's all."

Staring at her he only half heard her answer. What would he have been, who would he have been, if his mother had chosen differently and Sonfranka had never been part of his life? All the things he had been, everything he had done, would not have mattered. So she had married a mechanic and did not complain about her life. She would have been a good wife to him, too, and he would be stuck somewhere with Nona in the *ofisa* and himself maybe teaching in a local lycee and he never would have flown. He never would have known the feel of a Krait or a batwing, would never have lost Plato but never would have loved her, either, would have been a whole different person. And would never have recognized himself now.

The room closed in on him, the air suddenly stuffy and full of *mule*. He had to leave before he became sick. He rose with some difficulty. "It was good to see you, Nona," he said carefully, reaching across the coffee table to shake her hand. "But I have an appointment. I really must go now."

Nona only sighed but said nothing. Cargo was grateful. His need to leave was almost a panic descended from some realm that held unrealized alternatives. Cargo let himself out, half stumbled down the single flight of dusty steps and back into the street again. He reached out to steady himself against the prefab wall, the cool contact with the smooth surface his only link to whatever reality was. Because reality had all shifted around him and become something else, something insane and unfair and he didn't want to acknowledge it.

He had never been *marhime*. He was not to blame for Sonfranka's suicide. She had been crazy, so crazy that her own cousin said so, and Nona Miller was not a cruel or vindictive person.

Anger rose, gaining momentum for all the years that it had been suppressed. He had always been angry at Sonfranka. And under all the emotions was the single small realization that Cargo had hidden from himself since he had first come home to Sonfranka's broken body lying wedged between the walkway and the maintenance undercroft.

He hated himself, had exiled himself, because he had to acknowledge that he had been relieved. Sonfranka, beautiful and willful and talented in the *bouzer*, had not fit in with any of his plans or dreams. She had been the strongest fetter that held him to a life he despised, and she herself had set him free.

"And when did you take up the habit of consulting fortune tellers? I can assure you that whatever you learned will be of no value where you're going." Dancer's ice-cold voice slid between Cargo's thoughts.

His first impulse was to grind his fist into the Akhaid's face, his second was to laugh. He did neither of these things. Instead, he pulled himself from contact with the wall, with Tel Hala, and with himself. The old mask, Cargo, who was Rafael Mirabeau and only incidentally Django Ynglesias, fell back into place.

"And you're twenty minutes early," Cargo said, arrogant fighter jockey to the core. "What's the matter? You think I can't read a chrono?"

"What I think isn't important," Dancer answered smoothly. "Ki Shodar is another story."

The first thing Cargo noticed was that his head hurt. Only after he had catalogued the pain was he able to observe that his mouth felt like one of Zhai Bau's infamous mining pits, that his hands were ice-cold, and that he absolutely desperately had to use the head. But that meant getting up and his head protested vehemently. The two necessities balanced for a minute, maybe longer, and then there was no choice. Cargo tried to slide his legs around and slip off the slick, hard surface while easing his head around as smoothly as possible.

In the long run it was wasted effort. When he tried to put his weight on his legs his knees buckled and he fell hard against the frame where he'd been lying. He struggled back to his feet and only through sheer will did he manage to stand and push himself far enough to lean against the wall as he shuffled the two meters to the door.

Nor did he realize that he was regaining control until he had finished and was staring at his own face in the mirror, resting but not supporting himself on the ledge. Then, slowly penetrating the thick fuzzy insulation that seemed to have replaced his brain, came the thought that there was something odd about all this.

Hospital, he thought, and was satisfied momentarily. He had been in hospitals twice in his life and both times had been thoroughly revolted. Only when he returned to what should have been the bed was he confused. There wasn't any bed at all, only a cold tray on supports. Cargo flexed his fingers rapidly. Cold tray, hands, head. He'd never been out before, but the symptoms were all standard according to what he'd learned in Basic.

Anger warmed him slightly. Pilots never travel out. Only civs, fat-assed merchies, and other unthinkable nonspecies went out for a voyage of any duration. Let alone a short one.

His hand went automatically to his face and was relieved that there was only two or three days' worth of stubble. Until he remembered that even hair growth was slowed out.

Even with his rapidly returning strength he didn't want to stand any longer than absolutely necessary. And he'd be damned before he'd sit on the cold tray. So of necessity he sank to the deck. At least he thought it was most likely a deck rather than a floor. The place had the raw, cramped look of a ship, not the open arranged space that he thought of as ground quarters. The fuzz was slowly clearing and the pain subsiding so that with some effort he could attempt to make sense of the situation.

Yes. Dancer. Dancer had taken him to a twofer. That was the last thing he could remember. He followed the thread until he could remember his visit with Nona Miller and Dancer's objective before deciding that it had been Dancer who put him out. His hand automatically went to the pill patch on his uniform only to find it empty. Not the first time, but he was sure that he had filled it before coming down. Everything had been so carefully planned for Stonewall's escape. Only there were no pills there now. And he had taken six before getting on the twofer. Even if the maze wouldn't accept him he couldn't sit there like mutant jelly while Dancer took the small craft out vac.

How the hell did Dancer get into the Three-B's? he wondered softly. Because that was the only way the Akhaid could have knocked him out. That, or in the maze. But he would remember the maze, he was certain of it, and there was not a trace.

Thinking was hard work. Almost too hard. He longed to lay down, even on the deck, and drift into sleep. He forced himself to remain partially upright. If Dancer had any other plans he wanted to know about them.

Only when someone did come in it wasn't the Akhaid. Only a guard in Cardia security uniform looked in, noted Cargo on the floor, and grunted. The sound startled Cargo back to consciousness. He blinked as the door banged shut, then opened again. The guard had brought a companion. He motioned with the symbol of his office, the thin rod that Cargo recognized as a sonic whip. Still feeling weak, he got to his feet. The guard said nothing, simply motioned again, and Cargo found himself surrounded and supported by the two.

Really had to be a ship, he decided, noting the configuration of the bulkheads and deck. But not like any ship he'd ever seen before. More a habitat, almost, but not fixed in permanent orbit. He was marched down a corridor that was painted, not burned, with large windows overlooking a tropical garden, complete with mist fountains and blue and yellow birds perched on the short palms.

Cargo would have liked to pause and enjoy the sight below but the guards hurried him onward. They turned into another corridor to a lift niche that reminded him of nothing so much as the Bishop's home. Not that Mirabeau would have ever chosen the geometric tiled design that decorated the niche or the low ceramic finished benches that ran the length of the hall, but the atmosphere of elegance was unmistakable. Compared to the fortress on Marcanter, this was a palace of sensuality.

They took the lift down only one floor and this time Cargo was escorted through the open loggia that seemed as much a natural part of the garden as the heavy scent of jasmine. There, where the cloistered walk widened, they came on Ki Shodar lounging on a pillow-laden divan.

Shodar did not glance in their direction at all, although Cargo had no doubts that he had heard their approach. Instead, he concentrated on the mango he held, extending a single perfectly manicured claw and peeling the blush green skin into an unbroken ribbon which curled on the floor. Only when he had finished the display did he deign to acknowledge their presence.

"So kind of you to accept my invitation, Mr. Mirabeau," Shodar said. "But, please, come here. Would you care for some tea? A mango? I'm afraid coffee is too pleasant for me to keep in any quantities."

Cargo knew that it was time to worry. The whole was perfectly orchestrated; the statesman and sensualist taking precedence of the military being was far more dangerous to him than the general had been. Mentioning the Akhaid reaction to coffee—a human might as well keep a supply of opiates around for recreation—that was supposed to be an indication of weakness, just as the business with the fruit had been a display of control. Cargo knew better than to trust either.

Years of training, of the Bishop's careful tutoring and innocent expectations together, flooded Cargo with a sense of familiarity. He forgot his crumpled uniform, the stubble on his face, the weakness that still had not completely disappeared. Instead, he slid effortlessly into the role the Bishop had prepared him to play.

"Your hospitality is too generous," he murmured, taking the seat Shodar indicated. "If, however, a cup of tea is not too much trouble for your staff I would be delighted to join you."

One of the guards brought over a complicated samovar, the other followed with a tray with two glasses in ornate silver holders. As the guards mixed the tea, hot water, and mint syrup, Cargo wondered if he was going to be poisoned and then decided that the question was insane. If Shodar wanted him dead, Dancer would have upped the chill dose. And even if the Cardia leader did his own killing, as rumor had it, Cargo knew with complete confidence that he would not hesitate.

Always indicate that someone else in your position might suspect foul play, but always take care that you seem perfectly trusting, especially when you trust nothing, the Bishop had said. *It is a generally admired trait among both species.*

The tea was served, sampled, and complimented before

Shodar dismissed the two guards, who promptly took up positions in the garden, out of earshot but well within range.

"You know, this garden was planned by my predecessor, but he never saw it. One of the greatest pities of his life, I should think," Shodar said, musing. "We were very young at the time of the revolt, Aliadro and I. Maybe younger than you are now. I never supposed that I would inherit President Ryio's floating palace when I sent Aliadro to burn it out of orbit. Well, *la plus que change*." He waved a hand in the direction of the garden, which seemed to have suffered no ill effects from one of the most admired feats of the revolt.

"It does seem fitting, though, don't you think, that Aliadro is buried here, next to the fountain?" Shodar continued. "Right near the spot where he died. There was a State funeral, of course, but my concordat at the time wanted him interred in some giant mausoleum. A memorial, they put it. I think my brother would have preferred the garden, though, and I admit that I made a private choice as a brother and not as a leader."

It took all Cargo's training and a little more to keep his face expressionless. Private decision as a brother. He didn't need the Bishop to explain that Aliadro had been as popular as Shodar in the beginning of the revolt, and maybe more so. Shodar must have been more than a little relieved that his brother hadn't survived long enough for the Cardia to really consolidate, or else Aliadro might well have been in Shodar's place. The Cardia leader wasn't about to set up his greatest rival as a martyr and object of public pilgrimage.

"An understandable choice in the circumstances," Cargo muttered with complete sincerity. "But I don't think you called me all the way from Tel Hala just to reminisce about grave sites."

Shodar met Cargo's eyes and smiled with cold approval. "The Bishop adopted Aliadro, you know. So in some way one could say that you and I are brothers. Perhaps that's why I let you go. I miss my brother, Verdun. And I need him. It's time that Bishop Mirabeau and I talked. He might not respond well to the usual appeals. But you, his son, the brother of my brother, can invite him. Tell him that I am sincere, that I have treated you well. And that it's time, I realize, to beat our swords to plowshares."

Cargo set his glass back on the tray carefully. "I'm afraid

that will be difficult," he said evenly. "The business about the genetic experiments upset the Bishop. He may not trust my word alone."

Shodar waved a hand again. "That was nothing. I will retract that. It was a bargaining tool. One needs as many bits of leverage as one can assume. Mirabeau understands these things."

Cargo smiled very, very slowly. "That may be," he said, unable to keep the pleasure totally out of his voice. "But you're forgetting that I'm just a fighter jockey and I don't understand these things. Or trust them. I'd need more of a guarantee than a few breaths of air to be willing to put my father at risk."

Shodar hesitated for the first time during the interview. "Very good," he finally assented. "Excellent. I don't even think Aliadro could have done it better. Guarantees. Well, perhaps we can work something out."

Moving languidly, Shodar keyed an intercom set into the wall tiles. Cargo didn't hear what he said, but less than a minute later Dancer appeared in impeccable dress blues, carrying an antique-style portabrief with heavy cream paper laid in the brass frame. Shodar took the brief, scanned the display, and made one or two changes on the screen. Then he printed the document and pressed the copy command. He collected the vellum pages from the frame and handed them to Cargo.

With the provision that all conditions herein are met and executed or answered and exchanged in kind, the Cardia forces, both governmental and military, shall immediately and without exception cease and desist all hostilities against the Collegium.

Instead of feeling relief, Cargo went on to read the demands and conditions. Something in the back of his mind nagged him that there was a trick hidden but he couldn't find it in the document. The terms and conditions were reasonable and fair, things that he knew the Bishop would approve.

Shodar put out his hand. Reluctantly Cargo returned the papers, which Shodar then handed to Dancer.

"So you have your guarantee," Shodar said. "Dancer will keep these documents until you deliver Andre Michel Mirabeau to me. Is that agreeable to you?"

"And where will Dancer be?" Cargo demanded.

Shodar's ears came up and forward with pleasure. "With you, Mr. Mirabeau. Surely you didn't expect that I'd want to split up such a fine team."

Cargo smiled and swore to himself in seven languages. Ki Shodar was way over his head, he was sure of it. Because, documents or no, peace treaty or no, Cargo was certain he was already in some perfectly disguised trap.

Chapter
11

Stonewall was glad Cargo had managed it on Tel Hala. Paese may have far more amenities and be easier to get lost in, but it didn't have the one thing that made Tel Hala such a perfect destination. For Ghoster as well, he thought, and it was primarily Ghoster he was interested in.

The one thing Tel Hala had was the largest, most complex, and oldest Walker nest in the entire Cardia. Documents of the Tel Hala nest and the great individuals who had passed through there—Akhaid and human, poets and musicians and diplomats and scientists and artists and even once a serial murderer— dated back to the earliest days of contact. And the nest had grown ever since.

Stonewall had read the brief three times before he had decided to break in and he still wasn't quite sure exactly how a nest operated. From his understanding he wouldn't even be breaking in. No one could. A nest, the Walk, were always open to all comers. No matter what those comers planned to do. The serial murderer who had come to the nest over twenty years before had slaughtered seventeen of the occupants before he had been caught. Still no one was ever barred. Even being murdered was an experience of the Walk.

The Walk made Stonewall uneasy. It violated his sense of the universe as neat and well organized, shipshape and clear with a proper place for each being. Only when those places were unclear was there trouble, he had discovered. And he himself was in the business of making the manifold tidy, cleaning up after various messes left by his superiors and generated by his predecessors. Gantor in particular, but Ghoster as well, and every being who had ever Walked.

In an Akhaid sense he could accept the Walk as a stage of life much like a nasty adolescence. He could even see them as similar in that both were stages that prepared the individual for the responsibilities of procreation and insuring the survival of the species through raising the next generation. With humans it was subtle, emotional, while among Akhaid the emotional experience triggered physiological changes that led to full maturity.

Maybe Walking was necessary for the Akhaid. Stonewall privately thought that the custom was a leftover from more primitive times and could probably be replaced by some medical procedure, but the Akhaid were not his people and he admitted he could be wrong. With humans it was another matter.

Humans had begun to Walk within a few years of contact. Leaving behind their families, their societies, their names, even the right to protection by local customs and police forces, hundreds and thousands and later millions of humans set out empty-handed to discover themselves in the universe. Most of them discovered only cold and hunger and oppression. Many discovered death. But the few who lived to complete the Walk and tell, those told tales of mystical experiences and revelations and dreams.

The Walk grew in stature. Walkers were called modern St. Francises, who left everything behind including his clothes in the Assisi town square and set off to find a new life. They were seen as the true followers of the Buddha, who had nothing but the contents of his begging bowl, and according to legend once ate a leper's thumb that had been dropped therein. The Walk was called the Vision Quest and the Night of the Soul and the March of the Heavens.

Stonewall and his ilk called it garbage and bullshit and other things too vulgar to repeat to his mother. So no matter how hard he studied the brief on the nest there was something that got in the way. Now he was going to have to enter one. The thought of the forbidden titillated and excited as much as it disgusted, and he managed not to acknowledge that fact. Only that if he was going to find an Akhaid, especially an Akhaid who was rumored to be among the Dancers, a nest was the best place to look for a trail.

As he descended below the living level at the Bridge Avenue station, Stonewall only hoped his intelligence was correct. He refused to think about the implications of his visit or what he might find when he got there. If he got there was more important. Nests didn't have addresses and buildings and terminal hooks to the mail. And they moved, whenever the authorities or the residents got restless. This nest had never been located in an abandoned building or on a series of rooftops or under the pilings of a bridge like the most famous planetary centers. A habitat offered the luxury of maintenance tunnels and ventilation shafts, access routes and storage niches. Plenty of room.

According to the specs he had received, Bridge Avenue was one of three stations in the chute system that opened below the living level and into the skin of the colony itself. And Bridge Avenue was favored by the Tel Hala Walkers for some reason Stonewall could not fathom. The lift cage passed the grass line, a scraggly layer of fading yellow, down through the topsoil and the heavy shelf of construction that underlay the colony. The lift kept going and it was dark. Stonewall couldn't tell if he was through the supports or below them and was toying with the idea of trying to touch the wall when all space opened below him.

Well, not exactly all space, he amended his thinking. Just all the space that mattered. No wonder Bridge Street had hosted the Tel Hala nest for over a decade, a nest so stationary that there were jokes that it had been assigned a mail code and precinct license. Here, in a dark pit illuminated by utility strings that glittered like fairy lights or distant stars, were the remnants of hundreds of chute cars, slabs of track, and odd fragments of what had once been a switching post.

The whole thing had the aspect of a Bosch painting of Hell. A habitat could not afford waste on this level, yet here it was, discards heaped together, preserved and enshrined in the lower depths. Then his eyes adjusted and Stonewall could see the sentient debris of two species scattered through the wreckage.

As the lift descended the smell assailed him and Stonewall no longer thought of it as some artistic abstraction, something that had more in common with Rodin's doors than life. The stench was overwhelming, unwashed bodies and rotting food, mold and matrix fluid and sewage all combined. He shuddered and retched dry inside the cage, one more twisted body added to the heap as the lift settled into a mesh platform.

Picking his way across the mechanical graveyard he detected a breeze and a lessening of the stench. A ventilation cross, maybe. He wasn't sure. He was sure that he hated habitats, this one included, and longed for the crickets of a warm and cloying planetary night. Here the jumbled remains of chute cars resembled the lot out back of Joe's garage, and he focused on those memories, of the summer nights sitting in the back seats of ancient vehicles drinking weak beer. Only there the smells had been mimosa and honeysuckle and tepid puddles rusting out steel. Then the vague images of South Carolina, Earth, faded and he was only aware of Tel Hala, of the nest that lay across the next barricade.

From here he could see the beings, human and Akhaid both, Walkers who stopped in this nest for a while. Walkers never lived anyplace, he reminded himself. They only stopped and then went on, their goal detachment and identification with all living things. Or so the propaganda said. Stonewall, who had lost his faith at the age of ten, tried to keep his contempt at bay. After all, he was going to need some help.

The nest itself was nothing more than a collection of light foam sleeping pads arranged in a rough rectangle around two firestoves. Probably discards from the looks of them, Stonewall decided. Besides, Walkers owned nothing. Whatever they had had been found. The air was decidedly fresher here, though maybe he was just getting inured to the smell. That didn't matter nearly so much as the fact that he was no longer gagging and could even contemplate opening his mouth to speak.

There were maybe twenty Walkers in the nest, most of whom were sitting upright on sleeping pads staring into space. A few were writing, and perhaps four were gathered around the far stove in what appeared to be conversation. Stonewall entered the marked area, strolled around the inner perimeter of the pads, and then went over to the stove. No one behaved as if they noticed him, though Stonewall was dead certain that his arrival had been carefully marked. Beyond Walker courtesy, or lack thereof, he had learned one very important thing. Ghoster wasn't in this nest. At least not now. Not yet.

Next to the stove he could see the four beings gathered there in the flickering blue flame. One Akhaid and three humans, all too thin, all four faces distorted by hunger and light and dirt. It took a moment for him to realize that only one of the humans was female.

"Is it that there are realities for every geometry, or is it simply that reality is only a symbolic representation of the geometry at hand?" one of them was posing.

"A geometry is descriptive," the Akhaid mused. "But in its abstraction it is more real than this place is, I suppose."

"But all a geometry describes is a gravity well, a pathology in spacetime," the human female answered.

The entire conversation was enough to make Stonewall sick. Not only couldn't he care less about geometry and reality, he found the speakers pretentious.

"I don't know that I'd call it a pathology," he interrupted, drawing their attention for the first time. "A pathology, as I understand it, is a disease. And since all matter has some gravity, then what you are saying is that all matter is a disease. And that is one load of pure bullshit."

The Akhaid's ears flew forward. "Precisely my point," the alien agreed rapidly. "If one observes matter in the universe . . ."

"You all are wasting your time," Stonewall drawled. "Observing, watching. How about living, doing something. Instead of sitting around in the dark like a bunch of fish bait worms. I'm not looking for any meaning, I'm looking for this Akhaid being, calls himself Ghoster sometimes and Orh-keru adzchiLo others."

The human male who had posed the geometry question in the first place whistled. "You are really far along the Walk," he said, his voice thick with admiration. "I mean, not even looking for meaning anymore. And then the whole symbolic idea of a Ghoster, someone who has reached the rank of Orh, that's something."

The only reason that Stonewall did not apply his fist to the young Walker's face was the stove between them. It took him a moment before he realized that he had learned something in the exchange.

"I have not seen that person in this nest," the Akhaid said formally. "But if such a teacher may come here, then perhaps I will remain. If you can tell us your reasons for believing such a thing.

"Now come on," the pompous young man interrupted. "There isn't any such being. It's all metaphorical."

"Tain't so," Stonewall interjected. "Ghoster's as much an individual being as any one of us, and don't go off on some tangent that's so much philosophical hogwash until I finish this time, if you please. He is a real being. And I think he might come here because I know he's somewhere in this sector and this is a pretty big nest. Just a guess, is all. Well, if he happens by, tell him Stonewall was looking for him."

"Stonewall?" the human woman asked. "Is that some kind of code."

Stonewall just shook his head in bemusement. He'd been away too long, had forgotten too much. "My call sign. Ghoster's his call sign. For pilots." He didn't bother explaining about Eyes, trying to keep things simple and on a civilian level.

"Wait," the Akhaid called softly as Stonewall stepped away. "I think I have heard of this individual. And I can send word. Stay here and wait. He'll come."

Stonewall hesitated. He'd forgotten about how much the Walkers traveled, hooking rides as supercargo on merchies usually, or getting picked up by generous strangers or whatever. But they drifted, floating from habitat to planets as if the vac couldn't hold them.

On the other hand he had absolutely no desire to stay in the nest. In fact, all he wanted was to get out of the place as quickly as possible and return to civilization. Showers, clean food, no slime mold on the mattress. The little things.

"Maybe if I get a hotel room," he equivocated.

The human man who had remained silent through the entire exchange offered an open palm. "We would be glad if you stayed. And we could not promise that the teacher would find you, should you go to the surface to live. Because we do not know the surface and will not know it."

The man had a voice that was almost familiar, deep and rich and soft in the quasi-night. A voice that brought back the sounds of home once again, many voices like that and dogs barking and beating wings and the soft splash of the water when they disobeyed their parents and went swimming in the creek. This person had to be from Earth, from one tiny section of that mother placed called South. Not far south, really, but called that. This being, too, knew the flash of mimosa and the cloying perfume of magnolia.

"Are you from the Carolinas?" he asked carefully, almost afraid no matter what the answer was. He wanted yes and no both. In all his years away he had never before come across someone from his own background, his own culture.

"Now I am from no place and going no place. And whatever was before isn't important anymore," the man answered, but the velvet softness and lilt in his voice gave away far more than his words.

Suddenly, on an impulse Stonewall regretted even as it formed, he decided to stay. If only to find out about this one being, trace the intricate ties of clan and blood to find how they were related. Because everyone was related, that was a given in the Charleston universe. And because he had to find Ghoster and because in the nest no one on Tel Hala would ever find him. But most of all, he decided to stay because he loathed the nest and the Walk, and Stonewall had never been one to walk away from a fight.

By the fourth day of waiting Stonewall had achieved a sort of compromise in his routine. Every day he woke well before most of the inhabitants of the nest, grabbed his fellow Southerner whom he privately called Wade, and headed upworld to the living. The first hour or so was reserved for the natatorium, which provided showers and soap and towels as well as swimming facilities, then breakfast followed by library search. Trying to get something on Gantor, or on whatever it was that Ghoster was a part of, anything. Stonewall knew it was perfectly hopeless but went anyway because it was part of his routine and kept him in touch with the rest of the universe. Besides, he could go to search and spend all the time going through the dailies. And it kept Wade out of trouble and aware of reality.

After lunch they returned to the nest. Wade almost always went back to sleep and Stonewall joined the group around the stove, giving them the latest news. In the afternoons he left when most of the Walkers reported to their street corners or whatever. This time of day Stonewall invariably ended up near the warehouse, the docking diaphragm, the station. He wandered as aimlessly as any of the Walkers until the shifts changed. Then he followed the workers off to Spin Street. Nothing much on Tel Hala, not really, but there was one pub that went annie/alkie and served edible food. The bartender there had actually heard of a mint julep and was willing to try to learn to make one.

Stonewall had been thrilled. It was the only hope of civilization in Tel Hala. He had been very careful in his instructions, showing the bartender how to ice down the metal cup, how the mint had to be bruised, not cut, and only with a wooden mallet. Never steel or, worse yet, aluminum.

"Yes, yes, yes," the bartender kept saying, glowing, nodding fiercely. "Like tea, I know."

But somehow the synthesized bourbon didn't quite taste like the real thing and the mint syrup hadn't come out quite right and the whole effort had been a major disappointment. Secretly he suspected that his honorable instructions had been somewhat altered to include the ubiquitous sweet tea of Tel Hala. What was worse, when he entered the place now the bartender immediately sent him one of those vile things, ersatz home and about as bitter.

Still it was a good place, friendly, with plenty of spacers coming through. And if most of them were merchies, they still drank like fighter jocks and could be talked into a game of Smash now and again.

He was becoming a regular, and no one questioned his habit. Sometimes a being might join him, most often not, but he was familiar enough not to be noticed. Exactly as he had been taught in operations. And, exactly as he had been taught, he had been at the rendezvous point between exactly the same hours every night in case his colleague needed to make contact.

On his fifth day in Tel Hala he was siting at his usual table, the second from the back, with the inevitable imitation julep and a rather reasonable couscous. It was still early and the place was half-empty. The dancer wouldn't arrive for at least two hours. If there was anything that saved the place it was the traditional dancers, whose nearly obscene gyrations were considered an art form here. The pub had one of the best, at least according to the bartender, who should know. His sister was the most revered dancing teacher in the habitat and was president of the licensing board for performers.

The center of the floor was empty, the bright rug rolled up until the dancing would start. The tables were only at knee height and surrounded by armchairs filled with tiny cushions that reminded Stonewall of his grandmother's drawing room. But then it was Tel Hala, he told himself over and over. On Zhai Bau he had eaten with chopsticks and hadn't thought twice about it, had removed his shoes without a qualm while visiting the Shrine of the Martyrs, and had joined the procession of Yorsi, the Akhaid water demon, with garlands piled on his neck and head. Tel Hala was just one more place with its own customs, its low tables, its dancers, its bright pink and light blue and orange color schemes. At least this particular place had managed to keep the orange a little darker and the blue a little less eye-searing than burn, unless it was simply the dampening effect of years' accumulation of dirt.

"Stonewall. Hello. It's been a long time."

Stonewall snorted and looked up. Steele had been his Eyes, once upon a time in a life that he barely remembered. When he had gone undercover in the batwing to flush out Ghoster. Steel had also been more than his Eyes for a whole lot longer. The Akhaid had been his partner for years, and they had gone undercover together more than once. That had been in the Fourth Directorate though, counterintelligence. This was Steel's first assignment in enemy territory. Stonewall conveniently forgot that this was his first as well.

"You know, Steel, there are moments when your timing is just damned awful, do you know that?" Stonewall began familiarly. "I mean, here I am, hoping for a peaceful evening before I have to return to that rat hole, and here you are the picture of elegance and staying at the best hostel on the habitat, I'll bet. And that outfit alone cost more than my entire operating budget for this project, or I can't recognize a Cosh-Nagor original when I see one. And since my daddy paid for plenty, I have a pretty good idea of what they look like and what they go for."

"I'm glad you missed me," Steel said, sitting. "And this is not an original. It's second line. Besides, *my* end of this is a little different than yours, wouldn't you say."

Stonewall rolled his eyes. "Sure would, darlin'. But where

I'm from, a honey trap by any other name is still the same old story. And I don't forget that you are personally involved."

Steel, usually as reserved as her sign, slapped the table forcefully. "I am not personally involved," she hissed. "That's over. And I was just doing my job."

Stonewall smiled nastily. "Just doing your job. Oh, darlin', then how come you and Ghoster made such a pretty pair and you never suspected one iota, not one trace, that he was the agent we were looking for?" He waited for a moment, held the anticipation while he sipped the vile thing that masqueraded as an honest mint julep. "Now I saved your ass on that one, Steel. Not just your precious job, your precious blue-grey hide as well. And you didn't have to brief with Gantor. So I figure you owe me good. And I need to work this job exactly right. So why don't you tell me how your end is going?"

"Aren't you even going to offer me a drink or a red?" Steel asked, defeated.

"You're a big being," Stonewall purred. "I reckon if you wanted one you could speak up for yourself."

He knew he was being cruel, but Steel had broken the unacknowledged pact of the Directorate. She had gotten involved with Ghoster, and to her bad luck he turned out to be the wrong one. Still, much as Stonewall knew she had not wittingly defied their code, he was still angry and felt betrayed. He'd gone over it logically with a shrink after they'd come back. Steel had not betrayed him. He should not feel jealous. Humans could hardly tell Akhaid females from males, let alone feel attracted to them. And he wasn't attracted to Steel, that was the funny part. Shrinks always turned everything into sex.

No, what the idiot shrink didn't understand was that they had been partners, they had been a team. Steel had lost focus on the task, and that had cost them plenty. Had cost him, in the bargain. There was a hole in his personnel file, and Steel had the nerve to still see the whole thing as her own private matter. As if they were finding her long-lost fiancé, not a traitor and a spy.

He couldn't forgive her for that. Maybe if he'd been the Christian his mama had wanted he'd have given it a better effort, but it wasn't his style. Revenge was slightly more suitable to his image. So he tortured Steel as much as he could and hated himself for giving in to the impulse. It gained him nothing and could hurt her dedication. He knew that, could write an article on it for the next *Issues in Intelligence*, but he couldn't stop.

"Are we really still partners?" Steel asked, more to herself than to him. Then she turned and met his eyes. "I came here to give you information. To wit, I have been doing my job, and a whole lot better than you've been doing yours, too. While you were traipsing all over the void, I put out rumors that I was looking for my old friend right here. Every Akhaid for about ten zillion light-years knows the story. Used one of yours, actually, something I dug up out of your library archives. Some strange old thing about this woman who loves this man and there's this war and she marries someone else . . . You know which one I mean. Worked just great. I think most of my neighborhood thinks I'm going to run down the main concourse yelling, 'Ashley, Ashley.' "

She hit it just right, and Stonewall was stuck needing to laugh with a mouth full of sticky sweet alcohol. Her mimicry of his accent was more accurate than he had imagined possible, and the image of the tall Akhaid dressed in hoop skirts and batting her whiteless eyes like some red-dirt Georgia belle was more than he could endure.

Steel's expression never changed but Stonewall could sense the amusement behind the facade. Nor did it particularly bother him. He was used to her constant teasing about what she considered a fascinating alien subculture. He was far more interested in what she had accomplished. When he finally managed to swallow without choking, he smiled encouragement.

"Well, the rumors and sending out word and all, it worked," Steel went on. "I have to admit that it was your idea, but you are in charge of this operation. Anyway, I have an answer. Ghoster is coming. I heard from him this morning, a message in my mail. He's very discreet, has had to be, I assume, given the fact that this is the Cardia. But he should be arriving sometime tonight."

Pleasure so keen it was almost sexual ran through Stonewall. Winning, this close to his goal, he could taste success in the air around him. It was physical, acute desire coupled with the fear that it might not happen. Ghoster might not come. Or might not agree to go along with him, which would mean using force.

Not that he cared, but Ghoster had been a match for him not very long ago. Stonewall remembered the games of Smash, the ease of the Akhaid's movements as he flung Stonewall across the beer-drenched tabletop.

Then again, his secret suspicions about Steel might be correct. He prayed they weren't, but he didn't believe in prayer. Too bad. It had been a good partnership, but Stonewall knew it was over. He couldn't trust Steel, couldn't rely in his heart on her integrity in this case. He was worried that, at the crucial moment, she would go over and join Ghoster against him. And, even armed, he was no match for both of them. Stonewall did not like that thought in the least, but he had to acknowledge that it was true. Ghoster alone he had a fair chance of besting, but Ghoster and Steel combined were more than he could handle. Besides, Steel had been such a fine partner for so long precisely because Stonewall knew he could rely on her skills, on her backup. Now that confidence was gone, and without confidence there was no hope of working together in the future.

"Well, I think it would be very rude to make ole Ghoster wait, don't you," Stonewall drawled, eyeing the remains of his pseudo drink with no regret. "Especially considering how very far he has come to see us, and how very anxious we are to talk over old times." With that, he touched his expense account to the glossy pay window set into the table and got up. "Madam, I hope you will be so kind as to lead me to your hostel. I haven't had the pleasure of its acquaintance as yet, being that my own accommodations are somewhat more Spartan."

Without a word Steel rose and turned gracefully and swept out of the bar into the night.

She led him, not to the chute, but to the private stand where two cars waited. She got into the larger one and held the door until he was settled. Then she leaned over the only control, the voice-box, and said, "Hotel Bekka." The car, keyed into the city maze, began to move rapidly out of Spin Street. Stonewall wanted to look around, but Steel blanked the windows. The silence between them was thick and uncomfortable, and the ride lasted a good ten minutes.

When they emerged from the car Stonewall noted that he was in a part of the habitat he had never seen before. This was farther in thought than in distance. The architecture here was chillingly beautiful in a way he had never imagined Tel Hala could be. The walls of what he could think of as both an alleyway and a corridor had been tiled in various cool patterns, each one intricate in a combination of white and blue and gold. The patterns, he saw, followed the demarcation of the individual units on the street. Overhead, the buildings met in a series of arches, creating the feeling of a cloister rather than the arcade it suggested.

Hotel Bekka was similarly elegant. A garden dominated the center of the building, hidden from the arcade street. Steel's room had a balcony overlooking the lush display of palms and orchids that perfumed the entire establishment. But on entering that room, Stonewall was not disposed to notice such amenities as the balcony or the rich carpets or the screen inlaid with seven different kinds of wood and copper, brass and gold as well. His attention was focused strictly on the being that sat perfectly calmly among the throws on the low sofa.

Ghoster looked at Stonewall carefully, as if checking him against some inventory, before he rose and, in a perfectly human gesture, offered his hand. "Stonewall. It's been a very long time."

Stonewall stared at the proffered hand but did not take it. A good Intel officer would, he knew. Just keep Ghoster in the dark, pretend they were still buddies from the old days. But his sense of honor prevented that. He would not, could not, bring himself to complete the gesture. There were certain limits beyond which he would not go, certain symbols that still had power. He acknowledged that he was what he was, and no matter how anachronistic, how utterly frivolous the code of honor he lived by was there was no changing it. It had lost his people wars and lost them their pride, had taken and used their wealth, but there was no help for the fact that Stonewall was a gentleman.

Instead of stepping forward, he drew himself up into a formal posture. "I regret having to tell you, Ghoster, but you are under arrest. I myself will see to your transportation back to the Collegium."

Ghoster dropped his hand and a look passed between the Akhaids. Stonewall didn't need to know anything at all about the expressions of that species to understand the betrayal, shame, and acceptance in that single exchange. He ignored it.

"What are the charges?" Ghoster asked softly.

"Espionage," Stonewall answered. "Attempted murder of a diplomat on a mission. And we'll want the details, naturally."

"Naturally," Ghoster agreed. "Steel?"

The Akhaid woman looked at her prisoner, her lover, her comrade, and then left the room without a word. Stonewall shook his head slightly.

"This is all rather confused," Ghoster said. "I came here to see Steel. And to see if I could find you. Because I need to talk to Cargo, and no one quite knows how to make contact with him. Except you, of course. You are working together, aren't you?"

Stonewall had the cuffs dangling from his left hand. In his right he palmed a miniature sonic whip. He let Ghoster catch a glimpse of the weapon as he came forward to restrain him.

"Are those really necessary?"

Stonewall swallowed. He still believed in one thing, in the correct behavior between individuals. No matter that his idea of correct behavior and another's were radically different. He knew that if a gentleman gave his word, using the cuffs was more an insult than a necessity. But he could not accept Ghoster as a gentleman, no matter how calmly the Akhaid was taking this. He snapped the bracelets on, noting as he did so that there was something peculiar about Ghoster's hands. Black rings had been marked in his skin on two fingers.

"Stonewall, I need to see Cargo," Ghoster insisted. There was a hint of desperation under the unperturbed exterior. "Let me see him and I'll give you whatever you want. Give you. Free. Everything."

Stonewall considered. He would like to take Ghoster up on it. He didn't relish turning over this being, for whom his respect was as grudging as his hatred, to Gantor's interrogation teams. That above all.

But he hadn't been able to take Ghoster's hand. He wasn't able to deal

"I'm sorry," he said with perfect honesty. "I can't help you. Cargo and his Eyes disappeared four days ago."

Chapter
12

Cargo needed a drink. Actually he needed two or three, a plate of blues and a week's vacation. Then, perhaps, he could face reality. Now he just wanted to blot it out. At least Dancer seemed unperturbed when he demanded where they could find something recreational and called Shodar's flagship a tub.

As a matter of fact, Dancer seemed positively abashed. Cargo had certainly not expected the Akhaid to simply lead him to rec 3, and was even more shocked when Dancer ordered two drinks, an annie mix, and then paid the bill.

Rec 3 was an unbelievable as the garden he had seen earlier, but on a different theme. Here were carefully pruned fruit trees in concrete basins lining what looked like real stone walls and restrained hedges marking out sections of what appeared to be a courtyard. A rose arbor ran along the far side and Cargo could smell the heavy perfume even from the distance. Something about the place reminded him of the cathedral, though perhaps it was only the quiet. The rec was almost deserted, which was only to be expected if this was the middle of the day, or some crazy hour just before internal dawn.

"Is the whole ship like this?" Cargo asked, mostly because he wanted more to snap at Dancer than to make conversation, but the part of him that had been trained by Mirabeau knew that was counterproductive.

"No," Dancer replied. "Only the core rings, where the old

governor lived. The crew's living quarters and work stations are about like any other. Maybe even a little more austere. But when Shodar took over, he changed all the recs and messes so they meet in one of the governor's gardens."

"It's very beautiful," Cargo replied, thinking of the Bishop. He would have appreciated this place as a work of art far more than anyone else Cargo could think of. And he would be unhampered by engineering considerations as well.

Too many years with Mirabeau had changed him, he realized. The peace and harmony of the setting took the edge from his anger. It was impossible to maintain that level of fury while fascinated by beauty. Besides, relaxing slightly as the two blues he had eaten took effect with the beer, Cargo could regard Dancer objectively for the first time.

True, Dancer wasn't Ghoster. But that hadn't been a fair comparison from the start. After all, Dancer had to be a little uneasy too, having been assigned to fly with someone who was essentially an enemy. It even occurred to Cargo that Dancer might be able to help him. After all, in the end they wanted the same things. Not that Dancer ever spoke, but Cargo didn't believe that the Akhaid could enjoy the killing any better than he did. Any better than anyone. The thought was something very new and very odd. It was also, he realized, probably very substance-biased.

"You know, we have a little problem" Dancer interrupted his chain of thought. "He didn't tell you, but I got the news. We don't know where your Bishop is. I hope you have some good ideas about that, because I wouldn't even begin to know where to look for a disappearing ex-Trustee."

Cargo knew that Dancer was almost as high as he was. There was a rasping throatiness in his voice that was a similar effect to slurred speech.

Cargo began to laugh. It started small in the back of his mind and escaped larger and larger until he was holding his sides, rocking back and forth on the heavily cushioned chair. The more he laughed, the more incongruous the whole situation seemed and the funnier it got.

In the long run, he knew, he was a pawn in play between Shodar and the Bishop. But the pawn had free run of the board, had been treated insanely well by the other side, and was now about to do what he might have prayed to do once in a particularly farfetched fantasy. Reality became blurred and unreal as the elegant rings of garden making their way through the void.

A sudden insight into the utter ridiculousness of the whole situation gave Cargo the answer. After all, if this were some entertainment show, something to amuse small children, the answer couldn't possibly be so coincidental and so obvious. It wasn't believable, which was precisely why it had to be true.

When Cargo caught his breath, he winked at Dancer. "How'd you get that sign?" he asked casually. Not an ordinary question, and generally considered rude, he hoped that their partnership gave him the right to ask.

Dancer seemed confused. "You know about the Guardians?" he inquired cautiously.

Cargo nodded, indicating that he should go on.

Dancer took a deep swallow and finished off what appeared to be an Akhaid equivalent to beer before going any further. "It's a very long story," he said hesitantly. "You know that Ki Shodar is the only survivor of a genetic engineering experiment that has since been banned in every civilized part of the manifold. Originally his brother Aliadro survived as well, but he was killed in the early days after the Cardia revolution. Anyway, Shodar gave me the name. Because he said I reminded him of Aliadro. His brother wanted to be a Dancer, to go study with the Guardians, but wasn't stable enough to do it. Because of the genetic mix."

"You mean you aren't entirely Akhaid?" Cargo asked. His mouth was dry with anticipation as he studied the being in front of him. Nothing about Dancer looked in the least bit human, any deviation from the Akhaid norm. And besides, the experiments had been banned. Shodar, if anyone, should have been very insistent on that. Nor, from his understanding, was it anything that could be duplicated in a basement by some home-based whiz-kid who'd read a couple of the papers. No, that level of viral splicing took equipment, expensive equipment at that, and labs and carefully controlled environments, and even then it had failed far more often than it had succeeded.

But Dancer was shaking his head vehemently. "No," he spat with disgust. "No, I'm not one of those. But there were donors. For the DNA. Two of those donors were grandparents of mine, as you would count it. So Shodar considers me his nephew or something like that. And he said that I should become the Dancer that Aliadro never could. So I applied. I went to the Guardians of Tzeryde and took all the tests and spent twenty-seven days under observation. And they said no and sent me back. So Shodar called me Dancer since it was the closest I'd ever come, and offered me any position I chose."

Cargo said nothing. He had heard a lot about Shodar, remembered the pictures he had seen of the bodies of the hostages on Luxor, but nothing had ever stricken him about the being as hopelessly cruel as this sign. Suddenly Dancer no longer seemed an enigma and a threat, but an individual who had had a rough time. "Why didn't you choose something different later on?"

Dancer's ears lay flat against his head. He swallowed two greens whole, and Cargo winced at the thought of the headache they would bring the next morning. At least for a human. Ghoster had always said it was the yellows that did it for the Akhaid, and Cargo had never seen one take more than one of those.

"You can't fight him," Dancer said softly, as if speaking to himself. "You don't know the whole story. I heard things, being in his personal retinue. I'm pretty sure some of them aren't true. But maybe some of them are. It wouldn't surprise me. How much do you know about the Cardia revolution?"

Cargo spread his upturned palms, indicating near total ignorance.

Dancer's fingers played over the order pad. Another pale green Akhaid beer appeared and Dancer drank it down deliberately. Then he set the empty glass in front of him. "There were three individuals who led the revolutionary forces. Ki Shodar, Aliadro Mirabeau, and Samantha Liu. They took the Ports of Dawn, secured their base against Collegium invasion, were declared governors by popular demand. I don't know a whole lot about exactly what went on before between the three of them. At the moment only one is alive and he isn't going to give you anything other than the party line. The three best of friends, total trust, total loyalty, enemies who killed Aliadro and Samantha and would have killed him if he hadn't stopped them first. Then the retaliations that brought around and consolidated the rest of what is now the Cardia provoked the

Collegium attack in response to Luxor. That's the textbook story."

"Which isn't exactly the whole truth," Cargo filled in for him.

"What is the truth?" Dancer replied. "If that's what everyone believes, maybe that makes it true. And certainly there is some truth there. And how would we know, either of us? Does Shodar even know the whole story? He only knows his own angle on it, and even then if he's decided that he doesn't like that he could convince himself that things were different. It isn't hard. You can talk yourself into believing almost anything if the motivation is high enough. Or so the technicians in security interrogations have said. And I think they know what they're talking about.

"Anyway, I heard that the textbook leaves out a lot of things. I can't tell you exactly who said this, you understand, but it was someone who was in a position to know. Someone you know and trust. The problem started with Samantha. She had been their major connection for money and weapons, as well as chief strategist. You know she was a chess champion before she became a revolutionary? Used to give lessons in a place called Yomi's, a chess parlor on Night Side. Place is closed down now. Anyway, supposedly she was a Collegium agent, or Shodar thought she was. It isn't clear which. You see what I mean about what is true and what isn't? Then she was found dead.

"At first Aliadro was the one pressing for an investigation. Ki Shodar insisted that she had been a spy all along and had committed suicide. Nothing was ever proven. The official version doesn't mention any of this. Anyway, the person who told me this said that it is unlikely that she committed suicide. Something about religious scruples, which you probably understand better than I do. But not a word about who killed her.

"And then Aliadro. The being I mentioned said that Shodar killed his own brother, and Samantha too. I believe that. And so does just about everyone else who works here for any length of time. Not because Shodar's mad or a sociopath or even cold. Just a being who chose to Walk with more pain than was necessary."

Suddenly the whole Cardia shifted like broken glass in a kaleidoscope and re-formed in a new and wholly unexpected pattern. Cargo took a deep breath and pushed his empty glass away. "Where do we find the Bishop?" he asked quietly.

Dancer lay both palms on the surface of the table. "I don't know. But since Shodar doesn't know it isn't technically part of the Cardia, and the transport wasn't far enough to have gone over into Collegium territory. So my guess is Tzeryde."

"How do we get there?" Cargo asked, hoping that Dancer knew what he was talking about. Beyond that he refused to think about it because it twisted more than any of his nightmares.

Dancer looked away. "Tzeryde is something like this ship. Almost a colony, but as mobile as a carrier. Something between the two. It isn't in any set location, and since the war began it has tended to stay somewhere on the frontier. On its own Walk. But you're supposed to be good at tracking. Your old partner Ghoster must have left a trail."

Cargo closed his eyes. The beer was warm in his stomach and the annies were floating in his head. Otherwise he would panic. Now, though, he drifted distant from the hatefulness of it all, only aware that Dancer had hit on something very profound and very true.

When they had been on the *Torque* where liquor was banned, he had told Ghoster about the *patrin*. It was an old Gypsy way of marking a trail, symbols scratched in the dirt on the side of a road or marked high in a tree where no one would look for them. Symbols that stood for directions and days and where it was good to steal food and where it was good to camp and where it was best to move on.

Cargo wasn't sure how Ghoster would have marked it, but it was obvious that Ghoster wouldn't have abandoned him. There must have been some kind of *patrin* all along, and it took a reeling high enemy to point it out.

A tape broke the silence, popular music by some singer who had more sex appeal than voice. Cargo winced. A chattering group of very junior officers took a table halfway across the courtyard, and were followed by still more.

"Shift must have changed," Dancer muttered.

Only two tables were still vacant. The music changed, replaced by an even more popular singer famed for the sweetest love songs ever recorded. They made Cargo sick. Still worse, they made him morose. Plato was gone. Beatrice Sunday. No, not gone, he told himself sternly. Dead. He had loved her because she was beautiful and brave and free, and it had killed her.

Suddenly he wanted to be anywhere but this rec lounge disguised as a courtyard. And he wanted to be far away from the Akhaid partner who was not Ghoster and wouldn't understand about Plato. He shoved himself back on unsteady legs and hauled himself to standing.

"If I listen to any more of this crap I'm going to get diabetes," he said thickly, then made his unsteady way to the entrance. He did notice that Dancer never looked him in the face, and made no attempt to follow.

In the dream he could smell Old Pulika's whiskey-soaked breath and felt the thick calluses on his granduncle's hands as the old man guided him learning the old ways. They were important, Pulika had insisted. At one time they had almost been lost and the people had become like *Gaje*, stupid and soft. He would not let that happen in his family, no, these boys were going to be proper *chals* that the *mule* could be proud to know.

So Pulika had taken them, himself and Two Bits and Angel, out to the park on Mawbry's to learn the *patrin*. Only in the dream the *patrin* was not the one Old Pulika had scratched in the dust or drawn high up in a tree or burned sloppily into the graffiti-dark walls of the chute station.

Here the park was enclosed in night and stank of excrement and unwashed bodies and stagnant water. Even in his sleep Cargo shuddered. Truly this place was *marhime*, unclean, by its own definition. And those who lived in such conditions were untouchable.

Cargo wanted to turn and leave this place, but Old Pulika held his shoulders. "Look," the old man whispered in his ear. "Find the *patrin*."

He had looked again. There were at least two stoves surrounded by foam mats, the cheap kind used for controlled habitat camping or a planetary beach. People sat on them or lay, asleep or dead he could not tell, Akhaid and human alike, all too thin and filthy. Walkers. He hated human Walkers. The Akhaid he could accept had evolved a tradition from their own biology, but the humans violated reason. He searched the Walker faces for her but they were all strangers. Even in his own dream he was terribly alone. And in a Walker nest at that.

A nest. *Find the* patrin. The stoves in the center of the nest flared, their combined flames burning into the darkness like stars scattered through the void. And they became stars and the stars began to spin, to dance.

Find the patrin. The stars danced across the void, changing places and forming combinations that changed even as he caught a hint of familiarity. But not all the stars. Some stayed fixed and he looked and named them off. Vega and Sirius and all the Crab. And it didn't even matter that they weren't all in the same part of the void. It was his dream, and if it defied one logic it constructed the next. None of the far galaxies moved, nor any of the brilliant and tiny stars. And then he saw clearly, saw into the whole series of interlocked rings that pointed the way.

Cargo bolted upright, awake. The logic of the dream hadn't left him, and he rushed to the small screen to confirm his guess. The *patrin* was *clear*, so simple that he wondered that he hadn't seen it before. That was the genius, though. He stared at the figures on the screen in wonderment, half tempted to run the sequence through time just to see how it unfolded.

Because the story it told could not be true. The nests radiated out from Tzeryde at set intervals. They changed as Tzeryde changed position, moving like iron in a magnetic field. And all the nests and all the Walk was not without direction. It was all a long and tortuous path to Tzeryde itself, calling those with the capacity to see to join the Dancers at the center.

In fact, it looked almost to Cargo as if Tzeryde remained stationary and warped the void around itself for sheer delight in variety. All beings and all created matter were chips of the kaleidoscope that was both its pleasure and its reflection. Then he shook his head to clear it. That was too crazy, he was still tired and taking things too far.

Besides, even if Tzeryde *was* the central point of the manifold, it wouldn't matter in his immediate quest. Enough to know where it was, with both Ghoster and the Bishop aboard. Both missions accomplished in a single stroke, a perfect ending.

Unable to contain his excitement, Cargo put a call through to Dancer. "I know where it is," he shouted when the light indicated that Dancer had switched on the intercom.

"You woke me up to tell me that?"

Cargo was undeterred by Dancer's lack of enthusiasm. "There's a pattern in the way the nests are laid out, the relationship of various Walker planets and habitats to others. You know there are just some places the Walkers don't go. And others. The Walk isn't some long aimless thing. It's got a point, and the point is a weeding out process for the Guardians."

"What?" Dancer asked, the disbelief coming clearly through the connection. "You got all that when I said look for the trail? You mean you didn't consult the nav index?"

The green light died as Dancer cut the connection. Cargo blinked and then swore very softly in Romany at the silent board. Nav index. Of course. He could double-check his calculations. But if he was right then he understood a whole lot more about the manifold than had ever appeared in the open literature.

The excitement his discovery had lit in the core of his being grew and became firm. Even Dancer's lack of interest in the discovery was only one more piece of positive evidence.

And then Cargo felt the manifold shift yet again, all around him although he himself remained unmoved. His own penetration of the mystery had brought him to some other place of being, and now he, too, was one of the immobile ones. The discovery brought him awe that turned to terror and wonder and a desire to Dance.

He handled the Three-B's gingerly before swallowing them down. Last time they'd been something different, and no matter how much he thought he understood, Cargo didn't trust Dancer. Which was a rotten way to run a partnership.

Still, the little red pills seemed to be working in the ordinary fashion, opening the DNA chip in his head to the microwave interface with the onboard systems. The mode's pure familiarity made it both enticing and troublesome. Cargo felt himself sinking and kept his mind clear and full of language. He didn't want to go to the deep levels, to the place where the maze was an extension of his mind the way the vessel was his body, not with Dancer riding right in with him. Even after their talk in the garden, or maybe because of it, Cargo was uneasy about this trip.

Really, he told himself over as the maze folded itself around his mind, the whole thing was nothing at all. A walk in the park, a game of hopscotch, a gold-brick one. The nav index had shown Tzeryde straddling the Cardia-Collegium boundary line, and just barely out of the way of heavy Zhai Bau shipping as well. Not exactly a safe position, and his worry was probably merely awareness of the fact that he would be cutting it very close to a couple of regular Collegium supply lines. But he knew where those lines were, knew the approach patterns as well as he knew them for Marcanter, knew that his friends and compatriots and former or current colleagues in the Collegium were too proud and too professional to engage a lone civilian-configured yacht as well.

Civilian-configured on the outside, that was. The equipment was the best military standard Shodar had available, some of it still experimental. Why shouldn't it be? It was Shodar's personal skiff, after all.

Which was another thing that bothered him. Perhaps the maze itself had been set, conditioned against him.

Nonsense. The maze had an uncanny habit of responding when he didn't want it to listen in the first place. Either he was slipping or this maze knew what no other had ever learned, and Cargo had to assume that he had been the one violating security over his own mind. There was no reason that Shodar's yacht would be programmed to understand Romany.

"You're getting the best because that's all we've got for this task," the hangar master had said sourly. "And as himself ordered it, there isn't much I can do. But I'll tell you this, you don't return this skiff to me with the shine still on and you're one dead hero."

He hadn't dignified that with an answer. Instead he stared straight through the hangar master and took possession of the craft.

It was beautiful, all right. Not the way a Krait fighter was beautiful, gaudy and brave, flaunting itself against cold vac, or the way the silent black batwing was beautiful, a shadow slipping across the stars. This was more like the Bishop's official transport, imperial and restrained and hinting at deep reserves of power tastefully hidden from view.

Like the batwing, the exterior of the skiff was sleek and curved, an abstract sculpture of the feel of flight. Only it was larger than the stealthcraft by a factor of three, and the only burn that marred its silver-grey finish was the marking numbers in regal purple. The elegance of the interior didn't interest him. Cargo recognized the expense and care that had gone into the construction, the fine parquet overlays on the bulkheads, the fluid Bachmeyed chairs and conference table all magged to the deck, even an ancient gold-leafed celestial map set in over what must be the head of the table. Mirabeau had trained him to appreciate such touches and to admire the good taste that had chosen them, but his admiration was merely cursory. What Cargo cared about were the controls.

Private yachts were usually dismal affairs from the pilot's standpoint. Not that he'd had all that much experience in them, not counting a particular grand larceny case many years closed, but he'd heard enough to have formed an opinion. Usually the mazes were simple directional link-ins where the pilot never went into mode and the only real interface was between the yacht-brain and the major port systems. He noted the bands in the control chair with relief. To fly without mode was to be blind, to be dead.

A collar hung casually from the board and Cargo picked it up and turned it in his hands.

"You don't need a helmet here," Dancer informed him. "This is not an attack craft after all. And we're on a long haul. You don't want to be tied in that chair the whole time."

Cargo grunted and ran his fingers over the soft cotton lining, neither blue for human nor yellow for Akhaid, but a rich solid black. He'd never seen that color coding before, and assumed it must be Shodar's own, or a switch system.

So he swallowed the Three-B's Dancer handed him and fastened the collar around his neck before stretching out into the deep padded chair. He didn't trust Dancer, didn't trust Shodar, didn't like the universe. And it was all irrelevant. Mode was the only thing that mattered, the merging of his thought/control/personality with the other levels of the craft, the "head" computer and the structural. And his partner. The Akhaid-human interface was the key to it all, in the end. The subtle tension between the two species created an energy that moderated and completed the circuit. And in that circuit Dancer was necessary, present, and held in threatening limbo beyond the membrane that both separated them and fed off the friction their interaction created. The membrane itself was a feeder line to the subtle levels of the craft's control.

Then the magtracks engaged and, with hardly a checklist or even a fam briefing, they were hurled away from the quasi-palace back to the place that Cargo knew was home. Back into the dark, seamless void.

Over the next several days, as he became more familiar with the yacht's capabilities and drawbacks, Cargo became home-sick for the elegant batwing or a sturdy Krait. For all its vaunted extra super state-of-the-art upgrades, there was no way to disguise the fact that essentially this was still a vehicle designed more for a politician than a pilot. The luxury of parquet and Bachmeyed paled considerably when maneuver-ability was thrown into the equation.

Cargo cursed softly and heard an echo to his right. Then he winced and took the mode still deeper. All he wanted was an Immelmann, a full circle turn on two axes. In theory that should be easy. In a Krait he could do it on three with only a flicker of thought. Here, he imaged the move again, trying to instruct the maze clearly as to what was required.

And the damned machine mind refused. Downright refused. Politely, no less. *This vehicle is not equipped with redundant burn lines for simultaneous maneuvers. Please refer to the NNR aerobatic model for advanced procedures.*

"Pig!" he shouted, slamming the handrest with his fist.

"Yes," the thought came through the maze, and it didn't belong to the skiff. "Would you like some more news?"

Cargo swallowed. "Sure," he thought. "Why not? What could be worse, right?" And braced himself because it couldn't have gotten a whole lot better. There was no way to fly this pig of an evil mother and nothing Dancer could add could make it different. A toy, a plaything to while away a couple of hours, or make sure of absolute privacy, that was all this thing was made for. Cargo didn't know who he was going to kill first, the hangar master who acted like the skiff was a pure jewel, or Shodar who had played the ultimate, final trick in loaning it.

"It's worse," Dancer's communication came through the ripple in the membrane deep in the maze. "Been working on the weapons systems. And guess what? Those cute little bluster guns, just made for ceremonial salutes that Shodar just had to have, not only don't they have spectral monitors and trackers, they don't even have ammunition. Nothing aboard. And if you think I can talk this measle-tongued, viral fluid maze into diverting power from mains to popguns, you deserve this can."

Cargo tried to damp down the flush of anger that threatened to erupt. Wouldn't do any good at all, he told himself sternly. Patience. There was a way around everything, every obstacle merely presented another set of options. Besides, there was always cover and bluff, and this thing was perfectly designed for that.

"That and nothing else," Dancer's track paralleled his own.

"We're seventeen hours from safe zone," Cargo informed both of them. "Maybe a little food and a little prayer and a little sleep on the subject, and God will smile on us and we'll wake up in a craft worth flying."

Cargo caught Dancer's unworded agreement under the haughty tone of the maze mind. *This is the finest small yacht ever built. Made with every provision for the comfort and safety of the passengers, this yacht will exceed all expectations . . .* But Cargo had already dropped the collar on the seat he had abandoned.

When they were both free and clear of the collars, Dancer stepped into the galley and pulled out a large tin of macaroni and cheese, dropped his ears nearly to his shoulders, and sighed. He grabbed a second tin and revealed chahert. At least this time they'd gotten their own cuisines, sort of maybe.

"Is that as awful as this is?" Cargo asked, poking at the rubberized mess with a fork.

Dancer's mouth wrinkled with disgust. "This is the kind of food they serve for lunch in a grade-school cafeteria. I need hardly tell you what we did with it at that age, and it certainly wasn't considered fit for consumption."

"You got to feel sorry for the being," Cargo said pleasantly, trying to decide whether to throw out the whole thing or try to gag down a couple of bites. "Raised as a University experiment, fed dorm food. So far as Shodar knows, this is home cooking. Proves the theory that sentients should not be raised institutionally. Or maybe that's why he's such a charismatic leader, who knows?"

Dancer swallowed, looked as if he were about to be sick, and took a long drink of water. "Have I ever told you of my theory? About the military and leadership and food. It goes, the worse the food in the culture at large, the better the military, the stronger the leaders. And that goes for both species. I, for example, come from a culture that has a relatively simple diet. Your friend Ghoster, an Atrash, no less, had to be suspect from the start. They eat at least four courses at every meal, and there's more sauce than food. The Atrash culture may be the most elegant among us, but they are also decadent. They haven't even had a flight team for twenty-seven generations."

Cargo thought about that, and wondered if it was simply a dig against Ghoster. Looking back at Dancer he thought maybe not. If nothing else, the horror of taking on a real mission in a showy toy had made the two of them work together. Cargo even felt at times like he and Dancer understood each other the way he and Ghoster had. Certainly the frustration was mutual.

A common enemy unites even the most unexpected allies, the Bishop had said. Only he had been talking about Paese and Marcanter in the Cardia against the Trusteeship Pact. Well, but nothing ever said that the enemy couldn't be a machine. Especially a machine with a mind and a personality that reminded him of nothing so much as a debutante he had been forced to dance with at the Beaux Arts Ball. Being Mirabeau's son had had its drawbacks.

His dinner was cooling rapidly, and two things Cargo had learned in the past two days were that there wasn't going to be anything better in the galley and that it tasted worse cold than hot. And he had to eat, unfortunately. Mirabeau had once told him of Buddhist monks who went for weeks without eating and walked barefoot in the snow, but Cargo hadn't gotten the hang of either one. He downed the stuff as rapidly as he could and hoped he wouldn't be sick again.

They didn't mention the problems with the skiff until the tins had been deposited in the trash. It had become a custom, firmly established in days, that only one major unpleasantness could be faced at a time. So the table was clear and Dancer faced him over the shimmering gold-tinted surface.

"Well," the Akhaid said. "What are we going to do? Seventeen hours to nose-bleed, no real guns, and a pig that flies in nice, straight, safe lines. You're the pilot. You're the boss. You got any ideas?"

Cargo closed his eyes for a moment and took a deep breath. His left hand unconsciously caressed the St. Maries medal from Two Bits' two pilgrimages. First to the festival, and then to the Wall. The he smiled softly. "We have a saying," he said. "*Si khohaimo may patshivalo sar o tshatshimo*. There are lies more believable than the truth."

"You would try to make them believe something that was not true?" Dancer asked.

Cargo's smile broadened. "No. I would succeed."

Chapter
13

They were nine hours from Tzeryde when the maze reported the patrol. Not in that manner, naturally. In its slightly superior feeling, it informed Cargo and Dancer that there was "traffic" in the general vicinity, and did they wish it to interface with the local port?

Cargo responded in the negative before he began grousing. "They're not supposed to be there," he thought out to both the maze and Dancer. "Heading yellow two-two-four-nine, blue one-zero-three, red x-ray seven, five-seven hotel. That's way out of the pattern. How many?" he demanded crisply from the maze.

Four.

Cargo took a deep breath. Doubles, then. Patrol groups usually split into two teams of two unless they had reason to suspect a threat.

"Why do I get the funny feeling that somebody was tipped off?" he thought to himself, although the maze and Dancer both froze without reply. At least Dancer's visceral reaction was satisfying. Cargo didn't think he could fake that, not through the maze, which was probably a pretty good indication that Dancer at least hadn't been the one who had talked.

And whoever had had forgotten that the cultured and civilized Mirabeau was the son of a knife-fighting card sharp and a *boojo* woman. Cargo didn't even contemplate the layers of duplicity here, nor which side it was coming from and to what purpose. He only knew it was directed against him and so he was left without a choice. Intellectually he could even accept the fact that it was probably not at all a personal attack, but that didn't change the fact that he could end up very personally dead. And he wasn't quite ready to volunteer for the Wall.

"How about playing the 'we're just civs and we don't know nothing' routine?" Dancer suggested.

Cargo's thought cut him off immediately. In less time than it took to consider the option Cargo had imaged his own perception that, along with knowing where to make intercept, the Collegium had also been informed as to their identities. And, he was equally certain, playing dead wouldn't work either. That one had been pulled once too often to be successful. Blanketing over his reasoning was another set of images showing exactly what they could do.

A flicker of startlement ran through the membrane as Dancer picked up on the overall plan. The flicker became something else, something harder with a different feel to it, a new taste. As if Dancer himself was no longer exactly the individual he had been just minutes ago. Then, well outside the maze, he heard a long, hoarse guttural sound. Dancer, laughing.

The maze, somewhere between condescending and slightly put out, demanded to know what was going on. It certainly had no part in the plan, didn't even understand the spectral prints used for most high-performance craft for navigation, let alone tracking for Eyes. Cargo ignored its pseudo-personality and simply requested information as to distance and closing between themselves and the pursuers.

There was plenty of time. He didn't even bother to ask the maze to calculate possible Eyes intercept. Either their plan would work or it wouldn't, but his physical presence was necessary for this part. He got up and pulled the collar off. The break from the maze was uncomfortable at best. Better than a Krait, though. In one of those, had he broken the connection that quickly, he would have been lucky to get away with a killer migraine. The skiff hardly touched him.

Dancer was already at work breaking up the gold-tinted glass of the tabletop. "Good thing it's not plas," he said without stopping. "Or we'd be in serious trouble."

Cargo didn't bother to answer. They were fortunate that plas, being cheap and plentiful, had not been used in Shodar's skiff. But there were other useful items besides tinted glass. The food tins, for one, every last remaining one of them. Cargo gathered them up from the galley and dumped them in the canister Dancer had set up.

Tins, table, foil, the shaving mirror, all sorted into their own cartridges, filled the carpeted living area of the skiff.

"I'm going to load up the first two," Dancer said. "But you're going to have to pull the heater rings on the tins. All of them. Or we won't get the infrared high enough."

Cargo nodded, didn't even bother to point out that he was perfectly aware of the full range necessary to cheat the Eyes. Because that was the only thing he could think of to do.

Once in what seemed like another lifetime he had been trained as a batwing, a stealthfighter pilot in a craft that appeared void and null. And he had learned about stealth and tricks and deceits, all neatly and naturally, no more complicated than the scams he had learned at his mother's knees. But the whole point of the batwing was that it never showed. Its graceful curves and honeycomb skin trapped and channeled sensing radiation and never gave a positive read.

What he was planning here was exactly the opposite. The Eyes needed a spectraprint in order to lock on to a target. Likewise, the high-performance nav tech was on a spectral triangulation. Screw the spectography and the only systems left to the Kraits would be life support and vis.

And no one ever wanted to come close in enough to fight vis. By the time a Krait came within that distance of even this pig of a craft, they would have overshot. The Krait couldn't slow down enough to fire at the skiff vis, not even if the little yacht was pushing full out.

Dancer held his collar draped over his shoulder but not attached quite yet. He concentrated on loading the plastic canisters, both originals and the ones they had filled, into the ceremonial gun's tiny tubes.

"What are the originals for?" Cargo asked perfunctorily. He was concentrating on making sure that the tins would read bright enough in the infrared that he wasn't even sure he cared about an answer.

"My own addition," Dancer stated. "Ceremonial. You know

what they shoot out ceremonial? Sparklers. That'll give the Eyes tummy-aches all right."

Cargo waited until he was certain that all the tins were warming and then twisted the mag locks on the canister before Dancer's statement registered. And then he laughed, hard gasping peals that threatened the integrity of his ribs. As Dancer pulled the collar into place and the canisters disappeared down the tubes to blossom into a majestic display of fireworks, Cargo laughed until he could hardly breathe.

Dancer was in mode, concentration deep in the maze. The Akhaid fired again, and the tins of mystery meat were catapulted into the void.

"I hope they had their Eyes on us," Dancer muttered. Cargo didn't hear him. The laughter had abated just enough for him to resume his position in the maze. And it was through the maze that he sensed the completion of his plan.

The sky bloomed around them, sparklers as well as their own spectral emissions reflected by the myriad particles of what had once been a terrible expensive conference table and mirrors and rations. Their slightly deficient maze reported increased traffic, possible meteors, maybe satellites, in any case a terrific mess and did the pilot want interface with port maze?

Cargo instructed it in the negative, asking only for running report, and was interrupted by the maze indicating with surprise the first explosion. Two others followed rapidly, the maze utterly confused by the readings it was getting from the environment.

Dancer tried to calm it down. "The reflections caused the tracking to overload, which made the Eyes go into a feedback anomaly and self-destruct. They just thought they were defective," he thought in simple sentences to the maze.

The machine brain was not pleased. They shouldn't be in an area with so much traffic, so many self-destructs. It advised them *very strongly, very, very strongly* to remove themselves from the vicinity at once. At once. After all, it had been programmed to respond to any situation with safety as priority one. This place violated every safety directive in the manual and it suspected that the human pilot was perhaps sleeping/dreaming, which was a state of data processing it did not understand and certainly did not consider competent.

Cargo observed the maze even while he was in it. The thing gibbered away, scrolling long columns of data through his mind, and he ignored it. He knew what was happening, both to the skiff and the four Kraits that, according to the flimsy evidence the yacht maze had managed to amass, were limping back in the direction of Zhai Bau. Even the victory did not leave him feeling pleased, merely sad and a little disgusted.

Damn all designers. They had too much confidence in their toys, forgetting that the more sophisticated the system the more that can boggle it. He could almost taste what it was like in those Kraits now, not nearly so comfortable as his own current Bachmeyed chair, but with power and intelligence in plenty flowing around him and all thwarted.

Spectra are unique. That was a grade school lesson, an axiom so basic that all the spectraprint mapping devices reported errors if they pulled a double match. Oh, there were provisions for reflection and such, but with all the fine tuning they were carefully selected out for natural reflection, or titanium, or aluminum and steel, or ice crystals, or any one of a million other things that were known to be floating innocently through the universe. What the print maps did not make provision for were mirrors. True mirrors did not exist in nature often, and not enough in well traveled and over-fought sectors to be worth calibrating. And so the Kraits, all of them, had been reading errors in nav as well as Eyes targeting.

And all the time the pilots must have known. Cargo thought of them, of himself, of all the fighter jocks he had flown with and drunk with and trained with and very nearly died with during his whole career. They knew. He would bet two months' pay on that easy and wish he could put down more. They knew they had been tricked through their machines, both the dependence and the inadequacy. But there was nothing they could do.

Meanwhile, the skiff, with a maze that compared to a Krait's the way a semifunctional goldfish compared to Mengesha Kha Loun, sneered and protested but made way steadily on course to Tzeryde. What the others were too sensitive to ignore the yacht was too stupid to notice. The reflected patterns meant only traffic and high concentration of obstacles, and that was all. It doubted its navigation and its telemetry not at all. That it doubted its pilot was due to the general mentality of those who bought private yachts, as Cargo had more than enough reason to remember.

He tried to force himself to dispassion as he watched the sensor readings indicate that the Kraits were limping on vis. They would have blown him to the Wall with no idea of what his mission was, or what Dancer carried secreted somewhere on that alien person. And then, slowly, the anger came.

In the heat of battle, wits or otherwise, Cargo had been deceptively calm. It was something he had learned from his parents and from Mirabeau and at OCS. It was something that had stood him well in the face of major examinations and high-rolling games. And usually, afterward, there was nothing left but the fragments of exhilaration still clinging to whatever had been won. This time was different. This time reminded him of other times far in the past, of Angel and of Ghoster and of Stonewall. Of a kind of dishonesty that violated even his somewhat elastic concept of propriety.

Slowly, carefully, coming close to the surface of the maze, he touched the shimmering membrane where he and Dancer interacted in mode. "Was it Shodar who told them?"

Dancer stared at him, through him, the opaque ice-green eyes unreadable. The Akhaid paused for almost a full minute and Cargo felt suspended, totally adrift through fantasies. None of this mattered. The universe was a bad dream and morning would come and it would all be gone. Plato would be alive again and Two Bits also, and Stonewall would laugh and they would all go to Stolie's and drink cheap beer and play Smash until the endless night enveloped them again. It was an image he clung to hopelessly as it shredded like a web of lies.

"No," Dancer finally said. "No. Shodar wants this to work. He doesn't confide in me, I'm just the gofer in this operation. But I know he wants it to work and I think I can guess some of the why."

"Then tell me."

"Better than that," Dancer said, and handed him the collar he had removed with such relief at the end of their encounter.

Cargo picked it up and looked at it, then shrugged and fastened it again. He could feel the maze-mind engulf him distantly, somewhere in the place where the dreams had been. Silently Dancer studied him, then handed him six little red tablets. Six. Three-B's weren't easy to come by in the Cardia, were rationed strictly by hourly use, were doled out carefully to guard against the generally preferred custom of upping the dosages to get even finer control. Dancer took a handful of the white Akhaid version of the drug—or rather that completely different compound that had the same effect on the alien physiology. Cargo raised his hand and swallowed them dry.

He went deeper into the maze than before, past the chattering idiot at the conscious gate level, down to the place where there were no words. Only thought itself, images and sensations, shards of memory and, and the membrane that shone more brilliantly than he had seen it in a very long time. Not since he and Ghoster had taken a batwing with its ultrasensitive barrier that was almost no barricade against the essential alienness of the other. It had been painful then.

This time it was cool, like descending into an ice cave, the raw chill coming from the unseen dark where the terrors rested. Not abated, simply glossed over and forgotten in the depths. But the depth was not Dancer. At the bottom of the pit was only himself.

Dancer sparkled around the parameters of his mind, there but not there, unobtrusive, almost gentle. And Cargo wondered if this was the place where Dancer killed him, with a touch so subtle that even he might count his own drift off into subconsciousness and beyond to be unprovoked. The gentle touch grew slightly more present in mode, a warming presence against the chill, a blanket the color of polar ice, the color of an Akhaid's eyes.

He saw Shodar in memory, but it was not his own memory. Here the Cardia leader looked tense, a tension that a human could not detect on an Akhaid face but that Dancer experienced as pain.

"It is absolutely necessary that the Bishop come here," the memory spoke softly. "Perhaps we can negotiate now. Before I have to go."

There was something about the inflection of the words that made the Dancer-memory string thoughts together like the satellites of a constellation. Negotiate now. He remembered other things, the rumors of attacks on convoys being successful and others of merchants lost and blown away. The worst was the time they had encountered a ghost, the remnants of a hull with half a name on it, the burn so deep that it was almost impossible to read. Lab took three days to chart the ship; it had been the *Mary Barnes* from Paese hauling food.

Then there were the news blackouts, the strange announcements, the stories of conscription gangs on the fringe worlds of Verde and Cheryshin. He should have seen it before. Cargo or Dancer, not sure which was who and if it even mattered, the membrane glowed stronger between them, no longer separating but linking in an energy net that was their own thought. Data passed freely and suddenly it was very clear, very easy.

The Cardia could not win. Shodar must have known that from the beginning. Perhaps if they had simply been able to hold their own the Collegium would have eventually compartmentalized them in its corporate memory and forgotten them. That must have been Shodar's original plan.

But the Collegium did not forget. Always there was someone to remind them, not to make war, but that they had not made peace. And that person was Bishop Andre Michel Mirabeau. Had his lobbying efforts been any less intense, had his own stature in the Trustee Palace been any smaller, and eventually the Trustees would have written off the sixteen planets and habitats that made up the core of Shodar's Cardia. The Collegium could afford to lose them, and the Cardia wasn't even made of the best sixteen anyway. Cargo/Dancer could have easily picked ten worlds more likely, or more useful to a splinter group.

The Deckmejians might be the dominant force in the Cardia, but they were simply the largest minority. Maybe they could have gone on forever, but they needed Shodar's leadership to pull together popular support. And from what he had said, from the feeling Dancer had from those words, Shodar wasn't planning to lead his rebellion very much longer.

The why of this had frightened Dancer and made him terribly sad. He could not understand why Ki Shodar, who was the leader and the World Walker, the only gene-splice construct to survive, who had killed his own brother for either betrayal or for fear, why Ki Shodar would walk away. It made Dancer feel a little like a child who had been abandoned by the core without the comforting touch/think of them.

Sadness trickled over. Shodar too close. A child thing, to grow out of, the touch/think, not for an adult, a thing killed in the Walk. The realization washed over Dancer with utter horror. Shodar had never Walked. And Ki Shodar had never been raised in the core, had never experienced the touch/think of childhood when it was the proper time. Any Akhaid who had gone beyond primary school knew that this deprivation caused severe personality disorders.

All the splice-life experiments had been treated alike, sterile rooms, no core. All the germs no one had wanted. And to the Akhaid members of the scientific teams that had created them, since they were not bound to a core they were not properly beings at all but expendable lab animals. To the humans their Akhaid phenotype made them alien, although their genes carried as much human coding as Akhaid. No wonder then that most died. The only wonder was that he and Aliadro had survived.

Aliadro had had a friend, someone who had been a teacher and a father and a contact with the universe and Ki had hated him for that. Because Ki Shodar had not been saved by a sentient being, however kind or alien. Ki Shodar had survived because of a puppy and three white rats and the mice, the experimental animals that lived in the lab down the hall from his own.

The anger and the bitterness, a lifetime's worth, had spilled over in that one touch. Dancer carried it now as his own, something new and terrible to add to all the other things life had handed him. In truth, Ki Shodar was the archetype, the hero-image of what Dancer had patterned to become. And so Ki Shodar was both his god and his executioner, and because of that he understood that the great one must go on, could not stop any longer in this place and fight this losing war. But to negotiate now might mean better terms. Maybe he could even declare a victory. After all, a lie becomes true if it is repeated often enough.

There was something else, too, something personal about the Bishop. But the name-image brought only torrents of hatred, a fury so clean and so penetrating that nothing could peel back the layers. Dancer/Cargo guessed it was jealousy. The Bishop had been Aliadro's father as he had been Rafael's and Two Bits' and even Angel's, even when Angel ended up bad. So it was the Bishop Ki Shodar wanted to use to achieve his own goals. Hatred, and a kind of just retribution.

Cargo grasped, tried to find himself inside the strange mix of mind that occurred as they locked. Submerged, drowning in the Akhaid's memories and overwhelmed by the differentness of it all, he fought to retain his identity. And failed. Dancer and Shodar ripped through him like the gales of Vanity, unnamed emotions from untapped sources became open wounds. Cargo, battered and subdued in the membrane with his Akhaid partner, became Akhaid himself. For one single, brilliant, eternal second he understood the alienness from its own point of view.

And then the membrane shifted, flared, and Dancer was moving away from him. The barrier came up again, functioning as it was supposed to. Cargo wondered how much Dancer had seen into his mind. There was no way to know. Only that he wished it could have been Ghoster and not his jailor who had shown him too much ever to go back.

Exhausted, Cargo pulled the collar from his neck and draped it over the armrest. It was wet.

It was drunk and rowdy time in Spin Street—early enough to be full of high spirits and late enough that no one on the street was sober, except for those who worked there. Stonewall always liked this part of the night, late and warm and full of promise, the lights clear and beautiful and enticing, the voices echoing between the facades an invitation to gaiety and laughter and a party that never ever ended. Spin Street was in business, and party was its business. Stonewall could never manage to get through the brilliant part of the night without wondering where all the others were and how they knew to go there and were they having fun.

Always he had wanted to be in those lights, surrounded by that crowd. He imagined that it must be very smug and warm in the special place where everyone wanted to go but no one knew how to get to. Once or twice that magic had worked on him and he was *there*, out of the known manifold and in a place where only the dimensions of blues and yellows, beers and brandy, defined time and space. And those there with him were all friends and beauties, shimmering beings who could do nothing wrong in the night, whose outrages and vague suggestions took on immediate reality in the pliant dark. The longing for that night, that magic, was an empty place in his soul, a place that he dared not touch but that made the lure of the night both poignant and cruel.

Tonight he was working. He had to remember that and not succumb to the temptations that glittered all around. Things that were not temptation during more sober hours, but took on a glamour when surrounded by the alluring music of laughter.

He had always wanted to be one of the magical people who lived the nights, and it had always eluded him. Sometimes he even wondered if those others whom he so envied lived in fact only in his imagination, and that every single creature that passed him in the street festooned with titanium chains and red and black and violet smudges left over from brushes with whores and party-goers and thieves were in fact as lonely and seeking as himself.

But he was working. He was always working. The glaze in his face was simply camouflage.

Just ahead, Ghoster turned into a doorway, disappeared, then poked his head back to the street. "This is it," he said to Stonewall almost impatiently.

Stonewall picked up his pace slightly. Just another bar, from what he could see. Nothing to distinguish it from every other bar in the universe with its scarred glass pay plates and undersized wooden tables and real-live bartender, there not so much to serve customers as to throw out those who were on the verge of wreaking too much damage, a delicate task not well suited to mechanicals.

Ghoster was waiting for him. Waiting for his card, actually. He, or rather the department, was paying. Not that Ghoster knew who or what was behind it all, and the Akhaid had already consumed enough annies that Stonewall knew he had better get a return on the investment.

All too bad, too. It would have been so easy to haul Ghoster in for desertion, if nothing else, then and there. A whole lot more satisfying, too. Or, Stonewall thought, to kill him. That had its appeal. The vision flashed through his mind, the tiny whip he carried in his sleeve pocket weighing heavily against his arm.

Instead, he feigned nonchalance, inserted his card into the pay plate, and led Ghoster to the table indicated.

"So I missed Cargo," Ghoster said thickly once a large plate of unmoulded blues appeared. "Loading rot of turtle dung on that. Need to see him, Stonewall."

Stonewall nodded, and his pale hair cast a halo around him

in the gloom. "I can't help you," he said regretfully. "Don't know where he's gone. I don't even know for sure, good buddy, if he's even staying with that same carrier he was on. Wish I could help you there. Maybe the Bishop knows."

If Stonewall was heavily disappointed that he couldn't arrest Ghoster immediately, he gave no sign of it. Instead he let the thought sink in, and then went on. "You know, I would surely be damned interested to hear about where you have been. There has not been one hair of a clue, like you had just disappeared. Now I told you don't be a stranger, and you are the only being I know on all this stinking little colony that doesn't even have a proper top-port, let alone a decent hotel. And you show up and looking for Cargo at that. I would figure that if anyone in the known manifold would know where to find Cargo, it would be his old buddy Ghoster."

Ghoster took a third blue from the plate and began chewing slowly. He waited until he had swallowed, and waited again until the faintly sharp aftertaste dissipated. Then, in a very good human imitation, he sighed. "You wouldn't believe it, Stonewall. And if you did, you wouldn't want to know. Really. It is something to do with the core, that's all. With the Guardians and the core and me and Cargo and the Bishop and . . ."

"Hold it right there," Stonewall interrupted. "You just reeled off enough names to make it sound like a whole entire season series. Besides, I'd rather get drunk than listen to all that old political trash anymore. It gets me bored, you know what I mean? I mean, who cares anymore? So long as I got a good batwing and a good bar and a couple of friends, I'm doing just fine. Nice and simple for this old boy. The simple life. No complications. Sounds like you got yourself in a mess of complications there for yourself, but I don't want to hear one word about them." Stonewall raised his glass and drained it, then called up another, only hoping that it worked. He drank this one only a little more slowly. Ghoster was too gone by now to realize that Stonewall was just faking it. The glass was pure tonic water, just like the textbook on interrogation instructed. That was one textbook Stonewall was pretty sure Ghoster had never read.

"We just didn't know," Ghoster said as if he hadn't heard

Stonewall. "The core, the Guardians, it was right, what we were doing."

"Insufficient data," Stonewall supplied helpfully.

"Yes. Insufficient data. And perhaps not quite understanding how alien you are," Ghoster admitted. "But the Guardians of Tzeryde are usually right, and, after all, we are trying to evolve something like a reasonable bispecial relationship, aren't we? And that's pretty new to us. To you, too, unless you're hiding something major out there."

Stonewall shook his head. "Ghoster, I just got lost, like as if the coordinates you gave me were so far off that I ended up like near M64. I mean, I am not tracking you at all, not at all."

Ghoster looked up and tried to focus. "The Bishop is on Tzeryde," he said very carefully. "He explained it all to the Guardians. Now we know that this military is not your Walk, that it is not necessary for your species survival. So we can stop helping there."

"That was right kind of the Bishop," Stonewall agreed. "Now, what all is Tzeryde and the Guardians and the rest of whatever it was that you said?"

Ghoster took a deep breath and tried to get it all out at once. "The Guardians are the official core of the Dance, which is a separate but higher core than the Walk. Tzeryde is the Place of the Dance, and the Bishop is there now. With Jakta, too."

"That's like the high Akhaid officials, right?" Stonewall double-checked.

Ghoster confirmed his suspicion, and Stonewall felt like his head had opened like a window to let in the air, the hunch was that strong. Pure and simple Godint, he thought, and tasted the thrill of knowing, perfectly and clearly, that he was right. Keeping that bubbling excitement from his voice and face was harder than he had expected, but he had been well trained and was even more motivated. "And this Tzeryde, where all is it?" he asked as if the answer didn't matter one way or the other.

Ghoster was obviously beyond hope. The Akhaid reeled off the coordinates absently and Stonewall privately thanked years of military procedure for the ease with which he was able to memorize the numbers. He couldn't wait to put the report through, get a team over to whatever this Tzeryde was as soon as possible. The last thing he wanted was to sit around longer with Ghoster. He'd take care of that bit of business later.

Lazily he stretched his long legs from under the table and got up. "Ghoster, what do you say about checking out of this dump tomorrow and getting ourselves over in those Tzeryde parts first thing in the morning?"

The Akhaid blinked. "We don't have transport."

Stonewall sighed. "Now, Ghoster, I am seriously disappointed in you. You know that we can borrow one of those pretty little Kraits all burned up pretty and pink and be under way before anyone knows that nobody authorized us to take it out. Hell, you done it before with Cargo, and gone them one better, too."

Ghoster's face closed and seemed to purse with thought. "Oh."

Stonewall just shook his head. "I'm going to get some rack time, and meet you out say at four hundred hours?" All Stonewall wanted was fifteen minutes to get in touch with the Directorate. Fifteen minutes and he could tell them about Tzeryde and where Ghoster was going to be. *Oh, no,* he thought, studying the Akhaid who was close to passing out. *No, you're not going to get away with this one, Mr. Ghoster. We're going to sew this all up good and tight, and break through with this Guardians of the Dance business without your little deserter hide.*

Ghoster smiled sloppily and stood next to him, reeling gently, laughing to himself. Without warning the Akhaid picked up a full pitcher of beer from another table and poured it all out over the counter.

Two large humans, somewhat put out, started after him, but Ghoster was already out of range. Instead, he had grabbed Stonewall's ankle and positioned the human so that the others would naturally take the rest of him.

"Smash!" Ghoster screamed happily.

The group from whom he had borrowed the beer roared. At least Stonewall had seen it coming. In the half second allotted he tried to relax and judge the length of the counter while the bartender got well out of the way. A bunch of spacers, military or merchie made no difference here, all heated up for a friendly game of Smash, was not something he wanted to break up. After all, the game did only so much damage. A frustrated crowd would do much more.

"Smash!" Ghoster said again. Then they tossed Stonewall down the well-soaked bar to see how far he'd slide.

Chapter

14

There was no mistaking Tzeryde for anything but alien, Cargo thought. In fact, he was certain it would be alien to most Akhaid, just as Jakta's mountain monastery was somewhere between incomprehensible and unimaginable to him. Shodar's bunker and palace were much more within his realm of experience. Here, though, he felt as if he had stepped out of the universe and into one of the Other Six. It was beautiful and this bothered Cargo terribly, because nothing at all should not be beautiful.

But light was not nothing, he reminded himself, and the glorious sculpture of light alone made the interior of Tzeryde perhaps the single most amazing art work in the manifold. Those who had built the ancient cathedrals of Earth had strived for this effect, but had been unable to eliminate stone and shadow. The light made the burned titanium bulkheads of every military carrier he had ever served on seem not only tawdry, but dull and insipid.

They were in the blue sector, named not for the sheets of brilliance that formed patterns on the plain white deck, but for the laser overlay that defined and interpermeated the softly glowing ambers and violets, the cool sea greens and all the colors of the Akhaid skies. As he sat the patterns shifted, the colors moving gently from one configuration to the next. It was like being in the middle of a giant kaleidoscope. Tired as he

was, and hungry as well, he couldn't keep his mind from
following the fluid light dance its way through the empty space
that was Tzeryde.

"You are still only on the edge," Jakta said quietly. "Inside,
in the center, the whole of Tzeryde, all the colors and all the
light together, spin around you. And you are the center."

Cargo remained silent. The Bishop had just introduced him
to the orange-robed monk who looked nothing at all like a
former Trustee. It was Mirabeau who had his attention in any
case.

The Bishop was changed. The frailness of age seemed to be
just a little less advanced, and the ashen cast to his skin was not
entirely gone but at least abated enough to show a healthy
ebony glow. His startling grey eyes sparkled as if he had just
heard a secret and wanted to smile and tell. Cargo thought it
might be a trick of the lights, but they shifted again and the
change remained even under the unflattering greens.

The Bishop smiled softly at Jakta. "I think this is impressive
enough," he said before turning to Cargo and Dancer. "Now,
what is this about Shodar inviting us back to the talks?"

"Not us," Cargo corrected. "You. Alone. That's what he
said, anyway. And I don't trust him or his offer, no matter what
anyone else says."

Mirabeau nodded. "Then you have heard some of the
rumors about him."

Cargo glanced at Dancer, who remained impassive. "Yes.
And after meeting him I don't find them hard to believe. But
are they true?"

The Bishop only nodded and closed his eyes. He tried to tell
Cargo what he saw, what he remembered, only it was clouded
by the telling, fragments of memory that might mean nothing
or everything.

He hadn't been there, precisely, had seen nothing. And there
was always the possibility that Shodar had been framed. But
Mirabeau didn't think that likely. He remembered Aliadro,
quiet and pensive those last few days between their success and
his death, as if pondering some vast and dark decision. But that
was simply Aliadro's way. There were times when Mirabeau
regretted introducing the youngster to Sophocles. He should
have realized that Aliadro had been at an impressionable age,
that the stark terror of the King, of the twisting of right and

wrong, would haunt a sensitive being throughout life. And so he blamed himself as much as Shodar.

Maybe more. He had started the action. All Ki had done was finish it, relieve the misery. No matter what the political objectives, Andre Michel Mirabeau firmly believed that Ki Shodar would never have become a fratricide had he never befriended a lonely Akhaid-appearing child. Who just happened to be one of the principals in the most significant interspecies genetic research project of the century. And the one that ended that line of inquiry for good. No, if he had never met Aliadro, never taught him the human classics, it never would have happened.

But it would, he acknowledged silently. If not Sophocles, then Tolstoy or Hemingway or LeBaur. And he had learned his lesson. From then on, all his adoptive children were steered toward mathematics. For Aliadro it was already too late.

Still, he winced as he recalled the room as he had seen it, shadowed and lit by only candles, the bedsheets torn and dragged half across the room. Stained with blood, too, but that was hidden in the dark, hidden by the other sight. Ki Shodar holding his brother's body, rocking back and forth as if to comfort him. And tilting that silver face with the eyes closed forward to hide the gash at the throat. All very primitive, too primitive for Mirabeau. And all very, very civilized. The death of Marat. All that was lacking was the bath.

He had stepped into the room, walked carefully on the mingled sheets and carpet, stepped down on something soft that was neither. And the memory of it still filled his mouth with bile and his body heaved in the recall. Like a pair of lilac marbles Aliadro's eyes had lain discarded in the folds of the bedclothes. Sophocles. Mirabeau knew then that whatever Ki Shodar had done had been a mercy.

The Bishop opened his eyes and looked at his son, at his friend. Cargo was pale and uncomfortable even under the rose-shift light. "So you saw him," Cargo muttered. "I'm surprised he didn't kill you right there."

Mirabeau sighed and knit his brow. "I was surprised, too. But that isn't the worst of it. The worst of it, for him and for me and for all of us, is that I forgave him. He hated me for that. I would be surprised if he doesn't still hate me for that. And I have always expected that he'd want to pay me back."

Cargo blinked. "That doesn't make sense," he said flatly. "Why is the fact that you forgave him any worse than seeing him kill his brother and all the rest? I can't believe that."

It was not Mirabeau who answered, but Jakta, and the Bishop was relieved. It had been hard enough to tell the events, to have to face his own memory of that night. He didn't want to try to explain any of it, not anymore. He had spent too many years late at night with brandy and his thoughts trying to analyze, to understand. As if something significant could suddenly come to light and change everything. So that Mirabeau could jump up and tell Shodar that it was all an illusion and there was no reason for any war, any trouble, any forgiveness. After all these years he knew that hope was irrational and he had carefully avoided the matter. It prevented him from drinking Cointreau, the scent that permeated the room where Aliadro died, and he could no longer look into Ki Shodar's eyes. Eyes that were so much the same as those disembodied spheres rolling across the sheets.

"Is this why we are fighting?" Cargo asked, incredulous.

"No," Mirabeau answered. "But it is the reason we can't make peace."

The light shifted again, the rose fading, merging softly into the following sapphire that strained around the clear blue laser beams that defined their space for the moment. Then the clear blue lines moved, too, swinging in great gothic arcs and focusing together to form a series of holograms far above their heads. It became a single giant flower, a corona, a galaxy full of stars. Only when the display disassembled itself and became again the familiar lattice-work of the blue sector of Tzeryde did Jakta rise.

"Come," he said to Mirabeau. "I am afraid we have been remiss in our duties. Our guests are hungry and we haven't even offered tea."

The music woke him. At first Cargo thought it was part of a dream, the background of the past. It would have fit in perfectly with the red hills he remembered so well, that had formed his flesh more than any other place, the hidden violence in the barren landscape that built a harshness into people's souls.

It was the violence that frightened him, not because it lay

incipient out in the parched earth but because it lay inside him as well. Like with his cousin Angel who had started no different than he but who had ended annie blind trying to rob a late-night pay plate. And his father. He mostly remembered his mother, beautiful and angry and too proud. His father had become only a series of discrete images, the sad music of the Gitano guitar, a flash of white teeth under a heavy black moustache, a strangely small heap huddled against a back alley wall with open knife wounds dribbling blood down the sewer.

Sonfranka never saw the red hills of Andalusia and never needed to. She was not Gitano, cut off and alone and threatened by the violence of the past. But her body lying broken and cast away under the fluttering red velvet at the *ofisa* window had only increased the anger in him, like the bullies in juvie. Nothing the Bishop taught him made him ready to forgive them. They had taught him a valuable lesson, the taste of blood in his mouth and of fear.

All the images came together, shards of this thing he called Cargo, called Rafael Mirabeau, called Kore Verdun, called Django Ynglesias. Pieces, fragments, but not the center.

The music went beyond into the center. The flamenco that was all death and sex and pain touched him in a place he didn't even know existed. A place that was beyond all the angers and the hurts and the little pleasures that he had called himself. This was some different self, far more basic and essential than the other.

Insistent and fluid, the music moved around him. The tune was familiar, a *sevillana*. And the light shifted also, mirroring the un-Akhaid harmonies of the piece. That was when he knew he was awake. The red/violet/gold pulsations surrounded him like raw flesh, the heart of some lab animal lying ready on a dissection table for a knife. Only he was inside.

An organ, or a membrane.

The light pulsations flickered at his thought. It was a dream, had to be a dream. It was only some very complex and admittedly beautiful computer-controlled schematic. It could not, not at all, respond to him. Not like in mode, nothing like the exchange/separation in the maze. Not at all.

The light walls became more brilliant, shading deeper into the colors of fire, of fear. Cargo knew it was only imagination. Hadn't he himself worked on similar effects to dupe the customers? Only his own weariness and the pressure of the past weeks needing an outlet before he went as mad as Sonfranka, that was all. Or maybe it really was a dream.

Since it was impossible anyway, he reasoned, what was the harm in thinking to it in what little Atrash he knew? Then he could go to sleep again relieved of paranoid delusions. As if a sculpture could think, could answer him. Craziness. But it didn't hurt to try, and when he failed he would have proven his point and no one would be any the wiser.

I am called Cargo, he thought in careful Atrash, groping for words he had nearly forgotten.

The light brightened around him and washed itself with gold. *I am first core,* the thoughts formed not in Atrash words but in something more primitive and human in his mind. *I am first core, but I have a name. The only core with a name. Tzeryde. I teach. Are you my new student?*

It was like the maze but beyond it. And then Cargo remembered that it was the Akhaid who had invented the maze. Humans had worked out the specifics of mode years before contact, but it had been a rather mechanical and sterile thing until the Akhaid had created the membrane and interfaces that made the maze so much smarter and more complete than anything that was merely machine or human or Akhaid could hope to be.

The thing that was Tzeryde was amused. He could feel it keeping a careful distance from him, a maze beyond anything he ever imagined existed. This core could come into his mind, overwhelm him, strip his brain down to the gears and reduce him to a breathing vegetable. But all it did was observe and wait.

Cargo considered it carefully, and then decided that caution be damned. He was sick of being cautious. It had saved his life plenty of times, and what did he have? No place, his best friends dead or in danger, his own people and family estranged over nothing.

Damn all caution. Damn all propriety. He was sick of it all, of this insane life and its obligations.

He looked at the golden sheets of brilliance woven into a blue laser lattice and defiantly invited it in. As the core/maze touched his mind, he realized that it had been waiting for him all along. For anyone who asked.

Crazily he began to laugh. The Bishop in all seriousness had often quoted that old phrase, "Ask and you shall be answered," but Cargo had never believed it. And here on an alien installation was a thing/being that behaved just like the Bishop's Bible.

A being, Tzeryde corrected him gently. *I am being, beings, all who have come here and are here and were here. That is core. This is first core. Maze is a new core. It does not have enough experience, but it will grow.*

Tzeryde instructed him as if he were in primary school still, but Cargo didn't notice. He was too astounded by what the core had implied. Part of him rejected it as a complete paranoid hallucination. Another part of him simply wondered about the mechanics in order to avoid the important questions.

Light is energy. Thought is energy. Energy can communicate. There is nothing but energy. Tzeryde is all energy.

The words stopped. Cargo felt the core opening deeper inside his mind, directing, in charge like no maze ever could be. But familiar, after a fashion. And then he remembered. Dancer's mind overcoming his, the infantile touch/think, had felt akin to this. But where Dancer was a single entity with only one pass through a very young and stupid membrane, Tzeryde was as old as the Akhaid and as great as the minds of the philosophers and artists and seekers and visionaries who had been Dancers and Guardians through the whole history of the Walk.

There was no resisting it, even if Cargo had the will. But he was enticed along down the rich compendium of images and ideas, reshaped abstractions, that overwhelmed him and finally became him as he became part of them and part of Tzeryde itself. And, to his great astonishment, became the first human to become one with the Dance.

Jakta and the Bishop could not touch the core. Only those who had been given the drugs, the Three-B's, and a whole range of annies for large parts of their lives could communicate with the core. Tzeryde showed him this, showed him its sorrow that it could not touch humans except through its own in mazes. As Ghoster's long friendship had made him ready, had brought him close into contact more than once before when he had been flying.

Because distance was not important to the maze-being. Once

an individual was connected to the core, that being was always of the core. Cargo did not quite follow the technical explanation, something to do with electrons and spin, but by then it no longer mattered. Nothing mattered except the joy of the contact itself. The core was hungry for beings, more of them, greater intelligence. At the center, Cargo was not quite sure that Tzeryde itself was not really another life form, a complete being that lived and fed off the exchange of energy with others. The speculation was not his alone. He could sense it echoed throughout the core, just as he could feel whatever was at the center of Tzeryde shift so that he couldn't catch a glimpse of it in its true form.

Organic or not, it didn't matter. The fact was that Tzeryde was a sentient living being, and a matrix for those who came together in the core.

Suddenly the Walk and the Akhaid and even Ki Shodar made a terrible kind of sense. All of them, humans, had been missing the vital piece of the equation, the cores. Even the Bishop didn't really know or understand. But once the missing piece was put into the picture the whole thing shifted, changed, and Cargo stared inside the knowledge.

There were millions of cores, maybe hundreds of millions, and together with the Akhaid they formed a symbiotic relationship of intelligences. Who or what the cores were or where they came from was hidden from Cargo, hidden from even most of the cores themselves, he supposed. That was no longer important. The fact that together they and the Akhaid had created a mutually dependent biology and culture was.

Akhaid infants were born with a think/touch instinct. Not really psi, but an entry into the Other Six, the theoretical dimensions of the universe that humans could not perceive. They were made part of a core as near to birth as possible with that first tentative reach into the universe. Which core they joined had something to do with parents and aunts and uncles and where they were born and even the medical attendants. Children grew and were essentially raised by the cores, by generations of earlier Akhaid whose thought patterns remained fixed in the light/energy patterns. Adults belonging to the core cared for the child's needs, and it was infrequent that these were the biological parents. And when the core decided it was time, the child was pushed out of the nest like a fledgling to Walk.

To Walk was to know the core, and that the one core of childhood was part of an infinite circle of every core and every Akhaid. As individuals sought out the stress conditions that would force the maturation of their bodies, they were also seeking out a new relationship to the matrix that held them, touching in over distances, being linked to secondary and even tertiary cores. Most of all they were finding their place as individuals and as working fragments of the central intelligence.

And in the center of the whole was Tzeryde, ancient and waiting, the never moving vortex of all movement. Tzeryde chose the Dancers, those who could link directly and consciously, but in the end every Akhaid was linked to Tzeryde because all the cores came together at its intersection.

Perhaps they were true beings not from another point in the timespace frame Cargo inhabited, but denizens of one of the Other Six, living in a completely different universe that touched his own only through the perception of the individuals who were in contact.

And so the Akhaid had given them the maze, the beginnings of a core, so that humans could begin to link into what the aliens thought of as universal mind. All the drugs and technology the Akhaid had brought had focused on this one point. Humans who had studied the Akhaid said they had a "maze technology." No human had understood just how true that was. Except for one thing. It wasn't a technology at all, it was a living entity.

He could feel Tzeryde's pleasure at his comprehension, pleasure at his participation. It had wanted humans inside for a very long time, it seemed, as long as it had known about them. Because thought was energy, and the more abstract and involved the thinking process the more delicately balanced and shaded the particle patterns it created for Tzeryde to enjoy. Properly the core ate thoughts, but it did not eliminate them.

And then Cargo saw the other thing, the thing he had missed so completely that he didn't even realize it was there to be missed. The core never eliminated its reservoir of thought. Every pattern was held inside it forever. No wonder the Akhaid had no fear of death. They had no conception of it. Within the eternal mind of Tzeryde every individual was immortal.

All the dancers of the Walk, all the killing and dying and keeping the war on, it all became part of a single overwhelming perception. None of those deaths were meaningful if there was no real death. And for the Akhaid the concept of death the way Cargo thought of it did not exist—could not exist. It went counter to their direct experience of the universe.

Tzeryde laughed. Not in any way Cargo could hear, but he could sense the trills of delight running through it, see the shifting colors of the light walls as they sparkled with internal hints of snowflakes and sparkles and the birth of stars.

"I always knew the Walk was wrong for us," the Bishop mused. "I just didn't know exactly how to explain it." He closed his eyes and seemed to drift off. Cargo was about to stand up when the old man spoke again. "I must be getting old, losing my edge. I've been here for over a week and I never suspected. The whole idea never even occurred to me. Maybe they were right and it was time for me to retire."

Cargo snorted. "Not when you're the only person Shodar will talk to."

Mirabeau looked up and his eyes brightened. "Yes. There's that, isn't there. I wasn't thinking. This whole thing about Tzeryde is so . . . so unexpected. Are you certain that it really is an other-dimensional being?"

Before Cargo could answer, Jakta cleared his throat softly, drawing their attention. Tzeryde sparkled around them, and Cargo could sense a faint radiation of excitement and hope. The core had broken full contact for the time being, but Cargo was aware of its current of thought, if not the thought itself. Tzeryde touched him now like a very light breeze, hardly present but still noted.

Maybe, Cargo thought, he had just become adjusted to what the colors meant. That wasn't satisfying. This felt more like the edge of mode, just as the drugs began to take effect. He wondered if this impression too would fade, if he would be left with nothing but the memory. He couldn't believe that. Nor could he quite credit that he could return to the enveloping warmth of full communication.

The Bishop shifted uncomfortably on the soft white carpet.

Tzeryde was light-filled and beautiful, but it was not particularly big on furniture, and this section was completely bare. The only amenities Cargo had seen had been a few lap desks, and even those were considered unnecessary in the visitor's sector.

Cargo looked at Jakta, completely at ease sitting on the floor no different than in his mountain monastery, and wished he wouldn't take quite so long. The Bishop was probably anxious to get back to his white leather wing chairs, although enough of a diplomat to hide it successfully from almost everyone.

"He can hardly be certain of anything," Jakta said softly as the hues around them shifted from pale ice-blue to red-violet. "Who Tzeryde is is not important, at least not to us, not now. What is important is that we understand what is wrong with Ki Shodar. No wonder he is unbalanced. It is amazing that he survived at all. No doubt due to excellent human genes. But not quite enough. What I don't understand is why he couldn't simply take a whole case full of Three-B's and join the cores the way you did."

Cargo nodded slowly. He was picking up Jakta's calm, centered movements the way he had earlier picked up the Bishop's approach to problems and Plato's accent. "I wondered that also," he started hesitantly. "Tzeryde doesn't know. I think maybe there are several reasons. First, that like any human, Shodar doesn't know the cores exist. His touch/think wasn't strong enough as a child to contact one, and no Akhaid adult would tell him anything so basic. Besides, the way I understand it, the natural communication is what determines which core one belongs to. So no adult would ever consider influencing that choice. The other possibility is that he knows, but because he wasn't able to reach out as any Akhaid he believes that it is impossible for him to do it. That maybe he lacks the physical ability from the human side."

"And you're the first human to make contact," the Bishop whispered.

Cargo smiled and shook his head. "No. Every time we go into mode we are in contact. Just that no one ever bothered to wonder quite with what. Or who."

The light blazed quickly gold and then settled into a sedate sea-deep blue. The Bishop moved his legs again, stretching them out directly in front and then kneeling. At least that position was familiar. Cargo sympathized. He wished he could cross his legs on his thighs and look as comfortable as the orange-robed abbot.

Finally Mirabeau arranged himself sitting on his crossed ankles and leaned back and braced himself with his arms. "The problem is whether the drugs will work." Miarbeau's voice had taken on the old timbre of command that Cargo remembered from his days in the Cathedral. "There maybe a physiological problem. From what I remember of the experiments, and I was rather well acquainted with at least one lab team, while the subjects take on an outwardly Akhaid appearance, several of their internal organs are actually composite and are not duplicated in any other living being. I remember something specific about the brain, about double sets of mixed neurons and an enzyme balance that would kill any other being. It could be that the drugs are harmful to them."

"To him, you mean," Jakta corrected softly. "Shodar is the only one left."

"To him," the Bishop acknowledged his mistake. "But someone must know if anything can help him. Tzeryde might know. And there should be records from the experiment." Suddenly Mirabeau was still. Cargo could almost see the thoughts falling into line, ordering themselves while the Bishop directed the future of the known universe. Like he always had. It was as if he had been suddenly imbued with the force and vigor and authority he had had twenty years earlier when he had been a Senior Trustee of the Collegium.

"Well," the Bishop said firmly, his gaze directed at Cargo. "We will invite Shodar here. Tell him that we have found a way for him to communicate with the core. With Tzeryde, if that will mean anything to him. In exchange, naturally, for an immediate cease-fire and a signed treaty by the end of the Akhaid year. You've met him. Do you think he'll agree?"

Cargo forgot to breathe. His throat was dry. "But, you don't have a way for him to link with the core. Only a few theories."

The Bishop chuckled. "By the time arrangements are made and he gets here, I'll have found one. Didn't I ever teach you to improvise?"

"You really think a head of state, a military commander in the middle of a war, will be willing to come in person? And to a place that's hardly on the charts?" Cargo asked, still somewhat taken aback.

It was Jakta who answered. "It has been done before. As your escort pointed out, the Cardia can't win. All they can do is play a holding game, and they don't have the resources to hold the Collegium off forever. Besides, Tzeryde and the Dancers are neutral. And perhaps it will be Tzeryde and not your Bishop or Shodar who negotiates anyway. You have said that the Akhaid and the cores don't understand what death is. Neither do we. But I think they are very good at games."

Cargo shrugged. "Then I'll ask that a message be sent," he said, before trying to get up in a single graceful movement like Jakta. He failed, stumbled, and had to brace himself with one hand while he untangled his feet.

"Just one last thing before you go," the Bishop stopped him as Cargo neared the thinned light that indicated a passageway. "Didn't Ghoster explain everything?"

Cargo wheeled around as if he had been slapped. "Ghoster? I haven't seen Ghoster," he choked on the words.

Mirabeau's eyes were wide and innocent. "He was looking for you. I told him to try Tel Hala. I suppose you weren't there."

Cargo swallowed hard and bolted out of the enclosing orange brilliance. Ghoster wasn't the only one on Tel Hala. And Cargo had not forgotten what Stonewall was tracking down. Of all the crazy, idiotic things—

He didn't watch the corridor change from orange to dark red, didn't notice the turnings and various indications of private spaces behind laser lattices that were no longer blue but hot red-violet. The place shifted and formed around him, leading him segment by segment to its inner heart.

Cargo followed the paths that opened for him. His whole mind was filled with Ghoster. Ghoster was the reason he was here at all, to save his old partner from Stonewall. And Stonewall was on Tel Hala. How could he have known?

But he didn't know. Only that both had converged on Cargo, that he was the center of it all. If he hadn't wanted to save Ghoster in the first place he wouldn't have been in the middle of this whole situation. Or maybe he would have been. Maybe it was his destiny, that no one else could have talked with Tzeryde before him, that his link with Shodar and Tzeryde and the Bishop all together had created a scenario that he could not have avoided.

Past and future shifted, fused. Choice and no choice led in the same direction.

And then Cargo emerged from the low corridor into a giant empty space filled with all the colors of the spectrum, all together but soft, diffused, no longer resolving into pseudo walls and ceilings. He was weightless, drifting through a sea of glistening energy, though he could sense and that made the hair on his arms stand on end.

He knew that he was in the center of the habitat structure, that this floating was due to the lack of spin in the center. But something more primitive felt borne up and enfolded in the gentle waves of Tzeryde.

He was not in contact but he could hear the voice of the being the same way he could hear the lowest notes of the antique pipe organ in the Cathedral, not with his ears but with the vibrations in his bones. And the notes that were too low and deep were asking him why he expressed such a strange favor. Truly Ghoster belonged within Tzeryde and was safe. The whole of the universe was safe, was contained in this one perfect space. And it was himself.

Chapter

15

In the soft brilliance that surrounded him he saw Ghoster. Not the living presence, but a reflection of his own images made complete the way the simple mazes of the batwings worked. Like mode but far beyond those capabilities, the stillness around him was plastic, waiting for him to mold his own thoughts into defined pictures.

The Ghoster of his image was in uniform, slightly lopsided as if he had visited too many annie bars in an evening or had indulged in a cup of espresso.

"Where are you?" he asked the image aloud, feeling faintly ridiculous and certainly not expecting any answer. A maze only knew the information it was given directly.

A flutter of emotion that Cargo could not identify passed through him, and then coordiinates appeared, coalescing out of the shimmering space that surrounded him. A section darkened like a briefing board and a map appeared large enough for him to drift through it and not touch the realistic projections that represented planets and moons and various small craft. Then the coordinates shifted into the map and shifted angle once again.

This time Cargo recognized the pattern. The large grey mass was horribly familiar. Only Mawbry's had that blasted and unrepaired microwave station still perched on its leprous white skin, overgrown by a functional new station that already looked like it had been attacked more than once. He remembered when that had happened, a daring raid so close to the Collegium itself. The three Cardia fighters that had taken part in it had been blasted back to electrons, but their attitude had been admired all the same.

Ships of various sizes and types and registries clogged the darkness that surrounded Mawbry's. He recognized at least two Kodian long-haul energy ships, a mini-carrier that would probably be a platform for only six or seven groups, a hideously decorated Table-Yum transport, and more shuttles than he cared to count. About average traffic for Mawbry's.

And there was one more, one farther off than anything else the display showed. From its configuration and burn it was nothing more than a light-and-lux, the well-shielded design preferred for transporting luxury goods. Nothing else so far out was shown, and Cargo couldn't decide whether he was sensing directly from Tzeryde or from the evidence that Ghoster was on that merchant vessel.

And, as he stared at the display, something else became very clear. They weren't heading to Mawbry's at all. Their trajectory was just the tiniest bit off. They were on a direct course for the Collegium itself.

Of course, Cargo thought. He had been stupid to even assume anything else. Naturally Stonewall would have to parade his prisoner around his superiors. Especially if that meant getting Gantor in public, making it impossible for him to continue in the Directorate. That was just like Stonewall.

Even more, they would have the instruments there, the drugs, the techniques to try and rip out Ghoster's mind. Interrogation, it was called. And the whole was only more horrible because they wouldn't understand what they got. The humans didn't know about the cores, and Cargo was certain that none of the Akhaid who worked on the Collegium would tell them. And the Akhaid, who would understand about Tzeryde, wouldn't believe that the humans didn't already understand the core's attempt at assistance, didn't already have such a symbiotic relationship of their own.

Only one thing bothered him. "How do you know?" he asked Tzeryde silently, his mind begging for some kind of answer he could understand.

But it was not the answer that was incomprehensible. It was

the question itself. Cargo caught Tzeryde's total confusion reflected in the play of the lights. *Where? When? These are not part. Parts are always parts.*

Cargo caught his breath. This was something that he would have to talk to his old professors about, the dimension where there was no when or where. Perhaps he could even define it mathematically, with the beauty and cold elegance inherent in that art form.

The map flared and hurt his eyes before it faded, bringing Cargo back to whatever reality it was that he had decided to live in. It was a reality where Ghoster was in trouble, that was the main thing. Everything else could wait.

Even the concept of trouble Tzeryde found difficult. Cargo didn't have time to explain. Besides, the core had encountered the idea before, and the emotion of fear from the Akhaid long ago, but it had not understood then and wanted to take this time to clarify this feeling.

Cargo found it difficult to deny Tzeryde, to tell the core no. The being was so innocent, if that word could be used to describe an entity as old and as experienced as the matrix-cum-collected experience Tzeryde represented. On the other hand, exactly the same could be said of Andre Michel Mirabeau.

Then Cargo recognized that his own lack of urgency was not his at all, but Tzeryde's. He had to shut his mind to it, to focus exclusively on Ghoster. Or Stonewall would win, and Cargo was not about to give up without a fight. Not when he was so close to understanding.

He wrenched his feelings back, imagined them in a cool steel box with a heavy print lock on the front. He had used this technique before with the maze on the Krait, when its priorities were different from his own. And it worked here, too, although he could sense the ripple of Tzeryde's surprise at being cut off.

He would explain to the core later, he would explain everything, he promised as he ran back into the corridors of light. Later. Now, first, he had to get to the Bishop. Only Andre Michel Mirabeau on an official mission from the Collegium had the authority to requisition either a batwing or a Krait from whatever force was currently in residence at Zhai Bau. He hoped devotedly for a batwing. Stonewall knew how to fly one and how to counter one, but it didn't mean that he could pull it off in some pig of a merchie.

The light shifted, played against itself, against the laser lattice that also shifted, and the corridor widened into an oversized cavern lit in deep blue. Against the reflective bulkhead of the skin were positioned banks of terminals, communications and information, flickering red in the twilight dark. The whole chamber curved along the perimeter of the habitat, following around until he could not see.

He was almost relieved. This was not the Bishop, but at least Tzeryde had proper capabilities. He had not seen any sign of even the most modest communications devices since he had arrived.

And then Mirabeau appeared out of a blinding wall of green that returned to midnight as soon as the Bishop had entered. He noted Cargo immediately and approached him as if he had expected to find him here.

"One of the Dancers said that you were here and needed me," Mirabeau said, and spread his hands. "What can we do?"

The batwing was everything Cargo remembered. The matte black hull matched the void, a statement in the cradles where the gaudily burned Kraits rested en masse. All sweeping arcs and soft undulations, nothing sharp to mark it in the darkness, the batwing was a beautiful thing. Cargo had loved them on Vanity, and for all he had given up war and the trappings of war, the beauty of the stealthfighter gave him pleasure. It was more a sculpture of the void itself than the angry fighters that violated timespace.

The Bishop had done more than well, had given him exactly what he wanted with a poetic twist. The carrier he was on had to be the *Horn*. The good old Horn and Hardart. When he had come aboard ghosts had lined the corridors, Plato and Two Bits and Ghoster and Fourways and even Stonewall as he had been then. As he had been as a batwing, not this strange android creature that played at intelligence for intellectual pleasure.

Nothing on the *Horn* had changed. Cargo found himself following his old patterns, even greeting individuals whose names he didn't know but whose faces he remembered. And he felt like a ghost himself, one of the *mule* that could not find their proper place and were tied to the living. Then he had found the head and thrown cold water on his face. The *Horn* was no different from any other carrier of its class. He would have been haunted by his memories in any case.

But the past was beyond help, and Ghoster was real and alive and part of Tzeryde, whatever that meant. And Ghoster didn't know that he could die, or worse.

"Your bid," an unfamiliar Krait jockey said.

Cargo sighed. He had barely left the hot room, impatient to leave the *Horn* and impatient to finish this business. No matter which way it went. The waiting was torture, and this time he didn't even have the excuse of massive paperwork.

He glanced at his cards quickly and made his bid, watched the toss and without a conscious thought picked up the points that had fallen. Two more hands to complete this sega and he was out.

"They weren't kidding," someone grumbled as he took the hand.

Cargo was too distracted even to smile. "Any report on that merchie?" he asked nobody.

The Krait pilot who had just lost half this month's combat bonus gave him a look that would have frozen oxygen and shook her head. "Deal," she said impatiently.

Cargo dealt, his mind more on Ghoster and Stonewall than on the cards. This was his seventh game, and they were all starting to run together. He glanced up at the blue display chrono on the screen. Not much longer. Maybe two more hours, he guessed.

He longed to take the batwing and launch early, burn it out at max and to the distance. That wasn't possible. The bat didn't carry enough fuel, let alone oxy and food, for him to stay out more than ten hours. More than that, it didn't have any room for him to even stretch, and there wasn't even a head. Ten hours was absolute max in a straight transport situation, and the batwing commander didn't want him to push it that far. Besides, if he got into an engagement he could use up several hours' fuel in that many seconds. Assuming that he might engage the enemy, even the three hours he had been given was cutting it a little close.

"First bid, ten, seven," the engineer on his right said.

"Ten, seven, seven, four," the next player increased the stakes.

Time. Tzeryde didn't comprehend time. Now and the past were the same thing. How many times had he sat impatient in the hot room playing khandinar and tensed for the alarm. It hadn't even taken a day for him to ferry the little yacht from Tzeryde to the *Horn*. He hadn't realized that they were that close. Or maybe the skiff was slightly faster than he had assumed.

Still, sitting on the *Horn* for a day and a half wore on his nerves. Only the batwing resting black in its cradle reassured him as the hours dragged by. The ace of hearts dropped and the king. Cargo took both, played his own double aces, and picked up the hand. An arm cut him off, the cards lay on the table, and a double-double fell.

The Krait pilot whooped with joy and swooped up the cards, laughing. Cargo blinked, reviewed his plays in his head. He had been right to drop the double aces, and four kings had already fallen. According to the probabilities he should save his three queens of hearts.

He looked at his cards again. He had been right. But the probabilities did always leave that chance and he had fallen right in. Or maybe, he wondered, just maybe this was Tzeryde. He was now something different, not the person who had played before. He searched his mind, trying to feel some echo, some resonance from the core. Because he didn't feel it didn't mean that it wasn't there. That thought didn't give him any comfort.

"Play again?" the engineer asked.

The winning pilot grabbed up the pot and shook her head. "I know when to quit," she said over her shoulder as she inserted her own disc in with the pot and transferred the entire three thousand seven hundred twenty-one to her account.

The engineer shrugged, then turned to Cargo. "You want to play another?"

Cargo shook his head and pulled back slightly, his eyes going to the chrono. The last hours were always the worst, the tension becoming unbearable until he wanted to go good and crazy. Instead he kept himself ice calm and mentally reviewed the batwing checklist in his head. It had been a long time since he had flown one, and while he knew that he would adjust quickly he needed to do something with the last few minutes.

The engineer snorted and shuffled the eight decks in massive hands. "You the one taking out that bat?" he asked conversationally.

Cargo nodded. Wearing civvies and without his wings, matte and black like the craft he flew, he could understand why the engineer had misgivings. But he had left the wings at the Wall, left them behind with another existence he had known on the *Horn*.

"Who's your Eyes?" the other asked again, trying to draw him out, Cargo supposed.

"No Eyes on this one," he said and watched the engineer's jaw drop open.

"But the maze needs Akhaid and human to work," the man protested.

Cargo just smiled. An hour with Tzeryde had taught him more about mazes than months of study and light-years of technical reports. Besides, who could he go with? Dancer? Or some innocent Eyes who wasn't involved in this whole mess? Or maybe some new being he couldn't trust, who would turn and betray him like Stonewall. Or like Dancer in an altogether different way.

Besides, he wasn't planning on using the Eyes. Taking out that transport would defeat his purpose. Instead he flexed his right forearm against the narrow sonic whip taped against his skin. He tried not to think about the knife in his boot, the long narrow blade so similar to the one that had killed his father. Primitive, after all. But then, sonic whips and Eyes and all the other trappings of technological killing weren't any more effective. A knife made a being as dead as Eyes.

"Well," the engineer said, doubt coloring his voice, "if you're going to do it alone, maybe you should get a head start. You got a double checklist to do, you know."

Cargo had to resist the urge to jump, to scream, to kiss the engineer on both cheeks like a long-gone relative. Instead he glanced back at the blue display. An hour and a half. If he went slowly and doubled on everything, and pulled the Eyes systems to his control, it would maybe take that long. Feigning utter sangfroid, he climbed the struts to the cradle and read in the sequence that gently dislodged the batwing from its mooring and set it on the magtracks.

The seat of the batwing embraced him as he strapped the stealthcraft to his body. He fumbled with his collar for a moment before he remembered that he was no longer wearing uniform and his Three-B's were in a packet in his breast pocket. They had been generous and Cargo, knowing the depth he would have to achieve with the maze to fly without Eyes, took eight. The helmet he had been issued fit well enough, but as the drug took effect he could feel the beginnings of a headache right where the biochip had been inserted. He missed having his own helmet with his name and, far more important, where the microwave link had been custom-calibrated. He forgot the headache as he opened into mode, but he knew he would suffer for it later.

He entered mode rapidly, plummeting into the expanded machine-core consciousness that included his own physical reality. Deep, linked with it, there was no membrane, no section of the fighter-mind that was closed to him. And he was in control. Without the balance of the Akhaid Eyes, to the maze he was god.

There was plenty of time. Together with the maze he went over the checklist twice, searching out any irregularity, making sure that every system was set for launch. Gently he expanded that list, opening the Eyes systems as well. The maze balked at first, trying to errect the membrane that separated the two areas. It failed and Cargo entered new territory.

Here was all color. The Eyes were spectrum-activated, but he had never known that their function was reflected in their operation. It reminded him of Tzeryde. And in full mode with more Three-B's in his blood than his body knew how to use, the thought of Tzeryde brought the link with that core swift and sure and solid.

The batwing maze cringed from the powerful intrusion as Tzeryde delighted in the mechanics of controlling the Eyes. The maze tried to build a membrane but only the attempt flickered momentarily before it was lost, shredded, and ignored by the linked beings Tzeryde and Cargo. It was Tzeryde that gave the maze its instructions, its targeting information, with far more certainty than Cargo could have mustered.

He rode, carried on the surging energy patterns of the being that merged him with the batwing more completely than he had ever imagined possible. It was his, it was him. There was no longer a need to think to the maze. Like his own body responding to his desire to walk or pick up a glass or close his eyes, the batwing became his body and the maze simply an extension of his own nervous system.

And he knew that Tzeryde observed with amazement how completely he subordinated the little maze.

Time. There was no time. Then he forced his eyes to see the display. Time had gone quickly, and the time was now. Cargo focused on the tracks, opening communications with the launch control. He heard the words, words that meant little to him. Instead, he felt the power surge in the lines as the mags came on and built to full strength, force increasing to the point where it was hardly contained. And then he opened up and reveled as the batwing thrust blindly into the void.

Freedom was dancing vac forever. No restrictions of time and gravity and mass, here there was only joy. Linked with him, Tzeryde also reflected the joy, a thing it understood. Here he and it were not quite equals, but at least comprehensible. Deep in the maze Cargo flew.

On a floating design with edges sharp down to the molecular level, the batwing slipped through the dark perfectly at one with the void. Matte and black it cast no reflections, and its honeycomb shield skin was made to trap any radio spotting transmission. Down near no-go the infrared mask was at full force and the craft would show null and cold even here. There was no way to see it unless it blotted out the stars.

He had slipped through a crack in the manifold, shielded in the Other Six. This speed, this power, this silence, was where Tzeryde lived. Dancing vac. In the back of his mind he heard the being that was Tzeryde agree.

There was no time until the maze reported the transport *Belle Pays* in their range. Not vis yet, but likely one of the glittering points against the backdrop of night. Not vis yet, but time to do something. Any closer and he was giving them the chance of catching him, vis, blocking a familiar view. He couldn't afford that.

For one brief moment Cargo panicked, wondered if Ghoster was still alive and if there was any point at all to what he was doing. He could turn around immediately, could forget that he'd ever had the chance. Very likely Stonewall wasn't alone. Also likely that Ghoster, even if he was alive, had already been treated with the drugs developed by the Sixth Directorate that would not only make him tell everything he knew, but would destroy his brain as they were excavating it.

Experimentally he focused on the Eyes. They were tracking a million spectra, each one with possible locks on target. Cargo found himself overwhelmed. How did Ghoster manage all this? Then he started to discard the obvious, and the maze eliminated all stars, bodies, and distant emanations. He asked for a reading on any possible targets with the coordinates Tzeryde had given for the transport.

Three, no, four sets glittered around him inside him. He could feel the Eyes pressing forward, ready to fire, begging to be let free. He held them back. The batwing was invisible to the finest military hardware. No lux runner was going to be better equipped. Probably they wouldn't have long distance detection at all—from this far out even the most sensitive instruments couldn't tell the difference between a police patrol and a super yacht.

He held the batwing on a tight leash, forcing it to approach closer than any military maze felt comfortable about, and then pushing it some more. He wasn't thinking anymore but acting on instinct, on the reflexes his training had given him, on intuition. Flying by Godint, by Divine Intelligence.

The lux transport kept on course without acknowledgment. Pure luck. Stonewall was as well versed as he was in batwing tactics; either the Charlestonian had gotten too arrogant or wasn't watching. Either one was bad, and his lack of vigilance angered Cargo. Stonewall was better than that. Or had been better than that once upon a time when they were both in the Second Directorate together. He shouldn't be able to sneak up on a trained stealth pilot so easily.

Not only were they vis now, but so close that Cargo could read the registry number off the transport's hull. The maze needed little guidance to match speed and course. The stealth-craft slid alongside the lux transport like its shadow in the noon light. Cargo nudged the batwing closer still, bringing it up to predocking position just behind the aft utility airlock.

And from there he was stymied. There was no way he could couple the two craft without cooperation from the inside. Well, it was time Stonewall knew he'd arrived in any case. Reluctantly he instructed the maze to direct its microwave antenna to the commercial craft's receiver farm, but as soon as he made the connection he heard Stonewall's words filtered through two mazes and his own mind.

"Yo, buddy, you think you can Sneaky Pete your way up on ole Stonewall, well you done pretty good. I'll give you that. So why don't you identify and I can open up this here hatch and break out the Jim Beam? You copy?"

Cargo snorted with disbelief, and then broke out in deep laughter. He'd forgotten that the batwing would give a Collegium ident on making contact with the liner, had forgotten as well that Stonewall thought they were at least allies if not friends. Even arranging for his disappearance on Tel Hala had reinforced that notion.

Maybe, just maybe, he could pull the *bouzer* on Stonewall. Walk right in and walk out with Ghoster, and Stonewall being none the wiser. That would serve him right. Cargo wasn't Sister Mary's son for nothing.

"It's Cargo," he identified himself. "And I've been dumped with a lousy bedbugging job. Got to pick up something from you, is all."

Even with the barricades between them Cargo could hear Stonewall's chuckle. "Welcome aboard, ole buddy. So you're finally living up to your sign, huh? Pure cargo work to be sure. Will wonders never cease? Bedbugging, no less. Well, if some Jim Beam'll make it go down easier I'll be glad to be of psychological assistance."

Cargo didn't respond. There was no real need beyond banter. With the security provisions met on both sides the mazes of the two craft went into their own interface and began the delicate docking procedures. Usually Cargo supervised. He didn't like to leave anything this tricky to a maze alone, but this time he was occupied with other matters.

What he really needed was the authorization fax. He swore under his breath and searched the batwing mentally. There was an official print in the Eyes station, but he couldn't get there. Besides, how would he change the white log copy to authorization green? And that wasn't counting the Bishop's signature, which he was pretty sure he could fake, and the Bishop's thumbprint, which he couldn't.

He needed to buy time. Somehow the maze caught his anxiety and began to slow down on the docking. Surprised, Cargo half thanked and half approved of it. Maybe the maze wasn't a machine, was a baby Tzeryde getting ready to take over half the manifold.

The maze seemed slightly pleased in response. Cargo would have sworn the maze acknowledged a blush and would have even projected red light could it have done so. But all the stalling in the universe wasn't going to help unless he could come up with the necessary papers.

He had once told Stonewall about the *bouzer*, one night when they were both drunk and patching up their first argument. He had wondered at the time why he had ever let on to the *Gaje*. Now he knew himself for an idiot, and had to rely on two things. First of all, Stonewall, for all his intel experience, didn't know a whole lot about the Trustees or how they worked day to day. There Cargo was far more informed about how someone like Mirabeau might word an official requisition or request and what it would look like.

Also, Stonewall didn't understand that Cargo despised him. That was his greatest advantage. There was one thing more, something he hoped for more than counted on. Stonewall had been drunk and annie blind that night on Vanity. Cargo rubbed the Ste. Maries medal and prayed briefly that he had forgotten.

His mother wouldn't have worried about any of those things, he realized. What had made Sister Mary so successful was that she could convince a stone to bleed. There was always a way around anyone, if you were smart enough to find it, she had taught him. And no *Gaje*, never, ever, could outsmart a Rom.

So Cargo thought about the authorization calmly. How had the Bishop ordered him? And then a smile broke unseen on his face. Thank all the saints in Heaven and all the luck that watched over him that the Bishop had insisted on a classical education. The Collegium was very, very traditional in certain ways.

Confidence surged through him. In the back he could feel a hint of Tzeryde, observing, confused and appalled and delighted all at once.

Cargo forgot the fax printer in the Eyes staion. Instead, he pulled out a letter the Bishop had written to him when he was still Kore Verdun. The old man's writing was densely black and ornate on the heavy vellum. But the paper had rag edges and was easily torn.

Cargo studied the results. Smallish, but not bad. Besides, he very much doubted that Stonewall had ever seen real writing paper before. And he was even more certain that, like most of their contemporaries, Stonewall couldn't produce the fluid, elegant script that all the Trustees used to pen their personal orders.

The docking was almost completed, the maze reported sadly. Cargo reassured it. He waited until the procedure was truly finished and there was no threat of unplanned movement before he took out the old-fashioned pen the Bishop had given him as a graduation gift. He composed the letter in his head thinking in French the way the Bishop would, and began writing in that language.

Then he studied the results. Not bad at all. He considered printing a translation in Indopean at the bottom, but stopped cold. None of the Trustees would do that. Something else would accompany a handwritten order, a thin flim with computer-generated translation.

The maze picked up his thought and executed it with an alacrity that was frightening. It barely reported finished when the alarm went off as the airlock opened.

The batwing hadn't been designed for docking and entering a small craft in vac. The coupling links had been an after-thought, and were precisely that difficult to get through. Two links, Eyes and pilot separately, fed into a single structure that attached to the utility outlet. There was barely enough room for Cargo to squeeze through, and he was on the slender side of normal range. As it was he wondered momentarily how his shoulders were going to make it, and while a good tug from the lux transport solved that problem, it left him with a torn sleeve and badly bruised deltoids.

"You always were one for an entrance," Stondwall chuckled as he dragged Cargo through the hatch. "Remember when you came to Vanity? And that long shaggy-dog story you told about how you single-handed outfought and outgunned four Cardia fighters? And now ole Cargo got put on a bedbugging task. My sympathy is with you. After all, I thought you had resigned."

Cargo squelched the urge to strangle Stonewall, on the grounds that someday someone wasn't going to be able to control him or herself and then the universe would be well rid of one obnoxious blond Charlestonian. It was a comforting thought.

Cargo handed the note he had written to Stonewall with a flourish. The other took it and felt the heaviness of the paper, pursing his lips as he puzzled momentarily over the words.

"Couldn't you at least have had him write in decent Indopean?" Stonewall asked petulantly. "Or get a translation. Not that it matters. I'd have to double-check and clear whatever it is anyway, so I figure I can ask when I do."

Cargo shook his head. "Didn't know you'd go and bother the Bishop when he's in conference with Jakta over the negotiations."

Stonewall flashed a knife-blade smile. "I need the authorization," he replied. "And a retinal scan or voice print. Even for you, old buddy, and I would trust tyou like I trust my own brother, I would have to get some real good evidence before I go turning over a prisoner as important as our old friend Ghoster, now wouldn't I? You wouldn't want anyone to call ole Stonewall derelict in his duty? It would ruin my reputation, to say nothing of my family honor."

Cargo's hands felt cold. What would his mother do, Sonfranka do, Sonfranka who was so talented that even crazy she was worth the same as Nona?

"I don't care what you do," Cargo replied, the old arrogance filling him suddenly with reckless bravado. "You could go declare war on Tzeryde single-handed in this pig for all I care. Just so long as you tell me where the head is."

Stonewall really did laugh then and pointed him in the right direction. Cargo disappeared immediately. Not that he didn't really need to use it, but the privacy afforded him some space to think over the situation.

He could feel Tzeryde with him, and Ghoster too. Now that Ghoster was so close and they were linked through the core, it was a little like the feeling of being in mode together, creating the membrane between the two. Only there was no membrane here, only easy and sometimes painful touch.

He prayed to every saint in heaven that he didn't believe in. No matter how much he wanted to avoid a confrontation with a person he knew, even a person he despised as much as Stonewall, there was no doubt that he would have to fight. Even now Stonewall must be sending the confirmation to Tzeryde, and the Bishop had too much honor to lie. Cargo loosened the tape that held the whip in place. He wanted it loose and easy when the time came.

When he emerged with his face still damp and his hands dripping to disguise the clamminess, Stonewall was waiting with a plate of crackers and caviar along with the promised Jim Beam. "Thought you might like a reminder of Vanity," he said.

Cargo took the other seat in the cramped quarters and tasted one of the crackers. The caviar was from Vanity, the best kind, the one luxury they had all become accustomed to living there. He refused the whiskey, however, and took only water.

"Flying in as soon as your confirmation comes," he said, gesturing to the bottle. "The thought is much appreciated."

"Mmmm," Stonewall replied. "You know, Cargo, if your Bishop Mirabeau didn't want Ghoster real bad, I'd have a serious problem right now. Because he is my very finest prize in the get Gantor sweepstakes, and I sure as hell don't want to lose. To say nothing of my own personal advantage, you understand."

Cargo tapped his finger against the water glass and didn't look up at Stonewall. "Mirabeau might be willing to help you," Cargo said slowly. "What you told me about Gantor, sounds like he isn't exactly the Bishop's kind of person. If you've got the evidence something could probably be arranged. I can't promise anything, remember, but there's a reasonable chance."

Stonewall's face went dead ashen white and his lips pressed firmly into a narrow line. One fist balled against his thigh as he contemplated the amber liquid in the bottle. "And then what'll I owe you?" he whispered through clenched teeth.

Cargo had the feeling that he was intruding on something very private. It embarrassed him to see Stonewall's raw, feral anger, and he knew that no matter what he said it would be the wrong answer. Stonewall and his damned antique code of behavior. He drank the water slowly, hoping to see Stonewall recover his normal color or relax a little or get too drunk to notice.

None of those things happened. Instead, the flashing yellow message light came on and Stonewall flicked the set to general audio. The voice that came over the speaker was all too familiar.

"This shall constitute personal voice-print confirmation that the being known as Ohr-keru adzchiLo, also known in the Collegium service as Ghoster, is to be immediately remanded into the custody of the negotiating team currently in residence on Tzeryde. He is to be delivered with all due haste as his presence is required to further our ongoing effort. Article seven twenty-one Collegium general code gives duly appointed Free Legates standing authorization under the Trusteeship to enforce such necessary changes as they see fit in order to attain a Collegium priority goal. By order of Andre Michel Mirabeau."

"Satisfied?" Cargo inquired.

Stonewall snorted. "I'll have to check it through the print scan. Not that I think it's a fake, just that I know you wouldn't want me to skim any of the regulations, now would you? And when this confirms we'll have to arrange the details. After all, you wouldn't hardly want to put a traitor like Ghoster into a powerful position like, say, the Eyes station on a Batwing. No, indeed, I certainly could not say that was a responsible way to act. We'll have to consider this very carefully."

Stonewall spoke very slowly and the print match went through without any delays for social niceties. At least pure machines didn't have ambitions and ego problems, Cargo thought with satisfaction. Or maybe not. Maybe they were just too alien to comprehend, more to Tzeryde's little siblings. Or some other order of being all together.

Cargo didn't know and his head hurt. The water wouldn't have done that. Either Stonewall had copied Dancer and slipped him something under the tepid mineral-flat taste of the water, or Stonewall himself was tying Cargo in knots. Cargo voted for the second. Stonewall always did have that effect.

"Look, why don't you take the batwing and I'll keep your prisoner on this tub till we get to Tzeryde," Cargo said heavily. "It'll take almost a full day on this pig's power, but you'd have the advantage."

Stonewall's smile was as threatening as the blade of the knife taped in Cargo's boot. "No, I wouldn't dream of doing such a thing. It's been a very long time since we really had a chance to visit. Now this little lux transport isn't the finest of accommodations. I would prefer to offer you the hospitality of my home, or at least a four-star hotel on Luxor, but my mother always said that it was the company and not the setting that defined the gathering. So why don't we all go to Tzeryde together?"

Cargo prayed that his frustration didn't show. "Maze taking us in? Then I'll take you up on your earlier offer."

Stonewall passed the bottle and Cargo took a long pull. As the warmth of the whiskey spread through his body, Cargo permitted himself to reflect on Stonewall's half-hunter form studying him with distrust. The sensation was pleasant. Better than pleasant.

He had pulled off the *bouzer*. Sister Mary's son to be sure. He had tricked Stonewall and the *Gaje* would never even know. The perfection of it settled into him and he tasted the way the words shaped in his mouth in Romany.

The universe had changed. Nothing had changed. The *Gaje* were still the same, and it was still the destiny of the Rom to use them. Only there were people like the Bishop. He had to consider that, Cargo reminded himself. Mirabeau had picked up on his plan and gone along with no prior warning. Maybe the Bishop was adopting the ways of the Rom.

Only knowing the Bishop, he probably had plans of his own. Cargo sighed and began humming tunelessly. Whatever use Mirabeau had for him or for Ghoster or for the entire universe, he had walked right into it. Probably the Bishop had already begun to formulate this plan when he adopted a group of Gypsy juvenile delinquents. Then Cargo shut off his curiosity and surrendered to the current pleasures.

Drink and sleep were enough for now. Whatever the Bishop wanted would come in fifteen hours when they arrived at Tzeryde. He passed the bottle back to Stonewall.

"Long time until we get close," he said. "How about we get Ghoster and have a friendly game of khandinar?"

Chapter
16

Tzeryde encompassed them in shimmering blues creating a halo around the Bishop waiting at the end of the crossover. Cargo waited until Ghoster had emerged from the tunnel into the colony before he turned to Stonewall. There weren't any words he had to say. "Good-by" was not enough and too strong all at once, and besides it was not a word the Rom used, but he had to look at least, to somehow fix the finality of the moment in his mind.

Stonewall studied him briefly, and then held out a hand. Cargo could not refuse. The gesture was controlled and dignified, formal and slightly antiquated, but at the same time Cargo knew how much it cost Stonewall to offer. He tried to meet him with a measure of courtesy. He had won. Ghoster was safe.

And when Cargo turned away he knew that Stonewall had won, too. Hated friend and half an enemy, there were still memories that would not permit him to reduce the other to a nonbeing. No matter if he ever saw Stonewall again, Stonewall had created him. Without the challenge and the chase, he would never have come to Shodar, to Tzeryde, to understanding the missed cues and mixed signals that gave the Bishop and Jakta such hope.

Stonewall had done more than he would ever realize, Cargo

thought, and would never be written up in history texts or honored by a public dinner. History had to be full of them.

Cargo nodded briskly and turned into the corridor that connected the transport to the habitat and entered the blue light. He did not look back when he heard the soft huff as the door to the tunnel closed. Tzeryde's pleasure was an emotional backdrop to his own myriad feelings. Jakta and Dancer emerged from the light at the Bishop's side.

"It's a good thing that Dancer was here," Mirabeau started. "You know that you were so intent on Ghoster that you never did contact Shodar with our invitation."

Cargo blinked. What invitation? Then it all came back. Damn. But there was the gentleness of teasing in the Bishop's voice and a half smile on his face. The old man was not displeased.

"It was better that the contact came from Dancer in any case," Jakta added kindly. "But while you were taking care of your responsibilities we were taking care of ours. Shodar is due in two days."

"If he doesn't change his mind," Cargo muttered.

"I don't think so," the Bishop answered seriously. "You see, the Guardians of the Dance had a long conference with Tzeryde. At least I think it can best be described as a conference. There is a compound that Tzeryde believes should work on Shodar. Provided, of course, that Shodar also wants the communication. But I believe that should not be a problem."

"And what about you?" Cargo asked. "Are you going to try to enter with him? You haven't had the years of drug therapy, the experience. Your body isn't young. It could kill you."

Andre Michel Mirabeau just smiled.

Andre Michel Mirabeau lay in the cradle of light. The colors shifted lazily, lulling him to sleep. To dreams, no doubt, that Tzeryde tasted. Since Cargo's discovery the Bishop had been constantly aware of Tzeryde the being as opposed to the Dancers and the Akhaid who inhabited the colony. They, like himself, were simply extensions of the known. It was the unknown that tempted him.

And temptation he admitted it was. He had had everything he had wanted in life, power and strength and a place in history. Only knowledge still held out the beckoning reach that he found impossible to resist, and he had finally given in to it. A temptation indeed. And he worried, vaguely, if following it was perhaps sin.

He turned on the layers of quilts that had been spread over the carpet so that he could lie in comfort. The quilts, too, were white, like the lap desks and the robes of the Dancers and the whole interior of the place. Only Tzeryde had color, and that being provided or withheld it from everything in sight.

A mature Akhaid with startling magenta eyes stood under a bright pink laser arch. The Bishop sighed and sat up.

"The one we call Ki Shodar is ready," the Akhaid said in Indopean thickly accented from some distant outpost.

"Coffee," the Bishop chuckled. "That must be one of God's great jokes. Coffee is the key to the universe."

The Akhaid's expression did not change. "Coffee and a series of annies that would kill any other being," he corrected. "And it was well done. With all the poise of the Walk."

The Akhaid set down a small tray, lacquered white, where what looked like twenty tiny red pills lay arranged to suggest a stream, and the single dark glass an ominous mountain. Two white-pink flowers lay in one corner, from Earth and very highly valued. It must have been nearly impossible to get cherry blossoms. Mirabeau had never been able to accomplish this feat. It was a miracle, he decided, and a sign.

When he glanced up from admiring the tray, the being who had brought it was gone. The Bishop was sorry about that. He would have liked to express his appreciation of the artistic effort. But it was time. Hating to destroy the beauty of the arrangement, he selected the Three-B's carefully, trying to keep the image in the tray as long as possible. The last six he scooped up all at once, and when he had finished the water and the pills, he sprinkled the last remaining drops on the cherry blossoms and arranged them against the dark glass in one corner of the tray. Not as suggestive as the original, perhaps, but pleasing.

He lay down again, sinking into the pile of quilts. They held him like a cloud, and he could feel himself spiraling down, away, out, encompassing not only Tzeryde but the nearer stars.

How beautiful they were, and how alive. Mirabeau wanted to hold them, set them spinning off, skipping across the void the way he had skipped stones on the ornamental pond when he was a boy.

And Tzeryde touched his mind, another star in the constellation he had become, Tzeryde of the many spectra, the oldest one as he was now the youngest. In that touch he knew something Cargo had not learned, and the knowledge awed him into stillness. Tzeryde touched him as an equal, a partner. They had a task to accomplish.

Shodar was within Tzeryde, his thoughts riding in the matrix, a set of harsh burn colors searing their way through the more harmonious rainbows of the core. Tzeryde welcomed the Bishop, and then Mirabeau locked in to the matrix that Tzeryde kept and rotated through it until he was in contact with Shodar.

It was not the way Cargo had described it. Cargo had talked about a membrane between oneself and the Other, or within Tzeryde the modulating effect of the core itself. Mirabeau found only the raw and raging essence of Ki Shodar, and that presence cut through him like a bank of Eyes. All the colors of Shodar were pain. All the colors were afraid.

Mirabeau reached out to that fear, that pain, as he had reached all his life. It drew him, called to him like a hunger in his own soul, and he rushed to appease it. To make it whole again. Because Ki Shodar, for all his gifts, was missing something. A section of his being, of his self, was gone, amputated by ignorance and cruelty.

Mirabeau wondered about Aliadro, whether he had been as crippled of essence as his brother. And Mirabeau knew the answer. He had been the answer, not just for Aliadro, but for Cargo as well. He had taught them, maybe not to link with some being like Tzeryde, but with the greatness in themselves.

In the end, in pure essence, Mirabeau believed. His faith was primitive under all the layers of education and sophistication, under the years of power and the lifetime of wealth. He believed, utterly and simply, in grace and salvation and the divine origin of the soul. It was not a being like Tzeryde he had taught his children to touch. It was, he hoped, the God beyond.

And if this Tzeryde seemed like an angel, then that, too, was good. He could feel Tzeryde flickering wonder, bound up in the Bishop's view of the universe. These hows and whys were new to it, tastes that were unfamiliar and thus biting while it desired still more. He could feel Tzeryde, but gently, kindly, he asked it to wait. The core was merely enthralled; Ki Shodar was in pain.

There were no words, hardly even images that any being could use. The level where the Bishop needed to heal was beyond such concrete and separate things. Instead there was only energy/color/music, all of them a single thing that tried to express itself in various ways, to be known. Always changing in expression, the flow of energy itself was as grand as the background hum of the universe and as vast as the eons.

The hard, harsh nexus that was Shodar shone firmly before him. Mirabeau embraced the titanium bright colors, rejoicing in their clarity and their beauty. His delight joined the flow of energy that washed through the matrix and inundated Shodar like a tidal wave in a fishing town. There was no power that could resist. The only choice was to become part of it, flotsam dragged from the beach and indelibly wedded to the sea.

Drowned by the flow, Mirabeau was aware of Ki Shodar not as anyone apart from himself, but as an element of the surge together. But where Mirabeau floated in his glory, Shodar was that which swam. He had been a marine creature washed on the beach, unable to breathe. Here, united in that matrix to infinity, he leaped and dove and explored what should have been his by right.

Ki Shodar was alive for the very first time in his life. This perfect freedom was what he had wanted, this great and abiding power of the void made his political achievements puny and laughable.

Mirabeau felt his being and knew him. And he knew, in wonder, that Shodar had finally become what the geneticists had tried to create. They had succeeded with the creature, they had only forgotten to open its eyes. Perhaps because, like Plato's people in the cave, they had no knowledge that their own eyes were firmly sewn shut.

The experimenters had cited genetic research as their goal. But there had been rumors about a "World Walker." The Bishop had never quite known what a World Walker was. Ki Shodar had believed that Aliadro Mirabeau had been the one. Now it was clear that he had been wrong. Either or both of them could have become a World Walker, uniting with a core like Tzeryde and the human-side soul through the Bishop.

Either of them could have, but it was Ki who had become the thing that he had most desired.

In that instant Mirabeau finally understood why he had killed Aliadro. There had been plenty of other reasons—jealousy of Aliadro's popularity in the revolution and political potential; hatred of Aliadro's status as the probable "World Walker"; it was even possible that he had killed his brother to save him from self-inflicted blindness, to merely finish what Aliadro hadn't had the courage to do. All those reasons were possible and all of them were combined in the Collegium's portrait.

It was true, Ki Shodar had hated his brother. But only because he had hated himself. Killing Aliadro had only increased that feeling, making him justified in whatever he did. When he had become a fratricide he had become exempt from any code of morality because he was already lower than them all. Not that he had believed it had mattered. Neither truly Akhaid nor human, what did their ethics have to do with him?

The rage dissolved in the fire of Tzeryde's light. All that was left was Ki Shodar, a singular and fragmentary being who was just learning how to be alive.

The Bishop sat up uncertainly. His body felt as heavy and limp and numb as the quilts that supported him. Slowly, very slowly, he reached out a hand and made a fist. It was his body, no dream state. Nor was he dead.

He had fully expected to be dead. He wasn't accustomed to the drugs or to mode, but whatever Tzeryde was it was neither of those things. His head was perfectly clear. He tried to stand, and the numbness and stabbing pain of returning circulation were additional confirmation he hadn't needed that this was indeed reality.

In the light around him he could sense Tzeryde. It was not like the open communication the drugs and necessity had provided, but he was aware of how the light was alive and sentient, intelligent and watching. And more than that, it was hopeful and excited and pleased. It had had many new tastes in the past days, become part of many strange and wondrous dreams.

The Bishop chuckled. "I have had a most rare vision. I have had a dream, past the wit of man to say what dream it was. The eye of man hath not heard, the ear of man hath not seen, man's hand is not able to taste, his tongue to conceive, nor his heart to report what my dream was," he whispered to the being that lived in the energy around him.

"That is not Sophocles," a voice said from behind a curtain of soft rose light.

The voice was familiar, haunting, and the being stepped out though the radiance to face Mirabeau. He was not surprised that it was Ki Shodar. Not the young revolutionary anymore, nor the brilliant and scheming runaway lost in the Night Side pool halls and chess parlors. Nor was this the Cardia leader whose feral, silvered face appeared almost nightly on the news. This, instead, was a fusion of Ki Shodar and Aliadro Mirabeau, the power of the one and the judgment of the other. Only there was still something missing, something wrong.

And then Andre Michel Mirabeau recognized what it was. He smiled. "You've done it all," he congratulated the victor. "Except for one thing. You have to forgive yourself. How can you take your place as a Master of Compassion if you don't?"

"I don't understand," Shodar said carefully, as if he had never said those words together before.

The Bishop struggled to his feet. Shodar did not come forward, did not offer any assistance, for which Mirabeau was grateful. He was old, perhaps, but he was still far from feeble. In fact, he felt better as he set his feet stable under his shoulders and squared himself to look Ki Shodar in the eye for the first time since he had entered the room where Aliadro had died.

"You have been given every advantage," he told Shodar. "After all, how can you become a Master of Compassion if you've never done anything to earn it yourself?"

There was no dawn or midnight on Tzeryde. Only the constantly changing colors, the play of light on light, sometimes brighter and sometimes pale and anemic, but even the infinite variety finally had a sameness that made Cargo sad. Or maybe some of the sadness was the dull internal echo of the core itself contemplating him and his next movement.

He looked at his hand under the sea-green haze that filled the space and passed for darkness. It became an alien hand, unconnected to his history, not his hand. And his face in the same light would be just as unfamiliar.

"Are you sure you want to do this?" Ki Shodar had asked the

day before, when he had informed them all of his decision. "I had counted on you to be a member of our realignment team."

The Bishop had looked shocked. "I had counted on you to be a member of *ours*."

Cargo remembered watching them carry in the leather upholstered wing backs and sofas from Mirabeau's official transport. Tzeryde was pleased that they were white. The days that had followed Shodar's contact with the core had been frenzied with activity. A table was on the way, a table to sign the formal documents on. With the exception of Jakta, neither side thought a lap desk appropriate, and so the documents drawn up so easily through Tzeryde were waiting for the final ceremony of acceptance by the Trustees. Shodar alone spoke for the Cardia, but even he had invited other members of various planetary and colonial governments.

"There's going to be so much to do," Mirabeau had told him as they watched the precious inlaid desk pried from its boltings. "I should think you would be named Legate in a few years. And think of what it will mean to millions, to build the structure of the relationship between us and the Cardia. Acknowledging them was harder than fighting them. Establishing relations will be harder still. Helping them realign their economy to become self-sufficient and take them off a war industry base will probably be the biggest challenge of the century. Even more than flying your precious Kraits."

Cargo had smiled at that. The Bishop knew him well enough to know that the temptation of a challenge was a hard one to turn down. But there were other things he had to do first. The Cardia economy would still be there. And if someone had already cleaned that up, there were still generations of undergraduates to mystify with the intricacies of probability, and millions of casinos that did not have his picture in the back office. No, the universe was still full of challenge.

"I trained you for this," Mirabeau had reminded him gently. "You are my heir, the only one still living. And I had such hopes."

Cargo reached out and touched his mentor's shoulder. Under the heavy tweed jacket he could feel the thin bones move. "No," he said gently, aware of just how fragile the old man was. "I'm not the only one. You have Shodar, too."

Andre Michael Mirabeau squeezed Cargo's hand. "Maybe

he will carry on my work. You are my son. But I've never stopped you from doing what you thought you had to do. I'm not going to start now."

Somewhere in Tzeryde, Mirabeau and Shodar were learning how to work together, Cargo thought. He stared at his hand, now dyed an equally alien blue. The black ring around the little finger was new, and it still startled him. Ghoster had done it before he had slept. Ghoster had been planning to lead him to the inner precincts of the habitat, the place where the Dancers stayed and studied, but Cargo had refused even when Ghoster had pointed out that the guest facilities were near full.

Cargo said nothing. He didn't require much, a quiet corner to curl up, maybe something to eat. It wasn't so different from the stories of how their people had lived very long ago, stories that Pulika had told them in the winter-rides deep in the void.

Now, waking, he knew it was time. The universe would manage very nicely for however long it took. He washed, and straightened the sturdy black suede suit the Bishop had provided. Like a Gypsy from the stories he would have only one set of clothes. According to Pulika that was a virtue.

He made his way out of the guest quarters. Led by Tzeryde he wandered alone until he came to the port lock. He could hear people around him, swearing workers probably carrying the newly arrived table to what would serve as the conference room, elegant accents of delegates, whispers of Atrash from behind the light. But Tzeryde, which was a part of him as he was within it, kept him shielded from their sight. Like walking through a thick fog, he thought. And then it was quiet.

The path he followed through the port lock was not the same one as the conference used. This was far out to one side, alone, and seemingly unused for a very long time. The mechanism needed a little encouragement before it yielded and Cargo passed through to the cradles just inside the skin. Only four cradles in the small hangar, and only one was occupied, but the craft that hung there just above the launch tracks was a song and a breath and a memory of perfection.

Matte and black, the batwing beckoned him. Its elegant curved surfaces undulated in the shadows. It was beautiful and proud and cold, a thing at home only in the void.

Cargo climbed in the pit. A supply of Three-B's waited on the seat. He swallowed two and waited. And when he touched the maze, Tzeryde's youngest, it regarded him with something like awe.

Quieted, he reached deep into it and felt it nestled down onto the tracks. Tzeryde itself flowed into the energy lines of the tracks as the outer lock opened. And then Cargo launched them out to start his Walk dancing vac.